ALSO FROM MIA HEINTZELMAN

THE ALL MIXED UP SERIES

(Each book can be read as a standalone)

Mixed Signals

Mixed Match

Mixed Emotions

All mixed up series boxset

STANDALONES

It's Got A Ring To It - Releasing Fall 2020

Wrapped up in beau

DARK ROMANCE

Devastated: Wastelands academy book 1

The Stack w/a Emmaline Zanthi

ACKNOWLEDGMENTS

All you have to do is check an author's Google search history or listen as he or she talks to himself or herself while writing to know that creating a book is a crazy venture in and of itself. For this book to reach this form, it took a tribe and village.

Thank you to my village, my family. Thank you to Mommy and Daddy, the tale-spinner and the bookworm. Since I was packed up on Daddy's back while he pursued a college degree, you have instilled in me a love of reading, writing, and telling farfetched tales. Thank you to my husband, Daniel Heintzelman, for understanding, supporting, and loving me during my sleepless nights and endless writing days. For telling me I'm good enough to jump! Also, thanks for not thinking I'm crazy when you hear me talking to myself. To Nina and Brooke, you fuel my passion and dreams. Whatever dreams you decide to pursue, I'm behind you.

And then there's my tribe. Special thanks to my editor, friend, and BWP, Margo Hendricks. Glad to have you as my partner in this rat race. To the Thursday Night Therves, my awesome critique group, you guys get me and I get you, and that's all that matters. Thank you to the Las Vegas chapter of Romance Writers of America. It's amazing to be part of a team. Your support, education, challenges, and retreats are the best.

To Colleen Reinhart, thank you for supporting an indie author. Your work is so beautiful and amazing. I love that your vision is vivid and bright. It makes me excited to read and proud to share my books with the world.

Finally, but certainly not least, thank you to my family, friends, and readers. Taking you along with me on this journey is an honor. Thank you for helping me do what I love.

MIXED SIGNALS

MIA HEINTZELMAN

LeviLynn

LeviLynn

ISBN-13: 978-0-9990493-3-4
Mixed Signals
Copyright © 2019 by Mia Heintzelman

Cover illustration by Colleen Reinhart
Book design by Mia Heintzelman

This is a work of fiction. Names, characters, places and incidents are either the product of the author's imagination or are used fictitiously, and any resemblance to actual persons, living or dead, business establishments, events or locales is entirely coincidental.

For questions and comments about the quality of this book, please contact us at miaheintzelman.com/contactmia/html.

miaheintzelman.com

For Daniel. Thank you for believing in my dream.

Mixed Signals

CHAPTER 1

J ulie Laurich swooped into the right hand turning lane at the corner of Fourth Street off Casino Center. As usual, she was running late. And as her luck would have it, she'd caught every red light from the freeway to her current spot behind no less than ten other cars with drivers who apparently had nowhere to be.

She on the other hand, had exactly five minutes to meet her best friend Liz at the Skyline Cafe. Two until her phone started ringing and she had to hear about being considerate of other people's time.

"Come on, damn it." She cursed at the light and considered laying on the horn. She quickly decided against it for the mere fact that in this town, road rage was rampant. A yelling match wouldn't exactly get her to the restaurant any faster.

Instead, she gripped the steering wheel and inched closer to the red beemer in front of her. The same beemer, which had literally moved about a millimeter in the last ten minutes.

Julie threw her head back and exhaled loudly just as a siren wailed on her left. She lowered her gaze just in time to see a cop car weave past a black pickup truck through to the far left lane and dart into the intersection.

Don't tell me it's an accident. Great. Just great.

According to the clock on the dash, it was now ten fifty seven. Three minutes to get to the restaurant. And that didn't include finding parking in downtown Las Vegas. On a hot ass Sunday morning. In May. At the Container Park, no less.

At this rate, she'd be lucky to be in her seat by eleven thirty.

Rolling her window down, she careened her neck out and stretched to see what was going on up ahead. What kind of emergency they were dealing with determined exactly how long she could expect to keep Liz impatiently waiting.

From the looks of it, a blue SUV had probably been tailgating the silver rice rocket and nicked the bumper, which likely belonged to the thin guy in all black who was currently yelling at someone in the crossover.

The car was nice, but whatever the damage was, it was minimal from Julie's vantage point. But, to guys like that, a scratch barely noticeable through a microscope was worth suing over. *I guess cash remains king here.*

She flopped back into her seat, frustrated. Calling the police meant this was going to be a while—a hot sticky while, with her bare thighs melded together and her makeup streaked. So much for trying to be cute. *Great.*

"It's just an *accident*," she yelled to no one in particular as she leaned against the headrest.

This was Vegas. Auto accidents happened basically every second of every day. Pretty much, if the sirens weren't coming from an ambulance or a fire truck, chances were, it wasn't fatal, and therefore, it was just an inconvenience.

In Julie's case, this bootleg fender-bender was an annoyance, although a distraction she *should* welcome. But it was still only prolonging the inevitable: her standing weekly appointment with her best friend during which she stood to be reamed a new one about her failure to resuscitate her flat-lining love life.

As another squad car zoomed by in a blur in the left lane, Julie looked over, but it wasn't the emergency vehicle that caught her eye. Rather, she'd caught someone else's eye.

In the middle lane, in the black truck, just low enough to see him looking down at her, was a gorgeous, fantasy-worthy man with *come hither* eyes.

Hello.

Good lord, this man was something like Superman meets Khal Drogo from Game of Thrones at a monster truck rally. Minus all the eyeliner and add in a head full of dark wavy curls and angel eyes. He was looking down at Julie with those molten brown eyes under a canopy of sweeping lashes. He might as well have been looking down from heaven for the way she couldn't bring herself to close her mouth.

On top of all that yummy goodness, *his* mouth was, for lack of functioning adult words, delicious. A full pouty bottom lip underscored a toothy grin. He was saying something, but she couldn't make it out with the thundering sound of her heartbeat pounding in her ears.

The way he propped his arms up between the dash and the seat and flashed her that crooked panty-dropper smile, he could have been saying anything. He could have been telling her to go to hell, or that she had a flat tire. He could have been saying she'd left the gas cap door open, but Mr. Cutie Pants was basically a mute. Albeit, a gorgeous mute with the ability to make her lose both her breath and track of time.

Julie freeze-framed him.

She'd snapshotted him in her mind in that sexy position with his lovely lips and twinkle eyes. All other noise and movement had ceased along with the traffic. For that split second, it was Julie and hot truck guy, and his lashes.

Heat settled low and tight in Julie's belly as she rubbed her forefinger over her bottom lip.

Come to mama.

She breathed the words. But then her snapshot moved and she

vaguely registered the sound of a car horn.

Julie blinked a few times as the guy's low bass-filled voice flooded into earshot. The words came out garbled and clunky.

"What? What did you say?"

He gave Julie an endearing smile before nodding and pointing toward the cars ahead in her lane. "It's just an accident. Looks like you're moving now."

Apparently while Julie was salivating over the guy, the cop in the intersection had begun ushering the traffic to open up the lanes.

Already, most of the cars in front of her had turned. The people behind her were now slamming on their horns, and by the scowl plastered on the officer's face, she was officially the holdup.

She couldn't very well ask the policeman and all the drivers who'd been sitting ducks for the last fifteen minutes to give her *more* time. Not even if it would just take two more minutes, three minutes tops, to exchange numbers with the hot guy a lane over in the black truck.

She couldn't do that could she?

"Yeah, it's really moving now," she said, unblinking, biting her lips. Still her foot hovered over the accelerator, but she couldn't bear to push down on it yet. *Say something. Ask for his number.*

It was crazy. She was downright silly to think of getting a guy's number in the middle of the road. But, that's exactly what she was contemplating doing.

Just as soon as she figured out how.

The guy pulled forward and Julie rolled alongside him. "Um..."

His gaze flickered between her and the road, but he was still smiling, which was a good sign. "Is everything okay?" he asked, all sparkly eyes and teeth glittering at her.

"I, uh...I was hoping to get your phone—"

At that exact moment, her phone rang on bluetooth, echoing through the car and drowning out her exchange with hot truck guy. Julie winced and checked the dash to see Liz's name and number scroll across the screen in neon blue. Without thinking, she pressed the phone icon to connect the call.

"Hold on a sec, Liz." Julie whipped her gaze back out the window, but he was gone.

She had taken her gaze off of him for a quick second, but that was just enough time for her to see the black truck drive through the intersection.

"You still there, Jules?" Liz's raspy voice bounced off the windshield.

Julie slowly pulled forward to make her right turn toward the restaurant as she watched the black truck disappear into the distance. "I'm here," she said flatly.

"It sounds like you're in a wind tunnel. Are you coming or what because I'm getting hungry? You know I'll start without you."

She slouched down into the seat with her chin low and allowed her foot to rest on the gas. "I'm pulling into a spot now."

CHAPTER 2

J ulie looked up to see the tail end of Liz's eyes rolling. "What?" Julie asked, her brows twisting into a grimace.

"Did you hear anything I've been saying?" Liz snapped, her cinnamon skin flushed from a mix of hundred-degree heat, and apparently anger.

"Um…"

"Exactly. That's what I'm talking about. You don't listen. Part one of the plan is to see who else is out there. You know, like a 'whole sea of fish,' or however the saying goes." Liz's hands flew up into widespread dramatic air quotes.

As much as Julie wanted to ignore her friend's advice, she couldn't brush it off right away. If this breakup was for real, Patrick might not ever come to his senses. In which case, why was she sitting around waiting for him, or planning to show up on his doorstep?

To say what? Hi? Was she really going to be sitting around waiting for him?

The more she thought about it, the more she thought about the digs he'd thrown. And in turn, the more incensed Julie became. Plus, if there were men out there like hot truck guy, casting her line for the other fish might not be so bad.

Liz snapped her index finger and thumb directly next to Julie's ear. "Before you go crawling back to that hijo de la gran madre," Liz said with a litany of Rs rolling from her tongue, "I want you to remember what he *did* and what he called you. Don't you have any kind of pride?"

That was easy for Liz to say. She had a gorgeous boyfriend who was dying to marry her and make a shitload of cute little Puerto Rican and black babies, and she was holding him at bay. In the last couple of months, no one had been beating down Julie's door. So, no, Julie didn't have much...well...maybe she did have an inkling of pride left.

More than anything, Julie hated how she only seemed to remember the good times. Patrick *had* walked out on her, and she was willing to take him back without so much as an apology. What did that say about her?

Boring. Sick. Tired.

The words rolled through her mind on an endless loop since the night they broke up.

"All I'm saying, Jules, is that you can't lay around all day watching romance movies on Netflix and ordering from UberEats. You look better *today* but it's going to take more than a new outfit and YouTube tutorials on contouring and brow-shaping to boost your fragile little ego."

"I know," she snapped back, those three toxic words infecting her. *Boring. Sick. Tired.* "What the hell do you want me to do, Liz? Do you think I like this whole pity party thing I've got going on? No, I don't. But right now, a new dress makes me feel pretty, okay.

And yes, I've been eating my feelings. Guess what? As soon as that waitress drags her ass over here, I'm going to order a stack of buttery, fatty, *carby* pancakes and scarf them down like a totally boring, slob lard." Julie expelled a haughty breath and cranked her neck back, her crown of natural chestnut curls springing to life over her silken brown skin.

It was a mouthful, but Julie had to yell to keep from crying.

"Speaking of which…that dress though. Yass," Liz said, dialing back her harsh criticism. She must have known that she was teetering on that edge between being a mirror and just being a plain old bitch. "I don't know if I could pull off orange, but you are wearing it, girl." She gave an appreciative smirk, batting her lashes, which was basically a plea for forgiveness of her brutal honesty.

"Uh huh." Julie pursed her lips, pushing her cheekbones high off their perch.

"I'm just saying that you're hot. I can't wait 'til *you* remember that."

Julie lowered her gaze and Liz continued despite her friend's bruised ego. "You have curves and flawless caramel skin. You're lucky enough to have ass *and* boobs. And don't even get me started on your eyes. What real person that you know has fucking flecks of gold in their eyes?" Liz's brows wrinkled as if such a notion was unfathomable.

"Every guy in this place…shit, every guy who has walked by in the past twenty minutes has taken a double-take," she continued. "So the hell what if you have a few extra pounds, get over it. We can get you in shape, but his ass does not deserve you, and you don't deserve to feel like your life is over just because he isn't in it anymore."

"Okay, okay." Julie scanned the crowd. Liz was loud and her tone tended to border on aggressive.

"It's not okay," Liz chided her. "Snap out of it. Shit."

Her eyes bulged and her hands shook in agitation, but Julie was the one who felt small.

"I need a drink. *You* need a drink," she said.

Julie giggled at how fast their little chat had gone form zero to sixty in two seconds flat. Hell, she *could* use a drink.

Liz raised her quarter-full glass to Julie. "To my beautiful best friend. May she find a man who is well-endowed..." she paused, and Julie reveled in the depths of Liz's perverted mind. "With a sexy, nerdy brain to turn her on. Let him have a body made for sin and a heart up to the task of caring for hers."

From your mouth to God's ears.

Julie stifled the urge to say amen as she clinked her empty glass since a waitress had yet to pass. It was evident that she needed help from a higher power. Maybe there was someone else out there. If her luck hadn't run out, maybe God could make traffic spark twice.

What was the other part?" Julie asked.

"Huh?"

"Well, you said the first part was to start checking out the rest of the fish in the sea. So? What's the second part?"

Leaning her head back, Liz wrapped both hands around her hair and twisted it up into a huge messy bun with loose tendrils hanging on the sides. "If you decide to put on your big girl panties, Derrick might still hook you up with his hot ass friend."

"Speaking of which..." Julie trailed off.

Liz halted her glass halfway to her lips. "Excuse me? Don't tell me you've been holding out."

A mischievous grin pulled at the corners of Julie's mouth. "If you want to hook me up with someone, find the guy I saw in traffic on the way here. I would easily drop my big girl panties for him."

"Nope. Nope." Liz closed her eyes and shook her head like she was giving testimony at church with one hand raised for praise. "Start at the beginning and don't leave anything out."

Julie recounted every detail from the instant the second cop sped by and she noticed hot truck guy all the way until he drove off into the proverbial sunset. All the while, Liz did not blink nor close her mouth.

"Girl..." the word dragged out and lingered on her tongue. "Damn. That's some kismet type shit."

"Right?"

"So what are you going to do?"

"What do you mean, what I am going to do? I didn't get his number. That's it. The moment has passed." Julie threw her hands up in the air and let them fall to her lap.

"Did you get his license plate?"

The question was logical, although kind of creepy. Julie wasn't exactly in detective mode at the moment. She'd been too hung up on the fact that their paths had crossed at all and the weighted feeling that she'd never see him again. But now, the simplicity of such a suggestion, made her feel like an idiot for not thinking of it herself.

"Uh, no. I was too busy answering your call, Miss impatient." *Duh.*

"Damn. We have to do something."

A sputtered laugh escaped Julie's mouth. "Okay Sherlock, we've got no clues. No plate. No name. All we know is that he's hot and he drives a black pickup with all the bells and whistles."

"I've got ways," Liz said, fingering her brow, staring into space with a narrowed gaze.

"Then, by all means. Please find my dream guy."

A middle-aged waitress with lavender hair and precision-lined red lips approached as if to save Julie from her best friend's relentless digging and deducing.

"Hi there, honey. I'm Jo and I'll be taking care of you today," she said in a deep baritone.

This woman was fierce with style for days. In this day and age, Julie had just about seen and heard everything, but for some reason, she wasn't expecting that voice on this woman. The way she embraced her uniqueness was awesome, but the Southern twang threw her for a loop. More than anything, it surprised her.

"You're going to have to drink these two down fast if you want to catch up with this one," she offered as she placed one mimosa in front of Liz and two more brimming flutes in front of Julie. "Can I get you anything else?"

In her large hand, a pencil lay perched at the ready to jot down their order.

"I'll take the short stack with a side of eggs over easy…and the—"

"Shit. I'm so sorry, honey. I didn't realize. Should I bring out two virgins instead?"

Julie looked up for the first time into the waitress' cool blue eyes. They were centered on her and overflowing with worry.

Liz and Julie eyed each other. They'd come to know each other on an organic level. Without a word shared between them, a look would communicate anything from emotion to full-on instructions. Now, their furrowed brows and pursed lips let on that they were both confused and borderline annoyed.

"I'm sorry?" Julie returned her gaze to the waitress, her brow pinched in bafflement.

"How far along are you, sweetheart?" She nodded her head toward Julie's stomach.

Not long after Patrick gave up on her, Julie gave up on the gym. In between her movies and food and crying, she hadn't found the time to lift a finger, let alone a weight, or leg, or her butt up off the couch.

She looked down now at her stomach. Not that it would've made a major difference, but she'd forgotten to put on Spanx and now her pooch curdled up into a round bagel formation beneath her fitted dress.

Julie felt the blood rush to her cheeks and the familiar sting at the corners of her eyes. "Not far enough," she muttered under her breath.

Before the damn waitress could say another word to show off her lack of home training, Liz took charge and wrapped the side-winding conversation up. "Thanks *honey*, we're good here." The words were pleasant, but the tone was way more vinegar than honey.

But the purple-haired Southern Belle didn't take the hint. She stood with her big feet rooted in front of her with a blank expression, the wheels still making their way around the empty space upstairs. Then the recognition pulled her eyes wide and her lips into a full-circle O.

Her eyes bulged as she sucked in the thick air between them. "Oh shit, I've gone and done it again. I have a horrible habit of sticking my foot in my mouth. You're not pregnant, are you?" she asked, all doe-eyed and innocent. She was looking down at them over the bridge of her nose, which only in that moment did Julie realize was crooked as a wayward tree branch.

Julie simply shook her head and pulled the coral blue cloth napkin above her protruding waistline. It wasn't hard to tell that the waitress didn't have ill intentions, but the words hurt worse than sticks and stones. *Because they're true.*

Perfect. Why not crush the rest of the small amount of dignity I have left?

The waitress cowered, shoulders slouched and her eyes locked on her notepad. "I'm going to go. Just let me know if you need anything. I'm truly sorry, I am."

Julie and Liz watched as she beelined across the patio and slinked behind the bar.

Liz reached over the table and set her hand on Julie's. "Jules," she looked her dead in the eyes as if she might say something profound. Not one to disappoint, she finished her sentence with a statement that only she could say and have it mean as much as a tidbit from Oprah. "People are assholes. They don't know when to shut their fucking mouths."

At the slight lift and fall of Julie's shoulders as laughter rumbled through her, she fell back against her chair and jolted up again almost instantly. "Well...it was going to be bad either way. Shit, you would've had way more problems than a few insignificant pounds if Patrick had knocked you up."

She had to give it to her girl, the woman had a way of putting everything out there on the table. She was right of course, but Julie's ego wasn't any less bruised.

"Shit...you're not, are you?"

Julie hurled her napkin straight for her face. "Bitch!"

Liz was her most crass and unfiltered, wild friend—and her best friend, for those same reasons. When the shit hit the fan, she had her back with love, and a much-needed dash of cynicism to keep it real.

"So...that happened," Liz continued. She pressed at a few flyaway hairs and exhaled like the world was on *her* shoulders. She gulped down the rest of her third or fourth mimosa. "Well, fuck." She sighed. "I guess we both know what the second part of the plan is, now."

"Detox? No, no...that apple cider vinegar diet?"

"No, dunce. Revenge body."

CHAPTER 3

Is that what I want? Revenge?

Yes, she wanted Patrick to end up fat and ugly in a group home for jerks, but that was highly unlikely based on his sharp jaw and cheekbones alone. Revenge wasn't it, but the prospect of him seeing the made-over, poised, put-together version of her with a sexy sleek body? It did sort of ring a bell.

"So you want me to lose weight to win Patrick back?"

Liz deadpanned. "Um, no." She slowly lowered her eyes to her phone and pressed her forefinger onto the widget to unlock the screen. Her Instagram feed came into view with a stream of before-and-after pictures of women who were anything other than stick figures.

"See? Real men love curves. You're never going to be one of those anorexic twigs, so wrap your mind around that first. I don't know why you would want to be, anyway, but, if you're going to find someone better than that asswipe—someone like truck guy— you're going to have to chisel it up a bit. Sooo...you're going to the gym."

She flicked her fallen tresses from one shoulder to the other, unleashing a massive bale of curls—a clear indication she was serious.

Before Julie could get a word in edgewise to agree or disagree, Liz halted her with that same pointed forefinger. "And not that little rinky-dink hole in the wall you go to, either."

As it turned out, Julie's gym *was* a hole in the wall. At least compared to Beast Body.

Wide-eyed and intimidated, Julie scanned the crowd the following Sunday. She had never seen anything like it. There was nothing calm, or quaint about it. She was surrounded on all sides by raw black concrete walls with five huge cement pillars holding up a matching exposed ductwork ceiling. A three lane crimson astro-turf track circled massive yellow machines and fitness equipment.

The place was like a dream set for the making of the next P90z fitness video. *Really, why stop at X or Insanity when this pit had every-thing to help you break a sweat? Or, a bone for that matter?*

What sort of threw her off though, was the enormous juice bar front and center with glittering lights and a cornucopia of exotic fruit.

She got the whole industrial metal meets asphalt, but the shimmer meets shine part of it didn't exactly mesh. Must have been an appeal to both the Olympic athlete *and* the yoga mom. If there were a Starbucks and a place to purchase Lululemon, people would practically be giving away their money—keep the change.

Talk about gymtimidation.

Julie sidestepped away from the door to let a chiseled Greek statue with teensy spandex shorts enter. Of course, he didn't even seem to notice her. Why would he? She fit in at this sort of gym like a pair of boots at the beach.

Talk about crossing a threshold into unchartered territory.

No doubt about it, this was nothing like her "hole in the wall." This *place* was a *crater* in the wall.

She was used to the unpretentious muted pastels of her lavender-scented circuit gym with regular weights, tension bands, and calming music.

Here, it smelled like a gym. A thick musty sock stench went hand and hand with its rough dark décor. The fruity sweet aroma from the juice bar was like perfume trying to mask the smell of cigarette smoke. It ended up only filling the air with the stench of musty fruit.

Drawing her arms into herself, Julie searched for signs of Liz's perky ponytail swaying among the sea of Baywatch beauties on the ellipticals and treadmills. One foot in front of the other, she stepped away from the door.

She scanned the room, finding a landmine of judgmental eyes. Each pair attached to an InstaFit body. In her own threadbare heather gray sweatpants and stained Regions West Bank T-shirt, she was definitely out of her element.

She was still inching around the corners of her mind trying to recall the source of the stain when Liz walked up behind her, giving her a start.

"Hey," Liz said, out of breath and chipper as ever. "This is going to be *so* awesome," she exclaimed, way too excited for Julie's current under-enthused state of mind.

They were standing in the middle of an aisle, flanked on either side by serious machinery, manned by the athletic highbrow elite of millennials. Julie's gaze traveled from them back to Liz, her brow pinched and her shoulders sunken.

What am I doing here?

No sooner did Liz point out the human statue who would be training Julie did she disappear.

Way to have my back, Liz.

She watched as her friend abandoned her to go to the juice bar where Derrick was waiting for her. They practically burst into giggles, as if this was some kind of laughing matter. Liz hadn't even given her the rundown on this Dane.

She eyed him sheepishly now. "So..." Julie said, her hands clasped behind her back. She swayed from foot to foot, in the hope that Dane would fill in the awkward silence.

"Let's get some measurements." His voice thundered as he placed his clipboard on the mat near his feet and pulled a bright yellow measuring tape from his gym bag. "You're going to need to lose that shirt. I can't get accurate measurements with that thing on," he commanded, a touchy edge in his tone.

She was new to whatever it was he was about to put her through. At her gym, people smiled and greeted each other. They were friendly. This was the first time they were meeting, so how could he be annoyed with her already?

As if she was just supposed to know to start stripping down in the middle of the gym. What if she hadn't been wearing a sports bra? What would he have said then?

For a second too long, Julie stared at him wide-eyed, afraid of what he would say once he saw her in the flesh, unfiltered. But, he hadn't even glanced back at her once. This was no big deal to him. If he really did whip people into shape, he must have seen bigger asses and flabbier pooches all the time.

Julie dug down deep in her gut and found the last ounce of gumption she had left. Slow and labored, she contorted one arm at a time to slip them from the sleeves before inching the stretched cotton fabric over her head. Julie quickly glanced around the room while she patted her flyaway hairs back into place, and no one seemed to notice. *Thank goodness.*

She returned her gaze to Dane who showed no signs of the severely repulsed look she imagined would be waiting for her.

In fact, the idea that everyone else was unfazed spread through her like contagion. Julie exhaled and stood that much taller. A sneaky little smile crept its way onto her face. For a moment, she felt good. Damn good to be standing in a den of skinny minis and she was somehow holding her own.

She had an urge to tell Dane so, too. Then, he picked up his neon yellow tape from the mat and measured her arms and waist first without so much as a word. It wasn't until he lassoed it around her bovine thighs that her fight or flight instincts began to kick in.

The numbers rolled off his rough tongue in foghorn barks.

Twenty-seven inches, he'd said in slow motion. "Two seven," he repeated, his voice a robotic instant replay.

It didn't seem so bad.

At least not to garner the disapproving look that finally met her gaze. And it *wasn't* so bad, until he guided her eyes downward. The measurement was for *one* thigh. The same, no *more* than, the waist measurements of the little size twos in the place.

Sure, she was about five foot seven and a half inches—five eight according to her driver's license—but twenty-seven inches was big even for her.

Julie swallowed hard as heat swept up the back of her neck and around to her ears and cheeks. This couldn't be happening. Her rushed breathing and tightening chest alarmed her, but it was the lightheadedness that sent her into overdrive.

She didn't know whether to lash out at him or break down, but she couldn't do it here. Not in this place. Her gaze darted around the room in search of an exit as the choking sensation wrapped her throat in a death grip. To keep her hands from shaking, she clenched and unclenched them into and out of fists.

She wanted to run and hide.

About the only thing that gave her pause was the fact that Dane hadn't moved an inch. He just stood there in front of her with his tape in hand. He waited, as if he'd experienced the kind of self-discovery process Julie was undergoing too many times to validate it with another step.

Dane might as well have wound his thick index finger in the air and told her to wrap it up because she was wasting his time.

Her nostrils flared as she exhaled the steam that was building up inside her.

She could run. But, that was what she'd done—what she had

been doing. When her dad passed away, she couldn't bear to stay at home with her mom and the flimsy walls that couldn't keep a secret. So, she'd moved into her own place where she could be alone. When things with Patrick ended, she'd hidden herself away from every-thing and everyone. And that's how she'd gotten here—by herself, buried inside a body she barely recognized.

Her left brow lifted in response and she sucked her teeth. With a narrow unwavering gaze, Julie allowed her shirt to fall to the floor as she crossed her arms over her chest, defiantly. She planted her feet wide apart. The rims of her eyes stung with stifled frustration.

God she could just scream, she was so angry. Still, she wouldn't let another man break her.

"Good."

It was a single syllable, but it could have been a match because it lit her nerves on fire the way it boomeranged her back into focus. She shot him a deadpan look, thinking about how *good* it would feel to give him a *good* right hook to the jaw, right about now.

"Excuse me?" Distaste lingered on her tongue.

"I said, good." He stood within an inch of her face. "Good. That's the response I want. I want you to be pissed off. Angry. I want you to want to kick your own ass."

What kind of drill sergeant reverse psychology bullshit is that?

A few speckles of spit landed on Julie's cheek, but she refused to move out of range for fear of what he might do next.

Oh, trust me Sarge. You don't want to see me pissed off.

"It's time for you to stop looking dazed with that weepy little look and get fed up. I want you to be angry enough with yourself to *do* something about it," he preached, and she was just about ready to say Amen.

But, was she ready to *do* something about it?

She inhaled and felt her chest stiffen, and in that moment she could have been The Hulk. She hadn't even started the workout, but she was sweating. Her pulse sped up and her teeth ground over each other. Deep below the layers of self-loathing and world-shaking aftershocks from her breakup with Patrick, her muscles began to quiver at the possibility of *doing* something.

With his calloused pinky finger, he lifted her chin. "Are you ready?"

He was talking about fitness and health, but he might as well have asked if she was ready to kick her sadistic habits.

Yes. On the inside, she was screaming, "yes" to the top of her lungs. On the outside, Julie must have nodded or given some gesture of consent because from that point on, she was metaphorically and literally kicking her own ass.

First she kicked it with squats and lunges and way too many burpees. Then, she kicked it on the elliptical. When she was done sweating out her insides, she literally kicked her own ass with alternating sets of high-knees and butt-kickers.

"You mad yet?" Dane taunted a little over half way through her workout. He crouched down near her left ear while she prayed her twitching muscles wouldn't give out on the last sixty-second plank.

"Tired," was all she could manage. She was out of oxygen, patience, and excuses.

Sick. Tired. Boring.

"Yes! Good and tired." He let out a wicked laugh. "I hope you get tired at the sight of those Ho-Hos and Twinkies I know you've got stashed at the back of the pantry. If it's not that, I know you have a sugary latte frappucino daily, heavy on the drizzle. Get tired of that."

Grande iced caramel macchiato espresso with whipped cream, heavy on the drizzle.

In that moment, Julie knew this was fun for him. He enjoyed torturing his clients—no, his victims. And it boiled Julie's blood.

In that moment, it was Patrick's sweaty, drunken face that she saw glaring back at her.

"I hate you," she breathed.

Patrick's face blurred back into Dane's, and he smiled back at her apparently satisfied with her reaction.

"This is how you crack the whip?" Julie questioned, her voice labored and shallow.

"I don't crack whips, I crack the mold, honey. The one that's got your beautiful body trapped beneath it. That's what I'm doing, sweetheart." His voice was strong and definitive, as if there were no question about his purpose. He spoke with a conviction that made Julie wonder why she'd had any doubt at all.

Although, the words *honey* and *sweetheart* felt as condescending as if he'd called her "little lady," as far as she was concerned. She was about as far from a "little lady" as she could be, and she definitely wasn't his sweetheart.

Julie craned her neck up at Dane from the middle of her scissor set, intent on dispelling any notions of her being weak-willed—whether she still felt like it or not—but he was mid-wave, calling someone over.

Given the fact that her muscles were crying for relief, she granted herself a much needed breathing break, allowing her legs to flop down onto the mat.

"Oh no, you don't. You've got two more sets before you get up." Dane pressed Julie back into her divot. "We're done when we're done."

The twists of his disapproving frown unwound as the heavy footsteps grew closer. "Look who it is..." Dane announced. "What are you pressing these days? A ton, maybe two?" he guffawed.

A deep-gutted roar joined in with his, successfully drowning out all other sound in the room.

"Seriously, though. From here, sounded like you were moving mountains with all that grunting and growling you were doing. Is that how they do it back East?"

Julie stretched for a better line of vision of the guy, who was behind Dane, but from her position on the floor, she couldn't really tell what he looked like since he was upside down. Plus, with Dane's big calf in the way, she couldn't get a full glimpse of the guy's face. All she could see was a head full of dark wavy hair and a black T-shirt with blaring red stripes and a goofy-looking elephant logo on the breast pocket.

That, and the fact that he was tall, given how far she had to crane her neck just to see his hair.

"Dane, I'm just trying to get on your level, man." A loud slap landed on Dane's body and Julie felt the vibration travel down his legs to his ankles where she was still holding on. The second she let go, Dane moved from his spot and turned toward his friend.

The guy's voice was low and filled with bass, in the sexiest way— the kind of deep rumble that settled low and tight in her belly. *It can't be.*

At the prospect that her luck had struck gold twice, the juncture between her thighs gave a hardy squeeze, throbbing at the same erratic beat as her heart. She stretched her neck passed Dane's foot. Still no decent view.

Move Dane.

The guy's voice thundered again, and again Julie's insides did acrobatic flips. It had to be him.

If it's him, I owe you big time God.

As the two men fell into a bromantic embrace, full of pecs and biceps and way too much testosterone, the smoke and mirrors faded and finally she got a glimpse of the guy's eyes over Dane's shoulder.

They were the same molten brown *come-hither* eyes and they were masterfully attached to hot truck guy.

CHAPTER 4

Julie exhaled a breath she hadn't been aware she was holding. Open-mouthed she ogled her Superman Khal Drogo hybrid—Super Drogo. Mesmerized by the ruffle of lashes fanning down at her in slow motion, she sighed. The man was gorgeous.

Hello again.

It was hard to pinpoint exactly what she was feeling, but if her dry mouth and sluggish heartbeat were any clues, she had to be dreaming. Time stood still and as Julie licked her lips and rested her teeth on her bottom lip, she realized that she didn't mind one bit. She was entranced as her gaze traveled down to his pouty, delicious mouth. *Yummy.*

There went her adult words again.

He stared at her for what seemed like forever taking her under his spell. That head full of dark wavy curls and angel eyes. The panty-dropper smile that tugged at the corner of his mouth. But the second he unleashed that twinkling toothy grin, she freeze-framed him again. The sexy image of him locked in her vault.

Then, it was just the two of them and his lashes again.

"How long do we have you this time?" Dane's thunderous voice broke the spell and hot truck guy tore his gaze away.

Luckily, since she wasn't sure how much she could handle of Super Drogo all at once.

Dane's voice echoed with joy and something resembling pride. "I want to be ready with a net to catch that trail of broken hearts you leave behind," he said, but at that point, Julie was only half listening.

"Yeah. You know how I do," Super-Drogo boasted. And just like that, the record came to a screeching halt.

Ew. Trail of broken hearts? A net?

If she wasn't listening before, she was now. Both ears perked up toward their voices, hungry for a hint that she heard wrong.

As her gold strike of luck would have it, she hadn't misheard. The more they talked, the more she understood exactly what they were talking about. Flipping over all the pieces of their conversation and putting them together, she didn't like the picture they painted of this guy.

How many women did he have that he needed a net? And how many hearts had he broken? Furthermore, why was he content to brag about it?

Dammit. Hot truck guy was just another sleazy gym guy.

She rested on her back, flat against the mat with her upper lip curled in disgust. Her brow screwed low over her eyes. It figured. Five unguarded minutes was all it took to see what kind of manwhore he was. Just another basic fuckboy.

"Nah, man. I'm back. Sick and tired of all this back and forth, you know? I'm here for a while. Got a whole bunch of kids waiting on me."

And scene. That's my cue. Drawing the line at deadbeats, she'd be damned before she sat there and listened to this. *Enough!*

Julie leapt to her feet in a haughty pout, darting toward the exit. For the life of her, she couldn't figure whether she was more disgusted with this guy's nonchalance about the hoard of kids he'd conveniently left behind, or the fact that she'd, for even a second, thought this guy could be anything more than a handsome face.

Once outside, she sat in her car without turning on the ignition. As rain began to drizzle onto the hood of her car, she felt sick. Disgusted with herself, more than anything. She closed her eyes against the sting of angry tears and shook her head. She hated the void that in her heart. It pissed her off that she would give anything, everything for another second with her dad. What she wouldn't do to play video games with him, or let him win at Scrabble even though he always hid extra letter tiles under the scorepad. She missed the smell of Old Spice on his stubbly cheek and the way he always knew just the right thing to say when no one else did.

How could this guy be so cavalier about kids when she had no dad?

Julie knew what a father's absence did to people. What it did to her. She knew how it felt to be a pebble left behind in that trail of broken hearts.

Deceased was completely different than absentee, but the void was all the same. Those kids were missing a piece of themselves.

She swallowed back the lump in her throat, blinking away the tears threatening to fall.

"Julie?" a muffled voice thundered at the driver side window.

Her heart nearly jumped from her chest as she jolted away from the blurry glass. A loud thump struck the window when a large hand pressed against it and wiped side to side.

"It's Nico. I'm friends with Dane." He offered. *Nico.*

She didn't recognize him at first, but the garish red stripes on his shirt flashed at her like a beacon with that stupid elephant logo. But, then she raised her eyes.

And there was the full picture. More than the pair of dreamy, chocolaty eyes she'd seen over Dane's shoulder. The ones that immobilized her in the middle of traffic. This was him, up close and personal. And he had a name. Nico.

She was mad at him, though. What kind of person left their kids on purpose? Not that she knew the circumstances, but Julie couldn't imagine a good excuse.

"Nico?" she tasted his name on her tongue. It was as delicious as the watery silhouette before her. *Stop it. You hate him.*

Down to her bones, she knew this guy was a Grade A jerk, but that didn't stop her from getting lost in the smoke and mirrors.

His face was a watercolor masterpiece of angular lines in brown and gold, softened by the rain. Through the streaks in the glass she took in the beautiful olive undertones of his warm tawny skin. A strong square jaw with light stubble and a Roman nose rounded out the symmetry. Then there was his mouth. That pair of full delectable juicy lips made him irresistible.

As if that weren't enough, Nico parted them to reveal a set of gleaming white teeth with a slight overbite that was sexy as hell, the way it sort of pushed his bottom lip out into a pucker.

Temporary insanity is what it was. What kind of crazy did it take for her to go from loathing this man to lusting after him in six seconds flat?

"Hey, are you all right in there?" His voice reverberated against the glass.

Given her current state of mind, she couldn't be sure, but it sounded like genuine concern laced his words. *The audacity. You're not a nice person.*

Even still, she couldn't deny that he was nice looking. She couldn't get past the fact that every word came in slow motion with sprays of water *splishing* and *splashing* off his taut muscles.

Julie licked her bottom lip and a fiery shiver blazed down her spine and settled between her thighs. Her pulse quickened and her toes curled inside her shoes.

For a moment, as she eyed his full lips and the sexy way his hair dripped at the temple, she had to remind herself that this wasn't some elaborate shower fantasy. This was the loser who had just bragged about his conquests, who had actually gotten a pat on the back for breaking hearts.

She didn't even know this guy, but she was determined to hate him. Not just on principle. The guy had broken hearts without the courtesy of sweeping up the shards. He left a trail in his wake for the next guy to pick up the pieces the same way Patrick had done. It wasn't the same, but her dad had left those pieces for Julie and her mom to pick up.

Whether she was armed for it, a war raged between her body and mind. No matter how hot he was, or how her body responded to him, she couldn't excuse that.

Julie pressed the button on her door panel to crack the window and a whip of crisp wet wind lashed across her cheek. "I'm fine. What do you want?" Her voice rang with a bravado she didn't feel.

"You—"

"I what? I walked out? So what. Who are you, the gym police? Did Dane send you out here because I didn't finish my session?" She laughed. "You've got to be kidding me."

"I was just going to tell you that—"

"It wasn't enough for you guys to stand there, right in front of me. Like I wasn't even there. Talking about—"

His large hand slapped the glass again and she stopped mid-sentence, her mouth gaping. "I don't know what your problem is, but I just came out here to give you your shirt. You left it inside," he said.

Julie's gaze flickered toward his hands where he was holding her rain-spattered t-shirt. She swallowed, but couldn't get past the lump in her throat.

He stared at her for a long moment before continuing. "Good luck with all that...whatever it is you're doing in there," he said as he pushed the shirt into the car, gave her a final look and walked away.

The second he left, Julie beat her hand against the steering wheel and screamed at the top of her lungs. Her mind clouded with an oily black haze. She was turning into a raving lunatic. And over what? A hot guy and a few extra pounds? Dane's taunting?

It couldn't really be what hot truck guy had said. Correction, what sleazy gym guy said.

"Don't cry," she ordered herself as her foot tapped incessantly against the floor panel. "Dammit. Don't cry."

She'd run out of the gym and didn't exactly know what she was running from. This wasn't about what some stupid jerk had said and she knew it. What did she care about this guy and his women and his kids? Nothing.

This was about her. How somehow she'd managed to construct an image and a persona out of a clear as day stranger. She didn't know him from Adam and here she was building fantasies around him. Around the man *she* wanted him to be.

Patrick's words sounded in her ears. *Sick. Tired.*

Julie was sick and tired, too. She'd built this guy up. Fantasized about him and his black pickup. It just seemed wrong to be proven wrong. *What a let down.*

She wiped at a determined tear now as it spilled down her cheek. Frustration bubbled into an anger that boiled inside her. It grated on her nerves as shallow breaths forged into panic. Her eyes stung at the welling tears and she dug her fingernails into the seat.

The windows glazed over as the drizzle outside came down harder, spattering raindrops over the roof of the car.

In the window crack, her damp gray shirt hung on the glass, stretching with the weight of the rain. Inch by inch, it slid through over the pane until she held it with both hands. But all she could see was wet eyelashes.

CHAPTER 5

S ometime between the moment when the hills began to blend together and the falling sun met the earth, a horn blared from behind Julie. She looked up to find herself dazing through a green light.

Damn. The detergent.

She either did a load tonight, or it would be bikini bottoms to work in the morning.

As she turned into the Walmart parking lot and slipped back into her damp shirt, it was still Nico who starred in her thoughts. Her mind had drifted from Patrick to her flab to the pile of laundry waiting for her back at home, before landing squarely on Nico.

Her mind was still reluctant to dismiss the man who'd pulled beside her in his big black truck and politely, but forcibly stolen her attention.

Even as she found her way to the far back corner of the store near the disposable plates and utensils, she couldn't get past the idea that she'd so misread him. *What is it with this guy?* She wondered as she finally reached the laundry aisle.

Deadbeat hottie couldn't be the whole story.

Detergent and fabric softener in zip bags and bottles climbed the shelves in bright oranges and greens. Absentmindedly, Julie lifted herself up onto her tiptoes and reached above the major name brand ones. She grabbed the free and clear liquid in a seventy-five ounce pink jug. The mountain fresh tropical flowerburst one had left a cluster of hives all over her body the last time. Now, she was strictly dye and perfume free baby detergent.

As Julie pulled it down, she knocked over a row of fabric softener on the shelf below. Righting them on the shelf, she shook her head deep in thought. Nico's smile was sexy as hell, but it was also kind. Like he'd be humble and gentle. He looked like the kind of guy who'd have a library card in his wallet and a good credit score. Likely a dog guy with a soft spot for a lazy snuggly cat.

And his truck? It wasn't showy with flashy rims even though it looked expensive. Deep down, she figured he had it for noble, neighborly reasons. You know, in case he might need to help a friend move, or because he worked for Habitat for Humanity in the summer and they hauled big loads.

He was supposed to be a *nice* hot guy. Not manwhore of the year. *Ugh.*

With everything neatly back on the shelf, Julie turned on her heels and started toward the end of the aisle.

"Is that you, Julie Laurich?" a nasally voice called.

Keep walking. You look like shit.

For the second time that day, her name had been called with a question mark hinged on the straggly end. Her gut urged her to keep on marching. It never failed that when she looked and felt her worst, she'd run into someone she knew.

Plus, this was an in-and-out trip. No basket, she reminded herself.

Still, curiosity won.

Julie pivoted in the direction of the strained familiar voice. Celeste Waltman. *I should have kept walking.*

Except, Celeste wasn't *just* someone she knew. At one point, Julie had called her a friend.

They had worked together as tellers, but were fast friends—probably *too* fast, when she really thought about it. Almost overnight, they were texting and calling and hanging out together on weekends. Pretty soon, Julie's friends became Celeste's friends, since she was new to Vegas and didn't know anyone. Road trips turned into weekend getaways and quick flights to San Diego and L.A. The two were inseparable, sharing clothes and makeup and money. Besties. Friends.

"Oh. Shit, I didn't know who you were," Julie said, pressing her free hand to her chest. She was far from relieved though.

Their friendship was fine. Until Julie began to notice that her buddy had turned into her mirror image.

It hadn't bothered her the first time. When she decided to chop off her locks and dye her hair black, Celeste turned up the next day with the exact same raven-hued bob.

The matching manicures and purses caught her attention, but still not enough to be worried. Not until the chiseled guy who bagged groceries at the supermarket next door to their branch showed interest in Julie. A little less than a week later, Celeste hooked up with him, and the clues slowly began to add up.

After inching away day-by-day, making excuses why they couldn't hang out, and "missing" Celeste's calls, the distance finally felt wide enough for Julie to slip away unnoticed.

"Hey, I thought that was you, but I couldn't tell from the back." Celeste tilted her head, her gaze stalling at Julie's thighs before a phony smile stretched the loose skin around her mouth into pronounced parentheses.

Julie only knew it was phony because they'd laughed together once back at the bank about telephone voices and customer-facing smiles which they plastered on to get good service reviews.

Celeste had demonstrated hers, complete with unblinking sparkly eyes, a tight smile, in which she bared only her top row of teeth, and a bubbly high-pitched send-off when she'd finished their transaction. At the time, Julie had called it her Stepford wife face because it was so robotic. A real *Invasion-of-the-Bodysnatchers* type habit.

The irony was not lost on Julie that at this low point she'd run into the one person who had literally tried to be her.

She stood before this not so strange stranger, a bottle of baby detergent weighing down her arm, broken-hearted, out of shape, and underdressed easily by comparison to Celeste.

There she was—tired with messy hair, in frumpy clothes that highlighted her perfect pear shape. And, she was pretty sure she reeked.

And then, there was Celeste.

Or was it? Long gone was the stringy-haired flat-chested plain Jane she used to know. Looking at Celeste's tight, unnaturally pulled skin, she'd obviously had a nip or tuck, or two. Everything was inflated, including her pouty red lips, and the boobs were definitely new. Had to be at least a D cup.

Julie stared in disbelief at the platinum blonde bone-straight strands flounced over her bronzed bare shoulders. Dizzying curves highlighted a cinched waist. A skin-tight white dress hugged her in all the right places.

Cute dress, too. But who gets all dolled up to grab paper cups and champagne from the grocery store?

Julie's brow creased slightly. "Hey—" she let the word drag, not wanting to seem too excited to see Celeste.

Somewhere deep down, the sight of this radiant long ago friend filled her with questions about winding roads and crossing paths. She and Celeste had met at a fork in the road and their paths hadn't crossed again until now, but to look at them, she wondered who had made the wrong turns. One of them was full of life in all its forms and the other was merely passing time in the wrong body.

They were both undoubtedly searching for flaws in the other. Celeste with her veiled digs, and Julie straining for a glimpse of the person she used to know beneath the expertly curated image.

"Oh my gosh. Are you...?" Celeste started.

You have got to be fucking kidding me.

Julie blinked. Then she blinked some more, but the ghost did not vanish. Just past the snowy strands tucked behind Celeste's left ear, he was coming right toward her. She spied him. With each step, she couldn't believe her shitty luck.

All sound ceased as he settled into his wide stride, heading toward her. On his lithe frame hung an expertly tailored black suit, in all its splendor. As always with Patrick, the devilishly opulent design was in the details. The diamond-encrusted cuff links and tie clip. The thin lacquered black leather belt and matching loafers. Ties and pocket squares that complemented his smoky eyes.

It figured—this new selectively adorned version of Celeste complemented his moneyed image.

Patrick wasn't good-looking by all standards, but he had that certain something. Ooh, she had a weakness for long lashes and dimples on a man, and Lord, this man had them in spades.

Before Patrick, she wasn't the biggest fan of facial moles on men, but he even made a discolored melanin pocket look good. Off to the left of his top lip, a small, perfectly round brown dot sat as a beacon of his masculine beauty.

It was barely noticeable, but at that exact moment, Julie's hands shook and her skin pulsed with a tingly numbness that spread all over until she couldn't move. Her stomach tied up in double knots. She was exposed and awkward and overwhelmed in the worst way. And, she looked like shit on a stick at the moment.

"Uh…" Julie panicked, looking for an out. She swallowed hard as her mouth dried into a cottony slur. "I've got to, um…go," she started.

"Julie, this is amazing," Celeste shrieked with far too much enthusiasm for someone who'd been given the slip.

Julie took a few steps back and when she'd nearly reached the end of the aisle, her feet planted to the ground. There was no fight or flight left in her. She could barely speak coherent sentences, let alone take accounting of her scarce arsenal of zingers for a fight.

And as much as she wanted to run, the sight of him after two months had just about disabled her motor skills. *I have to get out of here.*

"Honey, this is one of my oldest friends, Julie," Celeste purred.

Honey?

Heat trailed up to Julie's cheeks as she tried to steady her breathing. Palpitations drummed in her chest. She was shaking on the inside, breaking on the inside.

Celeste was who he had chosen and they were nothing alike, if not polar opposites. She could be a lot of things but she couldn't be superficial and flashy. It wasn't in her blood, which at the moment was boiling.

In that moment, Julie really looked at Celeste. All the changes she'd made. Changes likely at Patrick's request. She had changed for him, too.

Sick. Tired.

She had a mind to tell him all the things she'd planned to say before he beat her to the chase. She was going to ream him a new one. Tell him what a dickless coward he'd been—*was* being now, the way he just stood there without saying a word, quiet and still. A damn deer in headlights with his bugged eyes and clenched jaw.

Beads of sweat glistened on his pale forehead, a haunted expression pulling at the edges of his face as if he'd seen a ghost.

Yes, it's me. Grow some balls.

Julie shook her head in disbelief. He was liar, a cheat, and a bastard. He could barely look at her for more than two seconds before his chin dropped to his chest.

Then, his hand slipped into Celeste's. A simple, quiet gesture. The kind of thing people do out of habit. By the ease in which he'd done it, Julie could tell they'd been doing it long enough that they didn't even have to think about it.

Her eyes zoomed in, laser-focused on their clasped fingers. His slender and strong. Hers dainty, though fittingly tipped with acrylic claw-sharpened points. Blood red.

A knowing stare flickered from Celeste, back and forth from Julie to Patrick. She knew something. Julie didn't trust it. This coincidence was far too coincidental to be happenstance.

No one had luck *that* bad.

Julie lowered her gaze to their interlaced fingers again. It took every muscle in her body not to lunge toward them and unleash two months worth of wasted fury, but they were perfect for each other: an asshole and bitch.

Julie forced a thin smile, refusing to give him the reaction he likely craved.

She had prayed for a sign and here it was as clear as day. Patrick was not the man for her.

A stab of resentment pierced her. As pissed as she was, no as incensed as she was, seeing them together only hardened her heart. She thought it would hurt her more than anything, but it was just the opposite. All the frilly nostalgia and longing just wasn't there. It was hard even to be jealous when she was seething with anger.

She narrowed her eyes and slowly lifted her gaze.

As Celeste jabbered on making introductions and throwing in all flavors of exaggerations about their short-lived friendship, Julie was thinking about addiction and signs that let you know it's finally time to quit.

This same nicotine patch commercial for smokers would come on all the time asking the same questions over and again. *Has your smoking habit begun to control your life? Are you worried about your health? Have your friends and family and colleagues told you that your clothing, hair and breath smell? Are you always trying to hide your habit?* That's how you know it's time to quit, the bass-filled voice would say in the most grave of tones.

Yes. To all of the above, Julie admitted now.

For far too long, Patrick had been her addiction. He was controlling her life to the point she was starting to worry about her health. Liz had made it clear that she stunk from sitting in the house moping over him. For the past two months, she'd been hiding it. This was her breaking point. There was no other choice but to quit.

"We're not telling anyone, either," Celeste whispered and winked. With her right hand, she lifted what looked like non-alcoholic champagne, and cups. Then, she released her left hand from his and rubbed it over her belly in a way only women do when there's a joyous celebration about nine months off on the horizon.

While Julie should have been watching the smooth curve of Celeste's hand, she couldn't help but focus on the blinding emerald-cut solitaire perched on a very special finger.

Mother fucker.

CHAPTER 6

The following morning, Julie propped her phone on the bathroom counter and waited for Liz to pick up. *Please don't pick up.*

She wiped the foggy mirrors and laid out her makeup, still in bra and panties as she got ready for work.

The ringtone continued to echo loudly against the walls and shower stall glass. Julie prayed for voicemail, but as soon as she finished dotting her face with warm caramel foundation, she heard the click of the line pick up.

"Okay, okay. Before you kill me, let me tell you what happened," Julie blurted out. She stood there staring at her polka dot face, her hand squeezing the blending sponge.

"Let me guess..." Liz's voice crackled through the phone. "This has something to do with Patrick, right?" Her tone was accusatory and peppered with a combination of annoyance and morning grogginess.

"No...well, kind of," Julie began. She was going to tell Liz everything, but she didn't want to start with Patrick. Her eyes were still puffy from crying, but that wasn't anything her concealer couldn't handle.

Plus, she was trying not to focus on him.

For the next twenty minutes, she contoured and highlighted the curved angles of her face as she recounted Sunday's events post introduction to Dane. She started with a recap of her training session and moved on to her reaction to Dane and Nico's conversation. By the time she brought Liz up to speed on her outburst in the car, Julie hit quicksand.

She got stuck on Nico's description.

She told Liz at length about his style down to his clean sneakers. She spared no detail about each of his muscles and the way his wet, tacky clothes clung to them, which led Julie's dirty mind to the full physical description.

His face still hadn't escaped her mind yet, but talk of his dripping hair and those big honey-dipped brown eyes—oh, and that heroic full-teeth smile—had steamy images flooding in like a sexy tsunami.

Halfway through her thorough description of his lips, Julie made the mistake of calling him "hot truck guy."

"Wait what?" Liz interrupted her. "Hot truck guy is gym guy, and gym guy is Nico?"

"Yeah."

"So, Nico is hot truck guy?" she asked again. Although, Julie still couldn't figure out what exactly was so confusing. It was like Liz couldn't quite wrap her mind around the concept that all three people were one and the same.

Julie blew out a sigh, eager to get back on track with the conversation. She had to leave in the next twenty minutes. "Yes. What don't you get?"

"Nico is Derrick's friend," Liz exclaimed. "The one I was going to hook you up with. He's from Vegas but he was working on the East coast, and now he just moved back."

"Shut up." Julie just about poked her eye out with her black liner. So, while she and Liz were at the café arguing about whether to hook her up with hot truck guy or Derrick's friend, they were literally talking about the same person. That kind of stuff just didn't happen. Not to her.

"Yes." They were clearly on the same page with the universe conspiring to get Julie and Nico together. "That's some crazy shit, right?"

Crazy was right because all she could think of was what a cool meet cute story that would be to tell people when they asked how they'd met. Except for the teensy problem with him being a player and a deadbeat.

"It is, but it doesn't matter anyway. He's a dick," Julie said flatly, her heart sinking even as the words crossed her lips.

After a couple minutes of bargaining and reminding Liz that she had to leave for work in minutes, Julie finally convinced her to listen to the rest of the story—the part that included Patrick. Liz opened her ears and closed her mouth while Julie gave her the full Walmart rundown. In record time, without sparing any details, she got to the ring and the baby.

As soon as she finished though, all bets were off.

"Puta! Ugh, that bitch! That asshole!" Liz spat.

"Exactly. Apparently," Julie stated, picking up a black tube of lipstick and removing the top. She twisted up a rosy pink shade and glided it on, continuing, "this psycho breed has been creeping with Patrick long enough to get pregnant and engaged. Hell, they might be married already at the rate they're going. She's such a stalker. I know she knows we used to be together. You should've seen her with her platinum hair and this get-em-girl white club dress she had on."

A loud thud cracked through the phone amplified by the smooth granite countertop in Julie's bathroom.

"Liz, you still there?"

"I hate him. Ooh, I hate him," Liz scoffed. "I've always hated him. This is what I've been telling y—"

For all of five minutes, her BF had held it in, then there it was. The I-told-you-so Julie had been dreading. And Liz was pissed. More pissed than Julie thought she would be originally.

It both angered and filled her with prideful pleasure. As mad as she was at Liz for blaming her, having her best friend on her side fueled her with the red-hot adrenaline she needed to actually do something about it.

"So now, not only am I *boring*, but go ahead and add gullible, naïve fool to the list. Oh, and for good measure, why don't I turn into a full tub of lard while he marries a woman who *literally* tried to be me."

A gorgeous family man hitched to my bootleg knock-off. Awesome.

At that point, Liz and Julie yelled and roared over each other. Liz shrieked about some questionable—and frankly illegal—plan to wreak havoc on their tainted lives. Words like "karma" and "cursed" flew rapid-fire from her mouth.

Like most things, her pain had become about Liz.

She on the other hand, just wanted to give up. Call it quits. Move on. Put a wrap on her sorry excuse for a life. But at the rate Liz was going, she figured she had better get on board with Liz's hot-headed scheme or she'd end up on the receiving end as well.

"Oh, he wants to play it like that, does he? Oh, I've got something for his ass," Liz thundered.

Julie nodded along as she made her way to her closet.

"We can't just stand by and do nothing. He's pissed *me* off now, and I'm not just going to stand in the corner while he walks all over your heart." Liz took a small breath and kept going. "This is what we're going to do…"

For the next five or so minutes, Liz laid it all out for her. The gym, as far as she was concerned, was no longer optional. Instead of three or four times a week, Liz ramped it up to six sessions a week for Julie, with no cheat day.

Apparently, Liz wanted her revenge hot and fast before her patience wore thin.

Julie knew, from the phone in the palm of her hand, Liz had scheduled her hair to be clipped, colored, and styled. Liz had even gone so far as to squeeze in some kind of Brazilian wax job—which Julie had ironically mistaken for a whack job—the first time Liz had said it.

Aside from all of that, her best friend managed to include the brows, lashes, and nails. Honestly, it would be easier to scrap herself as a whole, and start all over again with the right blob of clay so Liz could mold into the fierce specimen she was going after.

The fun and games were over. This was clearly business now. *Or, was it personal?*

Julie had the nauseatingly disgusting privilege of hearing every gooey, smacking bite as Liz scarfed down her regular egg and cheese burrito. Still, with her mouth full, she continued doling out orders.

According to Liz's plan, by Friday, Julie would have already met with an esthetician, revamped her entire wardrobe, and brightened her townhouse with colors sexier than what Liz called the "boring beiges. She had considered them neutral and inviting before Liz debunked that theory. If she was going to make Patrick regret ever leaving her and find someone new, she wasn't going to do it living the same old gray...beige life.

It was a lot, but secretly Julie liked the idea of some kind of change taking place.

After accepting the calendar invites, Julie pulled one of her black blazers off a hanger and paired it with a bright orange blouse from the spot in the back designated for giveaways. She was pleased with herself for already embracing the new brighter, sexier Julie.

"Okay. I've got to wrap this up for now. I've got to get out of here, or I'm going to be late. You know how Elise watches the clock. I've got to beat her there—"

"Wait, wait, wait, wait, wait," Liz's words skidded hot and slick into the middle of Julie's goodbye.

She'd already made plans to change her body, home, and diet. What more did Liz want?

"Tonight. What's the earliest you can get out?" Liz asked.

"Uh...I think, maybe five-fifteen or five-thirty. Why?"

"Girl, your little nine-to-five is killing me. You might have to fake a bad case of the bubble-guts and slip out. We have plans at six-thirty and I need to get you all dolled up in time."

"For what?"

Liz let out a sneaky little giggle and sang, "That's for me to know and you to find out."

BY THE GRACE of God and three green lights in a row, Julie made it to work on time. Well, five minutes late, but earlier than her manager, Elise.

She'd been working for Regions West for the past two years as a personal banker and had managed to stay on Elise's good side. Every request she accepted obediently with a "yes ma'am" or a "right on top of that."

All part of paying her dues.

If she'd learned anything from working in customer service, she knew to nod and agree and figure it out along the way. Julie never bothered Elise with the details of how she got it done, she simply did it. And that was the key. When the time came, she would be ready and positioned to answer when opportunity knocked.

According to the grapevine—and her eight ball— it wouldn't be much longer until she heard that loud knock. Shannon at the Fort Apache branch had recently told her that Logan from the North-west branch was moving back to California, which would open up a branch manager position. It would be a small branch, but that was fine by Julie.

It had been over a year since the last position came available in the company. So naturally, when Julie logged into her email that afternoon and saw that the latest job posting for a manager opening at an affluent branch was only ten miles from home, she didn't hesitate. She pulled her always-ready resume from her desk and marched toward Elise's office.

With a light tap on the glass door, Julie announced herself. "Elise."

To anyone who didn't work for her, Elise Tisdale might come off as a tight-lipped, rigid, curmudgeon. At first glance, there was nothing but hard lines beneath a helmet of a bushy brown hair and steel-rimmed glasses. No makeup. No frills. Just business, inside and out.

The second she opened her mouth though, she puts sailors to shame with that slick tongue.

She was the kind of person who wanted what she wanted when she wanted it, and you had better get it quickly if you didn't want to suffer her wrath. She was fair and firm, and always first for sure. She led her team, not necessarily with an iron fist—usually, with a manicured black foam finger—toward an unyielding victory.

Seeming to sense her presence, Elise curled a long slender finger at the door without lifting her gaze. "Come on in. I'm just pulling the final numbers for this month. These stupid surveys are killing me," she hissed.

Traces of New York stained her words, her eyes still trained on the computer.

"What do they want me to do, pull a piece of chalk from my pocket and draw the lines for more parking spaces myself?" Finally, she peeked up at Julie who positioned herself at as comfortable a distance as possible.

Everyone in the branch knew to leave a good bit of distance between themselves and Elise. The office itself was small, but you could easily suffocate from Elise's curiously strong, musky perfume.

"I know." Julie concurred. Starting the conversation off with a disagreement couldn't possibly fare well for her cause. "They're always complaining about the parking. I think it's the carryover from the post office next door—"

"Just a second. Let me finish this line. I've got to get this out before my conference call starts."

Her fingers hit the keys to a rapid staccato *click-clack*.

All of two seconds later, Elise's beady eyes landed on Julie. She paused for a beat when Julie failed to begin, then raised her shaggy brows and cleared her throat.

"Uh…yeah. I, um wanted to talk to you about the opening at the Northwest branch?" Julie took a deep breath.

For goodness sake, why did it sound like a question?

She tried again. "I'm interested in the branch manager position at the Northwest Branch."

While she didn't think Elise would be whooping and hollering for joy at the prospect of losing an employee, she'd expected more than the blank stare burning a hole right through her. Sure, she'd have to recruit and interview and select a candidate. And if she was lucky, the person might be of use within a few months.

Still, Julie figured there'd be an element of flattery to have someone who she'd trained and groomed be considered for a promotion.

Was that too much to ask?

"I see. And you believe you're ready for all the hats a branch manager has to wear?" Elise sucked in a deep breath and leaned back in her chair, arms folded over her chest. The accusation in her tone was unmistakable.

Julie gritted her teeth and shifted on her feet until she stood what felt like at least an inch taller. "Yes," she said plainly though not with as much confidence or conviction as she'd hoped for.

"I'll admit, Julie, you are a tremendous asset to our team. You make your goal every month, you coach the tellers, and you're operationally sound. Don't think I don't appreciate all that you do, but there's so much more to being a manager." She inhaled and folded her hands on the desk the way she always did right before she doled out a bale of bad news.

"As a manager, when we do well, I give my team all of the credit. But, when we fail, *I* am the failure." Elise's voice lowered to a strangled proclamation.

For the slightest moment, it wasn't clear whether she'd been trying to warn Julie or confess her own struggles. Then, she swiveled in her chair and positioned her body square with Julie's.

"Listen, Julie. All I'm saying is, it's different when you're not only accountable for yourself but for an entire branch. I don't want to set you up to fail."

Julie's shoulders slumped. From her first day as a teller to her promotion to personal banker, she'd always had her end goal in mind. She was supposed to be growing her own branch and grooming her own staff for their roads to success. She knew about accountability and teamwork. That's why she bit her lip and ground her way through the grind every day.

As a manager, Elise had to understand that, she had been in her shoes once.

"I understand. I still want to go for it."

At Julie's firm words, Elise rose and turned on her sensible square-toed black heels. "If you feel that's something you need to do, then do it. But, I want you to remember what that means for this team. The void you'll be leaving this team."

Elise narrowed the gap between them and leaned in near Julie's ear. "Without you, there's no way we'll be ranked in the first quartile," she whispered.

A few hours of grinning and bearing it later, Julie checked her watch. Almost four. At least two and a half hours since she'd had lunch. *Perfect.*

Julie screwed her face into the most pained grimace she could muster. She held her stomach as she doubled over and dragged herself into Elise's doorway.

Somewhere between the flummoxed musings of her heart and

mind, Julie conjured up the one person she needed to hear from: herself. Minus the nerves, and add in a healthy serving of gumption.

"Elise, I need to leave. I'm not feeling so well. I think I have a bad case of…indigestion."

CHAPTER 7

Julie took one long look at the table tucked in the far right corner of the restaurant along the back wall, and her jaw dropped. "There's no way!"

She and Liz stood next to the empty hostess station waiting to be escorted to their party, but she was still shaking her head in disbelief. This was getting to be too much. She'd agreed to meet new guys, and dinner didn't seem like the worst idea, considering she'd skimped on lunch to give herself a believable sickly pallor when she lied to Elise.

Everything in my life is over the fucking top.

The lights were soft and muted. Lovely. The din of a few dozen conversations mixed in with bluesy elevator music and the clank of silverware against gold-rimmed flatware rooted her in place. She stared across the room still dumbfounded.

The tides were turning, but definitely not in her favor.

She knew her life needed an overhaul, but to go this far was the last straw.

Julie glared at Liz, who stood beside her with a smug look on her face, and stormed over to the packed restaurant door. The smell of fresh-baked bread and hearty Italian food with robust and tangy seasonings rushed through, warm and welcoming despite her hasty exit.

When Liz came flying out behind her, Julie stared at Liz with her mouth agape. Questions laced between her perfectly arched brows. "Am I a good person?"

Julie paced the sidewalk. "I mean, just tell me, Liz. Have I done something so wrong with my life to deserve this?" She was also talking to God, if on the off chance he was listening.

She pinched the bridge of her nose between her finger and thumb. "My life is literally circling the bowl, and I'm so over it. First Patrick, then Elise cock-blocked me at work today. Did I tell you that? That bitch basically told me that she won't promote me because she'll fail without me."

Liz let out a loud gasp. "Are you fucking kidding me?" She was leaning on the painted brick ledge of the restaurant storefront window with her legs and arms crossed.

"No. And now, just to add insult to injury, as if my life wasn't laughable already, *this* guy is the one you thought would help jump-start the new Julie? Nico?"

Liz tilted her head to the side, lips screwed into a knot as she watched through slitted eyes as Julie paced the sidewalk.

She tried to ignore the annoyed twist of Liz's face. Though, under the weight of her friend's stare, a flush of heat crawled over her skin. She knew that look well--the contemplative side eye and the pursed full lips that screamed disapproval.

Every time she mentioned her crappy life, Liz gave her a pitied look as if to get a good view of what a *woe is me*, pathetic woman looked like.

They were basically playing the quiet game. Julie was usually the certain failure who couldn't stand the thick silence and would speak first, but she could tell Liz had something else to get off her chest.

When Julie arrived to her apartment earlier, Liz had welcomed her with a curt "hey," which was so unlike her usual bubbly greeting. She was a hugger and an ear-to-ear grinner when she was with friends. No matter how long it had been since they last saw or talked to one another, they shrieked and made a scene as if it had been years.

Add in the fact, that she'd cracked her neck at least two or three times and Liz had basically been a mute the whole car ride over. It was obvious that she was peeved about something.

So, Julie let her have the floor.

"What the hell is going on with you lately? I thought you'd be happy. Amused, at least. The way you talked about him," Liz trailed off letting the words hang in the air. "The way you described him down to his pores and painted that whole masterpiece image of him for me on the phone earlier, I thought you'd be happy."

Under any other circumstances, she would be happy. It was just that at this juncture in her, like when everything was on a downward spiral, fairytales were too risky. And outside of Nico's looks, everything she'd heard from his lips said he wasn't exactly fairytale material.

"He's actually not a complete tool. Plus, he is really as hot as you said he was," Liz explained. The hotness factor always the trump card.

Sure, life sucks, but if you're going to be screwed, let it be by a hot guy.

"If nothing else, maybe you'll hook up and dust off the cobwebs, so you can finally move on."

Julie walked the few steps over to the window. In between the second N and the A of "Nona's Finest Italian" written on the glass, the pair of friends peered at the intimate booth in the back against the wall.

"Look at him," Liz ordered.

Derrick and Nico were seated at a white-clothed table under the glow of dim lights. Derrick sat on one side and Nico sat across from him dressed in a slim-cut white button-down beneath a navy blazer.

"He is really cute," Julie admitted and tilted her head as if deciding which was the best angle to really get a good look at him.

"Yes…he is."

"He does have a nice face…and lips," Julie continued, almost persuaded. She sighed. "And there are those eyes again."

The two women's faces hovered close to the glass, like kids watching puppies in the pet store window. "And even from here, I can see that they're all dreamy and chocolaty," Liz added.

"Yeah," Julie breathed.

Not quite touching the glass, she traced her fingers down from his eyes to his lips. Maybe, it wasn't *such* a bad idea. She could just get her feet wet a little. He couldn't be any worse than Patrick. Nico *might* be a manwhore, but he had already seen her without her shirt. Maybe he liked curvier girls. And what specifically was so wrong with a man with experience?

Liz interrupted Julie's inner debate. "Are you going to make out with him through the glass…or should we join them inside?"

It might have been the twinkle lights strung between the trees, or the fact that the sky was all lit up with stars, but the air of romance danced around Julie. Her skin buzzed with excitement, seemingly to the same rhythm as the butterflies afloat in her stomach. Suddenly, the idea of spending the evening in a five-star restaurant with a good-looking guy and good friends didn't seem so bad.

At the very least, it wouldn't be boring.

"Think there's anything upstairs?" Julie asked without taking her eyes off of him. If there was even a hint at an intellect, this could work. She would *make* it work.

"He's *actually* not an idiot. Derrick says he's a college boy and has a good job. Might be a momma's boy, though, but you could wean him out of that," Liz said, as if it were the same as convincing him to change his post-gym underwear.

"Nico and Julie," Liz muttered, as if testing their names together on her tongue.

"I know. It's so hot." Julie sighed. "I've already tried it a few times. Nico and Julie have a nice ring to it. Depends on what his last name is though," she mused, feeling like a teenager again, doodling and trying on names like outfits.

As she said his name to herself, inside the restaurant, Nico and Derrick looked over toward the window.

She wanted to cower and duck away, but where was that going to get her? Instead, she hiked up her big girl panties, smiled, and gave them a small wave. She could play with the beautiful player for a night. "Let's go in."

The way Nico's eyes appraised her as she and Liz approached the table left her thankful she'd given Liz free rein to play dress-up. After a few minutes of going back and forth, they'd settled on a black pencil skirt with a waist-cinching low-cut red blouse that gave her at least the semblance of sexy and classy. She'd opted to forgo a jacket, even though by this time of year, the air conditioning in every restaurant was on full blast.

She allowed her eyes to wash over him for the longest moment. A few chill bumps in exchange for those hungry eyes was well worth it.

Both men stood chivalrously to allow them into the booth, but she couldn't tear her eyes away from Nico.

He was taller than she remembered. Much taller. He had to be something close to a foot taller than she was because she was wearing heels and he still stood head and shoulders over her. She studied his sharp features and his clean cut dark hair, and though she didn't think it possible, he was more handsome than she imagined. Magazine Photoshop gorgeous. Catalog smolder perfect.

Her heart stumbled and struggled to beat as a tightness squeezed low in her belly. This wasn't the shower fantasy she remembered from the gym parking lot, but even dry he made her wet.

"Hey, Jules." Derrick leaned in for a hug. "This is Nico Farfalla. Nico, this is my lady, Liz, and her friend Julie Laurich."

While Derrick made the introductions, Julie and Nico exchanged a perfunctory handshake, but their mutual stare never wavered. His large hand was warm and strong, his deft fingers long and gentle at once.

"Have we met?" Nico held onto her hand while he narrowed his gaze in question. He bit on his bottom lip, almost like he was picturing her face in a different setting.

He doesn't even remember me.

Julie could barely concentrate on his question while her hand was still in his. Her hand burned in all the places his skin touched hers.

Liz slid into the booth beside Derrick, but Julie stood planted in the aisle as she waited for a waiter to pass.

Behind him was a fleshy woman in a royal blue wrap dress with poor spatial judgment. She tried to squeeze in between the narrow opening in the aisle, and her hip sent Julie into a tailspin.

With her left hand, Julie latched onto Nico's shoulder for balance. If it were the other way around, they'd have gone tumbling down, but he was as unbending as a cactus in a desert windstorm. And as steady as he was, his unwavering grip left her shaken somehow.

She hit the hard wall of his chest with both hands. With only the thin fabric of their shirts between them, she was hyperaware of the man underneath the shirt. The hard muscle dunes climbed and dipped over his chest. He smelled fresh and soapy and a little bit woodsy, which made her think of him in the rain again—damn the shower fantasy again. She had to quell the urge to rip the shirt right off of him.

When she met his gaze, a pair of bottomless brown eyes was trained on her, but she quickly looked away.

A smash and dash was sounding better and better by the second.

She looked at him again. Though, with Nico, she wasn't sure she'd have the willpower to dash. If she was going to do this, she'd have to pull out all the stops.

"You might not recognize me in all these clothes, with makeup and all this fabulousness." She fanned her hands up in broad strokes, freeing them from his grip, toying with him. "But yes, we've met. Twice. Briefly."

The right corner of his mouth lifted into a sexy grin and a

delightful low gravelly laugh rumbled from him as he slid into the booth beside Derrick. Somehow it made Julie happier to know that she had been the cause of such a beautiful sound.

"So, Julie?" he said, patting the space next to him. "Seriously, are you going to tell me how we met, or are we going to have to play twenty questions for me to get it out of you?" That smile trailed the hard tawny line of his jaw to the softened corners of his eyes.

"I'll give you a hint," she conceded, sliding in beside him. She was enjoying this game far more than expected. She parted her lips. "Both times there was a car involved. Most recently, there was rain and a car and yelling, but it wasn't a lover's quarrel."

"Ah. A riddle." He played along, resting his cheek on his forefinger, which Julie found to be adorable.

She playfully leaned in closer to Nico, her nose fighting to choose between the earthy aroma of pasta and buttery bread and the inviting woodsy freshness of Nico's cologne. They were so close their knees touched. Quickly, she shifted, moving her legs away. She was drawn to him.

He squinted his eyes and studied her for a moment. "That was you in the car last night?" Recognition colored his beautiful face. "The one going crazy in the gym parking lot, with the stained shirt?"

"How lovely of you to remember. Last I checked, a gentleman does not remind on point a woman's less ladylike moments, but to each his own," she chided him. *Ah sarcasm.* "But, to answer your question, yes, one and the same." Julie laughed as she watched him struggle to reconcile the two mismatched images of her.

"I do clean up well. It's okay for you to say it. I'll admit, I looked *and* felt like shit yesterday."

Nico raised his eyebrows. "Yeah, but I knew there was potential. For sure."

At his honesty, the four of them joined in laughter.

"Right? That's what *I* said," Liz added as she gave Julie a half-ass kick under the table. "Bet you never thought you'd see her again, did you?" She glanced over at Julie and winked.

CHAPTER 8

Nico fit in with their group seamlessly, Julie Thought. He understood their dry sarcastic humor and corny jokes. Derrick, who would usually tick off all of the reasons why she shouldn't see a guy, somehow had nothing to say. Due in part to his friendship bias, she suspected. Afterall, Nico was his pick. Still, it was strange for him not be giving side eye glances or snarky comments about any guy she dated. He was basically, the older protective brother Julie never had.

Derrick had never gotten along with Patrick, nor had he spent any significant amount of time in her ex's presence. So, to see him fully engaged and laughing with Nico warmed her heart. Deep down, in the future Julie hoped that her and Liz's guys would be as close as she and Liz.

Now, they going were back and forth about whether Michael Jordan or Lebron James was the best basketball player of all time. They shot off stats and compared longevity. Once they got to championships and rings, the women added Kobe Bryant and Magic Johnson into the mix, only to be instantly shot down.

Nico was arguing Jordan was a better all-around athlete since he played baseball and basketball, when a waitress came over to take the table's order. A primped and plastic waitress who just so happened to look like Celeste. She introduced herself to everyone at the table. Something like Carol, or Sheryl. It was hard to be sure. She was talking to everyone, but hadn't actually managed to look at anyone other than Nico.

Meanwhile, Julie was busy watching this imposter Celeste devour Nico like man meat with her hungry eyes. Goddammit. Was she jealous?

Why do I even care that she's looking at Nico? Ugh, check yourself, Jules.

Whatever her name was, she was thin and had legs that began at her armpits. To add insult to injury, she was at least two cup sizes bigger than Julie, and she had pair of sparkly blue eyes that could throw any red-blooded male off his game.

The waitress muttered something about the specials of the day, but Julie barely heard a word. She was too busy measuring herself up against the leggy woman, until Liz's eyes indicated that she had caught on, too. The "don't even think about it" look written across Liz's forehead meant the guard was on duty and ready to attack. Her slitted eyes trained on the waitress, daring her to even glance in Derrick's direction.

Like the wise man that he was, Derrick averted his gaze. He wasn't stupid. He was used to Liz's shenanigans, so he studied the menu like he'd be quizzed on the ingredients the next day. *Smart man.*

Luckily for him, the young waitress had her eyes set on Nico. She made her way around the table with a strained smile as she jotted down Derrick's veal parmesan. She moved on to Liz who ordered the fettuccine Alfredo. Under Liz's watchful eye, Julie reluctantly opted for the low carb special—filleted chicken breast with broccoli florets and a light lemon-pepper glaze.

When Carol or Sheryl reached Nico, he seemed to be her stage cue to pull out all the stops. In a matter of seconds, she blossomed into batted lashes and a silvery voice with a seductive giggle. "What can I get for you?"

By the way she said it, it was apparent to everyone—everyone except Nico, who had yet to look up at her—that there might not be a limit to what she was willing to *get* for him. *Something not on the menu.*

Julie couldn't blame her. Nico was hot as hell. She couldn't keep her eyes off him either. And for some reason that made no sense to her at all, Julie was jealous and feeling more than a little bit territorial.

Nico ordered the spaghetti Bolognese and a round of limoncello shots for the table. And, ignoring a woman who basically offered herself up on a platter, he paid Julie the kind of compliment most women dream about.

Right in front of the girl. Right in front of Liz and Derrick and the whole restaurant, Nico dropped the full weight of those brown eyes on her and smiled. She would never admit it, but Nico's hotness factor shot up for her instantly.

"What?" Julie murmured. She could feel heat crawling up her neck and settling in her cheeks. *I'm blushing.*

"It's just that...every time I look at you—"

"What?" she asked, almost defensively, afraid of what he was going to say. Her stomach roiled and her throat was uncomfortably dry. Fear crept in at the thought of what he saw when he looked at her.

"I just...I have to smile. You're gorgeous."

Julie had braced herself for a few possibilities to finish his sentence. Maybe looking at her made him want to throw up, or cringe, or make sure his eyes weren't playing tricks on him. But make him smile? Gorgeous?

She'd been in the man's presence for all of thirty or so minutes and he'd given her more compliments than Patrick had in their two years together.

Julie shook her head. "Thank you. I...just...thank you."

Her eyes darted to Liz, who knew exactly where her head was, but her friend only offered a sympathetic smile.

Derrick on the other hand, who'd been quarantined off in the corner, took it as his opportunity to dive in head first the second the waitress skimped away.

"My man." He lifted his hand for a high five. "That's what I'm talking about. I was worried for you at first, but now I'm thinking I might have to take a few tips from you."

Nico gave a shaky laugh. "I'm sorry? I don't know what you're talking about."

"Please." Derrick dragged the word out and peppered it with sarcasm. "These two would usually be on the second round of twenty questions and have your balls in a vise grip by now, trying to figure your intentions. But you're over there holding your own. Got your eyes trained on the menu. Didn't even give a cursory glance at the waitress. Then, you lay it on thick like gravy and we haven't even gotten our entrees yet." He raised his hand for a fist pump which Nico did not return.

Out of habit, Liz punched Derrick on the shoulder. "Seriously, D?"

"You got me all wrong, Derrick." Nico flicked a glance at Julie. "I just know what I want. I know it's not some disrespectful waitress who thinks it's okay to come onto me when it's clear I'm here on a date. I don't need to see her face to figure that out."

Oh you're good, guy. Julie stilled herself for the windfall of bullshit.

Ever on the same page, Liz pursed her lips. "Uh huh. That's the story you're sticking with?"

"What? What? That's so hard to believe? That's me. I just want to be me, you know. I've got three brothers, a sister, and a mother who all keep trying to shovel me into some idea they have for me, and I just want to be me."

Julie gave a sheepish nod. "I could see that." The fact that she'd said it aloud shocked her.

"Um...I was just thinking. I'm kind of in the same boat, is all," she stammered, trying not to stare at him. "My mom and my aunt want me to be one thing. They're constantly comparing me to my cousin. And at work, my friggin' boss wants to keep me on a leash to pad her paycheck. I don't even want to get into the rest of the dirty pranks God's been playing on me lately."

"Exactly," Nico agreed.

The way his eyes bore into her, Julie thought he could certainly see through her. See that she wasn't the outgoing, sassy woman with the flirty jokes and confidence that went with the clothes. And no matter how endearing his words, he couldn't be that sweet guy. He couldn't possibly be that...nice.

Julie wished she hadn't already gotten a glimpse of the real Nico at the gym, wished she could unhear everything about the man who needed a net to catch all of his women with their broken hearts. She fought off the urge to meet his eyes again and turned her attention back across the table.

Derrick took Liz's right hand in his and pulled her under his arm. "I feel you, Nico. I've always known how to separate what I want and don't want. Once you know, it's like tunnel vision. Blinders on both eyes, you know?" He leaned down kissed Liz's hair. "I keep telling this woman, I want to start a life with her and make a boatload of babies. She's it for me."

At his words, Liz shot Julie a wide-eyed stare through clenched teeth.

None the wiser, Nico turned to Liz and said, "That's awesome. You guys look great together." She only offered him a tight-lipped smile that failed to reach her eyes.

"I could see myself having a couple down the road. I don't think I could handle a boatload, though," he referred back to Derrick's earlier comment. "When you grow up in a full house, or when you get to the double digits in nieces and nephews, it kind of changes your perspective on kids, one way or the other."

A loud choking sound erupted from Julie.

"You all right, Jules?" Liz reached for her hand.

"Yeah…I uh, I just drank the water too fast, that's all."

Derrick kissed Liz on the head and took a swig from his water glass.

"Be careful. Stuff's dangerous," Julie warned Derrick with a wink.

By the time the food arrived, the awkwardness had died down, save for light exchanges between the couples. They began to eat and allowed the silence to ease the tension. The shots arrived and Julie thought Liz might kill someone when Nico made a toast to boatloads of babies.

Before it could get anymore awkward, the ladies excused themselves to visit the restroom where Liz proceeded to vent all of the frustrations she had kept bottled up until that point.

"Where in the hell does he get off talking about babies and marriage, huh?" Liz blurted out the second the door closed behind them.

"He just loves you."

"And being with me isn't good enough? He can't respect the fact that I want to wait? That I don't want to end up another stereotype with a bunch of babies before I even figure out who I am?" she blustered through a stream of rolling Rs and melded words, hints of her roots surfacing.

Her hands slammed down on the porcelain sink as she huffed and let her head hang low. "Jules, I don't want this right now." Her words were strangled and desperate.

"Then tell him."

"I have. But he doesn't listen. He thinks I'll change my mind."

Julie shifted from one foot to the other. Who in the hell was she to be giving any type of advice? All she could think to say was what Liz had told her over the countless times Patrick made her feel worthless. "Make him listen, then," she said.

"How? How do I make him listen when I love him? And I don't

want to lose him. I just don't want what he wants right now, you know? But he keeps pushing."

She swiped at the trail of tears rolling down the curves of her cheeks and buried her face in her friend's open arms.

"I don't know what to do," she breathed into Julie's neck.

"You know what you *have* to do."

Before the guys became suspicious, Julie cleaned Liz up and mopped away all the traces of her frustration. When they reentered the dining room, the staff had cleared the section of tables in the front of the house to make room for an old-school parquet dance floor and a single spotlight at the center.

A few spread-out couples swayed to a low elevator-style ballad, but most of the patrons sat in surrounding tables as if they were waiting for a show to begin.

Back at the table, the guys stood and asked the ladies for a dance. And while Nico seemed genuinely pleased to see Julie, Derrick stiffened at the sight of Liz's reddened face.

"Everything all right?" He searched her eyes.

"Yeah. My, uh, contact got stuck," Liz explained.

Nico honed in on the palpable tension between them. "Maybe Julie and I will sit this one out. If that's okay with you, Julie?" He slipped his hand on the small of her back and led her to their table.

"Are you having a good time?" Nico asked, his voice low and measured. He was tracing lines through the condensation on his water glass, but Julie caught his gaze and found as much hesitation in it as there was in his tone.

"I am," she said. "I'm just worried about Liz."

He looked over to the dance floor where Liz and Derrick shuffled in choppy forced steps, her head on his shoulder, and his large arms draped over her lithe body. "Everything all right with them?"

Julie thought she heard relief in his voice that her worries weren't related to him. "Same as everyone. There's always someone who wants more than you want to give at the moment."

He seemed to consider her words, then he looked over to her

and covered her hand with his. She inhaled sharply, startled by the move. When she met his eyes, there was something genuine and sweet in them, and she felt herself relax. Those eyes made her want to be closer to him, get to know him.

She wanted to say something, something profound, or sexy, but when the music stopped abruptly, the trance was broken. Julie tore her gaze away in time to see the crowd had tapered off to the edges of the dance floor.

She nearly shit a brick. "No." Her eyes bulged from their sockets and her mouth fell open. "He's not doing this."

As Derrick began a shaky speech on a microphone handed to him by the leggy young waitress from earlier, he dropped to one knee, and Julie knew he was doing the one thing on which Liz wouldn't budge.

CHAPTER 9

Julie drove Liz's car in silence, save for the low hum of a gut-wrenching ballad ironically about breakups. Liz was curled in a ball in the passenger seat, her knees heartbreakingly pressed to her chest, her head tucked into her arms. She hadn't said a word since they'd left Nona's.

Liz and Derrick had broken up too many times for Julie to count, but something about this night felt final. Like goodbye.

She wanted to say something to make her best friend feel better, but for the life of her, Julie didn't know what to say—or do.

The red lights came one after another. Blinking beacons of clarity. If Liz needed a sign, it couldn't have been much clearer that she needed to stop. That much Julie had down. Her only clue, really. That was going to be the first piece of advice she gave her friend. But what else?

She was no good at this sort of thing—words of wisdom, pep talks, uplifting quotes. That was Liz's thing. Still, she kept running over profound tidbits she could give her whenever she came up for air.

Julie quickly glanced at the rearview mirror, biting her bottom lip before returning her gaze back to the road.

Stop. That was about as far as Julie had gotten by way of advice each time she pulled up to another red light. Except, what did that mean? Was Liz supposed to stop and think, or stop and go back, or just cut her losses while she was ahead?

Glancing over at Liz again, Julie decided she likely hadn't seen one of the red lights. Liz wasn't looking for signs from the universe right now. Her body seemed to sink lower and lower into the bend of the seat.

Muffled sobs and the gentle rise and fall of her friend's back made her want to reach over and hug her as tight as she could. But she knew what it was like to need that time to settle down. The time to bawl and make a way through all of the tangled what-ifs and whys.

Besides, what was there to say? What would really make her feel better?

"Liz?" Her eyes flickered between the road and the rearview mirror as she touched Liz's shoulder. "Got about five more minutes. How you doing over there?" she asked, glancing in the rear view once more.

At her side, Liz whimpered, but said nothing.

Rather than saying anything more, Julie turned the radio off and let the windows down. The desert breeze perfumed with that same air of romance drifted in her general direction. Well, it kind of floated in her direction from the black pickup truck still tailing her. The same truck where an annoyingly sweet Nico sat behind the wheel, with a heroic determination to ensure her safety home.

He and Julie had stood in front of the restaurant, arguing over how she'd get home. Liz had picked her up after work and she was supposed to take her back home. But what was she going to do? Tell her to suck it up and drive herself home when she'd just turned down a proposal from the man she loved? No.

For the umpteenth time, she assured Nico that she'd be fine. Once she'd dropped Liz off, it wasn't a big deal to call for an Uber or a Lyft. She'd done it a million times and she didn't need him to chaperone her. Still, he insisted and she finally snapped at him.

Up until three lights ago, Julie was pretty sure that he'd gotten the picture.

Through the rearview mirror, she peeked at him for about the twentieth time since she tried to lose him. She had swerved and jumped lanes, even gone as far as speeding through a yellow light on the verge of turning red. Even after three consecutive right turns brought them back to the same traffic light, he was right there, watching her through *her* rearview mirror.

He seemed like a nice guy. A real sweetheart. But then, so did that guy who roofied that girl in that New York nightclub and stuffed her into a shallow grave. She watched *Forensic Files* and *Criminal Minds*. Hell, she watched the news. She could be this guy's next victim.

Her mind was still sifting through a thousand and one signs that Nico might be crazy when Liz lifted her head, jolting Julie's thoughts. Her best friend was in pieces. Her eyes covered with black mascara sludge.

God, she had to think of something uplifting and supportive to say.

This is it. Half-hatched mutterings of reassurance and a few motivational quotes she'd read on Instagram floated in one ear and out the other, but they were all too rehearsed and impersonal. *Ah, what would a real friend say?*

She had no clue. This was Liz's territory. Julie had always been on the receiving end of their little pep talks. Liz was the one who always knew just what to say to light a fire under her.

"Uh...it's going to be fine." Julie settled on safe and simple. She couldn't go wrong with that. "Trust me, Derrick'll probably be waiting at your place when we get there."

Liz twisted in her seat and rested the back of her head on the window. Through the rays of streetlight piercing through the window, a twisted smirk pulled at the right corners of her eye and mouth, in the sort of regimented, unnatural way puppets move on command. "You suck at this."

"Huh?"

"Jules, you're no good at this, so just stop. You have no idea how to console a person. I'll be fine. What you need to be worrying about is that hot little daddy who's been following us and what you're going to do when you guys get back to your place." She gave a great impression of a smiling raccoon.

"I'm worried about you."

"Why? I'm good. Derrick and I will work this out some kind of way. But you? You need to get your shit together," she said. "You're probably over there, ready to call *America's Most Wanted* on him, when he's just trying to make sure you make it home safe. Need to get your mom out of your head and let him clean those clogged pipes of yours," she said as a giggle spilled from her lips.

Julie couldn't help laughing as Liz shook her head disapprovingly.

"What? What do you want me to do?" Julie managed between stuttered laughs. "He *could* be a mass murderer. You don't know."

Even as she said it, she couldn't help laughing at herself. The two of them burst into contagious giggles. Coming up for air in between bouts as they alternated from breathless heaving to all-out howling shrieks.

As always, Liz was right on both fronts. Julie sounded ridiculous, likening Nico to a psychopath—and a smash and dash might be just what she needed to unclog her pipes *and* her mind.

"Look, if you don't get your paranoia together at some point, you're going to end up haggard and alone. Shit, that boy is hot. If I wasn't all caught up with Derrick, *I* would push your ass out of the way."

In the face of Liz's kidding, Julie attempted to bring the conversation full circle. "For real, though, in all seriousness, he's hot, but he's too sweet. *If* this is the real version of him he showed us tonight. What the hell am I going to do with a nice guy?" she asked as she flicked on her left blinker.

"Uh, first you said he was a player and now you're worried he might be too nice?" Liz rolled her eyes. "Quit overanalyzing everything and just use him for the only thing men are good for. At least get some good sex out of this bust of a night."

I'm going to let that one slide. That's the hurt talking.

Julie's brows scrunched low over her eyes. "Oh, okay, like that's going to work. You know he's probably just a poser. I didn't get the manwhore vibe once tonight."

"Yeah, because you're so good at picking 'em," Liz teased.

"Jerk." With her right arm, Julie swatted the air at Liz. "Seriously, though. Not everyone has a stone wall around their heart and steel balls to walk out on a lovesick dude in the middle of a proposal. Nico's too nice and you know it. I'll end up breaking his heart."

Liz jolted upright. "Like Patrick did yours?"

"Ooh, that was low. Even for you Liz, that was low." Julie brought the car to a stop and put it in park.

For a split second, Julie cut her a serious side-eye.

Liz broke their stare first. Her shoulders lowered along with her eyes. "Jules, all I'm saying is that maybe you could stand to open up a little bit. Stop trying to mold your life and everyone in it around this plan in your head." She exhaled. "Can you just try to live in this moment for once?"

As much as Julie wanted to deck her friend for that little dig, she *did* know. She did need live in the moment for once. For the past few years, she'd been forcing her goals and happiness into unachievable deadlines, and where had that left her? Husbandless with a dead-end job.

She hated when her family pigeonholed her, so why was she doing this to herself?

Without a second thought, Julie leaned over and hugged Liz. "Could have done without the shade, but thanks, you jerk." She smiled and handed Liz the keys.

The lights of Nico's truck glared against the glass as he pulled in beside them.

"Think you can make it from here?" Julie asked as they exited the car, just as the driver side door of Nico's truck slammed shut and he walked up behind her.

"I could ask you the same thing." Liz nodded and winked as she bounded up the steps to the front door of her apartment. "Text me when you get home," she yelled to Julie from the second floor landing. "Oh. And Nico? I'll cut you if you hurt her. Bye!" She gave a chipper wave.

When the door shut with Liz on the other side, Julie turned her attention to Nico.

Immediately, she felt the blood rush to her cheeks. "Sorry about that. She's just...protective," she explained, hoping he hadn't read too much into Liz's warning. Neither of them could predict where things might go between them beyond this night.

If she thought being face to face with Nico beneath the dim lights of a romantic Italian restaurant was a lot to handle, she'd drastically underestimated the effect of low lights and street lamps upon a good pair of cheekbones and a sharp chin.

CHAPTER 10

Nico's eyes were illuminated like warm honey puddles and Julie's insides clenched with heat. All she could do was stare.

"We had better get you home." Nico placed his hand on her lower back as they walked around his truck.

She licked her lips and ogled this guy who'd transformed under the shadow of night. If she was going to hold off waiting on fate and lose her granny panties in the process, seemed to her he'd be a great start.

Right about that moment, Julie would've given an arm and a leg —and quite possibly her left kidney—to know what was going through his handsome head as they walked the few steps to his truck in silence. Every bit the gentleman, he opened the passenger door for her.

"Can I help you up? It's kind of a high step."

Julie anchored one hand on the interior door handle and the other on the frame and gave herself a mental countdown. On three, she hooked her heel on the step rail and hoisted herself up. The second she heard the loud slash of fabric ripping, she cursed the unforgiving fit of her pencil skirt. When Julie tried it on earlier in the evening, she'd wondered why she hadn't worn it more often. Why it had been banished to the back corner of the closet to collect dust mites and an awkwardly placed hanger crease.

It all came rushing back to her. The last time she'd worn it, her circulation cut off and her thighs were left raw from the constant rubbing.

Julie's hands flew to her backside and remained there as she plopped down onto the front seat. Her mouth agape, she shook her head and squinted her disbelieving eyes.

"I give up. I can't. I really can't do this anymore," she confessed.

Nico backed away. "Uh, if this is going to be anything like last night, I'm thinking I might need shatterproof glass." His voice was teasing and full of humor.

When Julie failed to bite the bait, he pressed harder for a smile. "Am I going to be safe driving you home, or do you need some time alone with the steering wheel again?" He feigned exaggerated worry.

While he was cute and she appreciated his attempt to lighten the mood, it was frankly too little, too late based on the past few weeks of her life. "Nico, you don't even know the half of it. I can't take another thing going wrong. I literally can't. Just take me home, please."

"Really? You're going to let a little thing like a rip in your skirt at the *end* of the evening get you down? Is that what I'm hearing you say?"

"Yes. As a matter of fact, I am. You don't know me and I don't need your sweet little nice guy act right now. We had a nice night and I appreciate you taking me home and everything, but this is clearly a sign that the night is over. I just want to get home, that's all."

"You're right about that. I don't know you. And this...this is not who I thought you were at all." His lashes seemed to have sprouted wings and flapped into a frenzy.

If she wasn't so pissed, she might've dwelled on how cute it was.

Daggers sliced through what inkling of hope there was left for the night. A blank-faced Nico read right through her, but only nodded in return. She was judging him. Had been judging him since the gym.

He promptly rounded the truck and buckled himself into the driver's seat where he sat completely erect, with no emotion visible on his hardened face.

"Where to?" he said without a cursory glance in her direction.

"Um...take the ninety-five to Durango and make a left."

The drive took all of twenty minutes, but for Julie, lightning speed couldn't have been any faster. If she was being honest with herself, it was wrong to take out her frustrations on Nico. He hadn't done anything wrong. If she was being honest, he was the only good thing about the bust of a night, as Liz called it. But he was there. And now, three days in a row, he'd seen her at her worst. Wrong place, wrong time.

When the truck came to a slow roll at a red light a couple of blocks from her place, Julie peeked over at Nico. In fact, she peeked over two or three more times, but the stubborn *ass* refused to look back at her.

"Nico?" She'd meant to say it nicer, but irritation seeped into her tone. He was giving her the silent treatment?

Without turning his head, he muttered a tight response that echoed her own annoyance. "Yes?"

Under the glow of the red traffic light, the edges of his jaw formed a skeletal grimace. Something about it was wicked and a tinge sinister, but she realized that could be her overactive imagination at work. Rather than let it run away with her, she addressed it head on. "So, now *you're* mad?"

"Nope. I'm just...taking you home like you asked." A neon-red vein popped at his temple as they inched to a stop.

"Okay, but you're not going to talk me the entire ride? That's mature."

"Says the girl who practically threw a tantrum because of a rip in her skirt."

He was right, but it didn't boil her blood any less. She was the one whose life had been flipped on its side and left spinning out of control. In her opinion, that gave her the right to be a little edgy. Most people would have spiraled a lot faster. So, screw him. Might as well lay all the cards on the table since the likelihood of seeing him again was about as slim as her soon-to-be-skinny thighs.

"What's your deal?" She armored up for the battle.

He glanced over at Julie under the green glow and eased his right foot off of the brake. Opening his mouth, then promptly closing it again, he turned back toward the road.

"Fine. Don't talk to me. It's just as well, but I know you. Or, at least I know your kind."

A smirk pulled at the right corner of his sexy little mouth as he shook his head. "Hmpf. Do tell."

"I love this whole chivalry thing you've got going on. Almost had me fooled, too. But I heard you talking to Dane at the gym. All your 'broken hearts' and 'bunch of kids' waiting on you." She searched his profile for any hints of denial, but there were none.

As she positioned her next point on the tip of her tongue, she realized the truck had stopped and they were parked in an open spot two buildings down from hers.

This was it. She could hold back and walk away now, or say exactly what she meant, for the first time. The idea rolled around her head for a beat. Then, just as he had done, she opened her mouth, and closed it almost as quickly.

It was his turn to deal. "Please. Don't stop on my account. I'm interested to know what else you think you know about me—about my kind—since you've got me all figured out," he said, with the trace of a sneer in his voice.

"Uh…" She couldn't see his face clearly in the darkness. Some-how, she imagined seeing his face would make it easier for her to unload on him. She wanted to look him in his eyes. On second thought, maybe looking him in those chocolate pools wouldn't help.

"Julie, you've got the floor. Might as well use it."

She slid her fingers into the door handle and hedged her body to him. *Why not?*

"What I really don't get, is why you felt the need to lay it on all thick tonight. That whole manwhore/ladies' man situation suits you, so why all the extra effort? Why whip out the chivalry card when you could've wiped your hands clean of me at the restaurant?"

When it was clear that Julie had spent her two cents, Nico worked in calculated moves to turn the engine off. The overhead lights illuminated the car with a soft white glow and finally she could see his face again. He made big work of reclining his seat, and propping his head up on his folded hands positioned on the headrest.

Air hitched in her throat and her breathing sped up. Good lord, he was good-looking. Not so much charming at the moment, but fuck. The way his heavy brows hung low over his hooded eyes and his square jaw curved with a muscular edge, it was too much. Every time she looked at him, she was back in traffic with those warm eyes looking down at her.

Followed deliciously by the slow motion shower fantasy.

She had to turn away from his full pink lips. Those kissable lips. She imagined all the things he could do to her with those dangerous weapons, and heat burned a trail from *her* lips down her throat to her neck to her breasts, before settling low and tight between her thighs with a hollow ache.

And in this big wide truck with the spacious back seat? God why couldn't he just shut up and kiss her? Better yet, why couldn't he be ugly?

"You about done?" he said, rousing her from her thoughts.

"Yeah...yes," Julie corrected herself. *Look him in the eye.* How embarrassing. He must have seen her drooling over him for sure.

She sat up straighter, even though he likely hadn't paid her too much attention. Clearly, he was oblivious to the NC-17 thoughts ransacking her mind at the moment. "Uh…yes," she repeated herself once more, though it still had the rising inflection of a question.

She needed to work on saying things with conviction. She needed to be more assertive like her cousin, Sophia. Julie's mom made it a point to mention it two or three hundred times. *Why can't you be more like your cousin? She knows how to say things like she means it, put herself together, put herself out there and make opportunities for herself, find a man.* No matter what, it always boiled down to a man in her mom's book.

"Good." He closed his eyes.

"Good? That's all you're going to say?" She was the one who had dragged the night into hell date territory, but seriously? He didn't even have the decency to deny it?

Placate me a little? Dammit, lie to me to save face.

"I'll tell you exactly what I tell my kids: 'ask the right questions and you'll get the right answers.' Since you've got all the answers before you've asked any questions, I'm good. Hope your night goes better than it has thus far."

Her mouth slackened and her eyes widened. She couldn't stop blinking as she set her hand on the door handle, both to steady herself and because she was ready to cut his whole self-righteous monologue short. *His kids. Asshole.* Ooh she could hear the smile in his voice, the smugness that bordered on goading.

This jerk was enjoying himself.

She was ready to hop out of his truck, too, but then, she made the self-destructive mistake of allowing her gaze to wander. As he stretched his legs and adjusted himself in the seat, she got a lofty view of the growing bulge in his pants.

He likes arguing with me. He's turned on by this. And she was turned on by the proof that he was turned on.

She bit her bottom lip hard and tore her eyes away. She chastised herself for acting like the Horny Harriet she was. It had been two months since the break-up, but even longer since she'd had her pipes cleaned properly. Let's just say, Patrick wasn't the best plumber.

And as much as she enjoyed her trusty ten-speed rabbit, there weren't enough batteries in the world. Electronic toys would never compare to the feel of warm, strong, deft hands learning the ins and outs of her body, working her into a painfully good frenzy.

"Shit," she blurted out. Not because she was frustrated—not counting sexually frustrated—but as Nico released his arms from behind his head and placed them back on the steering wheel, Julie's gaze maddeningly found his hands. His tawny, muscled, able hands.

Those kind of hands could definitely make her feel good.

She wasn't just mad at him. She was mad that he'd ruined her chance of a glorious walk of shame. Her pink buds were flaring up. Ten minutes into their ride in his truck, and she was willing to overlook everything in exchange for a one-night friendship with benefits. She was sort of curious, and strangely hard up for him.

Nico reached for a button on his door panel and popped the locks.

Not now. Now, she was pissed. "What? Are you...dismissing me?" She cocked her head, laughing nervously.

"Not at all. I got you home safe, now I'm just bidding you and your *ripped* skirt farewell."

CHAPTER 11

Nothing good can come from waking up at four a.m., Julie discovered. Especially when you're running on five hours of sleep because your wired mind incessantly replayed every second of a disastrous double date. Albeit, with an annoyingly hot guy—no less than a gazillion times.

Julie pressed the snooze button on her phone. She was awake, but unfortunately, she was still horny as hell.

She was still contemplating the female equivalent of blue balls as she slipped her hand back beneath the sheet. She squeezed her eyes shut against the glow of her table lamp.

"Nico, you've been a bad, bad boy." The star of her night's fantasies licked his lips and Julie's body tensed. "Yes, right there," she moaned, imagining his hands on her.

Even in her fantasy, his hands were so much better than her own. She remembered hers pressed against his chest in the aisle at Nona's. As she trembled and rubbed at the ache between her thighs, her breath shallowed and her heart beat erratically against her chest.

She was just about to...

Ugh, damn alarm.

It was useless. Nothing she imagined could compare to having him there.

Julie withdrew her hand from the sheets and touched the button to stop the alarm. Begrudgingly, she sat up ready to take on Liz's list.

Today, she had Julie scheduled with the skin magician. Julie was getting some kind of facial, which could only take place at the butt crack of dawn to fit her rapidly filling schedule. So, despite the ever present low-hanging bags under her eyes and the pasty pallor of her ghostly morning face, she slunk out of bed to go regenerate. Layers of herself.

Out with the old, and in with the new and improved version of Julie Laurich.

The way Liz had explained it, the facial appointment was supposed to be the best-spent hour and a half of her life. This esthetician...or was it a dermatologist? She hadn't been sure what the difference was between them when she'd Googled the place. But with Liz's recommendation and a five-star rating on Yelp, Julie decided that the title didn't matter.

Either way, the skin magician was supposed to work wonders on her complexion. Brighten and tighten her up.

When Liz first mentioned the appointment, Julie dismissed the idea altogether. Her skin didn't exactly glow with radiance, but she didn't have any pothole pimples or rosacea, either. Still, she figured a deep cleaning would shrink her pores and make her look that much younger for whichever lucky guy got to be Patrick's successor.

Now that it had been confirmed that he was even more of a douche than she originally thought, this whole revenge-body concept *had* to work. Even if she only got the chance to walk by his wagging tongue, that would be enough, she told herself.

And so, at four-thirty in the freaking morning, she trudged into the pristine serenity of the esthetician's office. She let her worries drift away with the waves of the waterfall soundtrack. The air was thick with lavender and eucalyptus and...coffee?

Julie inhaled, closing her eyes. Hazelnut?

A bright-eyed receptionist with mousy brown hair and pouty pink lips welcomed her by name. Julie liked her immediately. She seemed like the type of girl who could give off the sweetest pageant smile if you were nice to her, but just as easily unleash a swift right hook if you rubbed her wrong.

In her best girly girl voice, she offered Julie a selection of freshly brewed green tea or mountain fresh Arabica bean coffee while she waited. She could have used some coffee, but she was kind of nervous and didn't know exactly what to expect from a facial. Google's results on facial peels only came up with price lists for every salon within a fifty mile radius and some YouTube videos that seemed more like informercials than anything close to what the real service would be like.

She didn't want to have to go to the bathroom in the middle of her facial, nor did she want to be antsy and wired while someone removed layers of skin from her face. To be on the safe side, she refused the coffee and the tea.

However, she did accept the invitation to be seated. Off in the corner, there were four cushy chairs. In the center of them was a table with a small rock waterfall fixture, a planter of succulents, and a miniature box of sand with a teensy rake and stones in it.

Julie settled in to the one with her back to the exit. Shifting to find a comfortable position in the chair, she finally got a good look at the place. The pictures online did not do the office justice. The walls were a toasty cream color that gave the place a warm feel and worked well with the earth tone color scheme. Rich browns, greens, and small pops of a rusty burnt orange streamed through the fabric of the abstract curtains and in the landscape paintings.

It was probably frowned upon, but she ran her fingers through the little planter of grass and succulents just because she was dying to see what it felt like on her hands. It was both soft and prickly, relaxing to the touch.

The place was beautiful in an understated simplistic way and it was clean. On the few occasions that Julie did treat herself to a massage or a mani-pedi, she found herself inspecting the level of hygiene. Flesh-eating diseases were a real thing and she needed every ounce of her skin if she was planning on renewing herself.

She wasn't worried about that in this office. Liz had vouched for the place, but being there helped to seal the feeling that she was in good hands.

Julie checked her watch. It was only four forty-five. *Not even five yet.* She still had fifteen minutes until her appointment. She sat into the deep curve of the chair, resisting the urge to curl her feet up into the crease and close her eyes for a few more minutes. Instead, she took out her phone. Fifteen minutes was plenty of time to really "thank" Liz for setting her appointment at such an ungodly hour. She probably wouldn't be awake, but a succession of buzzing chimes at the witching hour served her right.

One after another, she flooded Liz's phone.

Julie: Good morning sunshine!
Julie: I'm here!
Julie: Are you up yet? Are you up yet? Are you up yet?

She swiped through the library of emojis and found an alarm clock and sent five in a row, one text at a time, followed by horns and megaphones and the dancing woman in the red dress. This was definitely an occasion to be celebrated. She was up against her will and it was Liz's fault, so her friend deserved a little payback.

Julie: Wake up!!!!!

Her insides filled with laughter at the image of Liz buried in a mountain of sheets and blankets, swatting at her phone. Julie knew she never turned off the ringer. Not since the time she missed the called for an interview with Pixar for a highly coveted graphic design job. When they filled the position before Liz woke up after a long night spent playing beer pong and drinking herself silly, it flipped a switch in her. After that, she basically slept with one eye and two ears open. Apparently, Liz decided that she could sleep when she was dead.

Sure enough, after maybe the twentieth or thirtieth message, the three ellipses appeared on the left next to Liz's name.

Liz: I hate you

Julie was jubilant at her response. Nothing like a good *I hate you* in the morning. Meant she was doing something right as far as friendships went.

Julie: There she is ladies and gentlemen, Miss Sunshine herself. The woman of the hour.

Another text with a row full of clapping hands went out.

Julie: I'm here
Liz: Where?
Julie: I should be sleeping, but I'm here at your skin magician. Ready to be radiant.

She knew she should stop with the emojis, but by now she was having way too much fun. Cheesing smile emoji. Poop emoji. Exactly how she felt, shiny on the outside, shit on the inside.

Liz: Oh, that's right. Low key, that place is legit the best ever. Um... and can you stop with the emojis already?

Knowing Liz hadn't had her coffee yet, Julie bypassed the small talk and capitalized on Liz's slow response time. She wanted to skip all the drama and the question she'd been dying to know since she got home last night—since Nico skidded off. But, first things first.

Hoes over bros.

Julie: Any word from D? Did he stop by?
Liz: Still blowing me up. Can't talk Yeti.
Julie: ?
Liz: *yet. Autocorrect sucks.

Julie nearly fell out of the chair. Without lifting her head, the sweet receptionist's gaze flickered over at her and Julie sunk down deeper into the cushion. She'd almost forgotten where she was.

The place was too relaxing. If she got any lower in the chair, she could easily fall back to sleep. Something told her it likely had something to do with her wanting to get back to her dream of Nico.

Liz: I can't bring myself to answer him yet. I don't know what I want
Julie: Who does? Call him already.
Liz: Ok…then you call Nico

Say what? Julie paused for a second. Without fail, she knew Liz would drag the conversation back to her, centered on Nico. Julie had been dying to talk about him, see what Liz really thought. What impressions she'd gotten. She wanted to talk about every word he'd uttered last night in finite detail. The dimple she'd seen peek from the hollow in his cheek. How they were sitting so close, they were basically on top of one another.

And the whole thing with the waitress? How he'd buttered her up and laid on the flattery so thick. She even wanted to talk about the drive home and how she was such a bitch to Nico. How he'd given her blue…no pink, balls. Pink buds.

But, the watered down way Liz wedged him into the conversation didn't exactly inspire that kind of talk. Liz was calling Julie out.

Julie: How do you know I didn't already?
Liz: How long have I been knowing you?

Since before I could get away with lying.
And that was her cue. Julie scrolled through her phone and settled on a clapboard slate emoji. Cut. She was not going down that road. Not at five in the morning. Liz was right, but that was besides the point.

Julie didn't validate Liz's question. Instead, she ignored it and switched back to talk about her chemical peel.

Liz was eager to get in a few more winks before she had to get going for the day, so she reminded Julie to ask for the mild peel, and to meet her at the gym when she finished around six. Without so much as a goodbye, she signed off.

Julie tucked her phone into the pocket of her comfy, cowl neck, zip sweater and let her head fall against the back of the chair. She closed her eyes.

Call Nico? Why would she call him after the way things fell out? Sure, he'd starred in her dream, but that was as close as she planned to let him get to her. He should be the last person she called. The last person she wanted to see. Really, what a poser.

The least he could do is 'fess up—putting on that whole sweet, concerned gentleman act.

She rolled her eyes and tugged at the hem of her sweater as she adjusted in the seat. Julie wanted to tell Liz to worry about herself and Derrick, and stop sticking her nose into in other people's business. But then again, she was dying to talk about every single second of her encounters with Nico's—all of the minutia that went along with them.

Nico? Ugh.
Those bottomless brown eyes flashed in front of her and she

could feel his hard chest under her hand again. The sculpted muscle dunes. A memory of his intoxicating woodsy cologne and the warmth of Nona's Italian restaurant flooded back to her.

Her pulse quickened and the hollow between her legs began to ache with need. Where in the heck was all of this coming from? She was like a teenager again. A horny ass teenager.

CHAPTER 12

E very second of the night before reeled in her mind and she was nearly back on the street in front of Liz's, beneath the stars with him. Until the receptionist called her name, dragging her mind back to the earth toned sanctuary.

"She's ready for you now, Ms. Laurich."

The woman escorted her to a cozy room with a cushioned bed in the center that looked like a massage table. This place continued to surprise her. It proved to be nothing like what she'd imagined. Julie had expected a cold, clinical doctor's office with sickly yellow walls and all kinds of sharp medical tools and zit poppers.

If anything, the next hour and a half looked as if it would be a much-deserved spa day more than anything else.

Once she was under the crisp, clean covers, she let their warmth tuck her in until her lids lolled at half-staff. She'd gotten so comfortable that she nearly missed the light creak of the door opening.

Julie exchanged tentative smiles with the doctor.

"I'll just need to go over a few things with you before we get started, but first, please fill this out for." The doctor passed Julie a thin clipboard with a single form on it. "It's mainly a few medical questions along with the purpose of your visit and you found out about us."

Once she'd completed the questionnaire, the doctor immediately went to work, preparing and smoothing and kneading at Julie's "moderately oily" skin.

It was a fair analysis. Very, professional and legit-sounding, Julie determined. Beads of sweat had been known to creep up a couple of times a day on her forehead and nose. No sense in disputing that.

So, she took it at face value. Plus, Julie couldn't help feeling like she'd time-warped into Seattle Grace—minus all the emergencies. The woman did favor Meredith Grey, if you closed one eye and tilted your head to the side, with her blonde hair and self-depre-cating smile.

"Relax. I'm just going to get started," said softly, sweetly as she engaged Julie in light small talk about the weather and the upcoming Memorial holiday.

The doctor seemed down to earth, like this sort of procedure was no big deal. Like she'd done it a million and one times. She even had a doctorly twinkle of confidence in her eyes, and teeth that competed valiantly with her stark white coat. All of which put Julie's reservations about the process at ease.

A simple chemical peel, Liz had said. She'd be in and out. People got them all of the time and were better for it on the other side.

As tired as she was, Julie decided she was in good hands. She'd catch up on a few Zs while the good doctor worked, and wake up transformed.

That was the plan, anyway.

At first, her skin tingled with a cooling sensation as the estheti-cian cleaned away the excess oil from her face wash and moistur-izer. Her eyes slitted open at the stretchy snap of latex gloves as Meredith squeezed her slender fingers in one by one. Still, Julie dozed. Rather, daydreamed, her mind filled with images and recur-ring fantasies of Nico in the shower, then her and Nico in the back of his big black truck.

She'd even gotten carried away with the vision of him picking her up for lunch from her new branch where she was the newly promoted branch manager. The fantasy reeled her in deeper as she relaxed.

"Soothing" and "mild" were the words Meredith had used when she explained the process to Julie. Better yet, when she pacified her. Damn near hypnotized her with claims of relaxation and illusions of unveiling her as a spanking new head-turner.

Dr. Meredith clicked on a small desk fan and let the feathery breeze cool over Julie's face as she ripped open a towelette and applied it to her tingling skin. For a few seconds, the air mixing with the application gave way to a refreshing faint fizzing. Sort of like effervescent bath bombs or peppermint tea. It *was* soothing.

"This is nice," Julie muttered.

Then, about five or so minutes in, the light tingling sensation escalated to a piercing million-needle scorcher that was anything other than "mild." And all of a sudden, she realized Meredith the skin magician would be true to her words. People would look at her alright. Only they'd stare and gawk, bugging their beady eyes out to see the scalded redheaded finch.

"What the hell is happening to me?" Julie said, terror in her voice.

"It's completely normal to feel a light prickle." The magician, no the evil sorceress, said. But her attempt to calm Julie was futile.

At the sides of her face, she could hear her flesh sizzle. Her eyes darted up at the ceiling in zigzags, then to Meredith, then back to the ceiling. The sound of her throbbing heart pulsed in her ears. She had to get out of there.

Julie bolted upright and nearly head-butted Meredith. She hastily tossed the sheet to the ground. She couldn't get out of there fast enough. She bee-lined to the restroom as visions of those naked, hairless dogs kept reeling past her shielded eyes. She ducked and weaved to avoid direct eye contact with other humans.

In the time she'd been in the white dungeon, the lobby had filled with people who must have been sadistic freaks.

With both hands, Julie burst through the door to the restroom and dunked her head beneath the faucet. After what felt like hours dousing handfuls of water over her raw skin, she came up for air.

It wasn't as bad as she'd imagined. Sure, she was still red around the edges, but her skin hadn't fallen off and she still looked human; albeit, a mad version with an affinity for way too much blush.

Through the mirror, Julie watched as the door squeaked open and the sweet olive-skinned receptionist who'd offered her the coffee earlier snuck in quietly.

"Is everything all right?" she whispered, her voice tranquil and delicate. "I brought you something."

Julie turned and eyed her tiny outstretched hand, but she didn't move.

"It won't hurt you, I promise. It's just an aloe vera wipe. Cools the skin and heals the tissue." She took two tentative steps closer to Julie, eying her with each move as if Julie were a rabid dog who might attack at any time. But it didn't deter her, as the girl reached out for Julie's face and waited for consent before touching.

"May I?" she asked.

Julie nodded, still apprehensive about the whole situation, but there was something gentle about the woman's voice. Something trustworthy.

When the girl's dainty fingers grazed her cheek, Julie steeled herself in place and studied her for answers.

"Don't worry. It looks like it was just too strong. You have such beautiful, delicate skin. Give it a half-hour and it'll be a cheery blush. People will think you're really excited about something, or that you went for an early run." She offered a earnest smile that reached up and pulled at the corners of her warm brown eyes.

"Thank you." Julie's words were barely audible, but the girl nodded.

Julie didn't know why, but she felt a wave of emotions wash over her. Mostly appreciation. The girl couldn't have been more than nineteen or twenty, but the way she'd tended to her, the way she was so careful with her feelings felt motherly, nurturing.

And in that moment, Julie missed her mom.

They used to talk a couple of times a day, but lately she'd been dodging her mom's calls. Though she meant well with her pep talks, they had a distinctly reverse effect since Patrick left.

The same words that used to give her a good ego boost left her deflated. Every compliment to her or dig against Patrick, or heaven forbid, mention of her cousin Sophia's upcoming baby shower, only highlighted what was missing in Julie's life.

No one wanted to be good at being alone. And if Patrick didn't deserve her, who did? Who was this great guy that Mom kept saying would come along at the right time?

She was ready *now*.

After a few minutes, Julie worked up the nerve to leave the restroom. She gave the girl a grateful hug, slipped out of the place in as stealthy a fashion as a woman with her worries on display could muster, and dialed her mom the instant the car door closed.

"Is that you JuJu Bean?" Her voice echoed through the car on Bluetooth.

Julie hooked a hard right out of the parking lot. "Yeah, Mom, it's me. Had your coffee yet?"

"Already on cup number two. Now, what are you doing up this early? You're all right now, aren't you, honey?" God she had missed the sound of her mother's voice.

"I'm fine, just checking in on you."

Julie pulled into traffic behind a red minivan moving at the speed of snails on hallucinogens. She'd just missed the green light. Damn, she was going to have to haul ass to make it to the gym on time.

"Uh huh." She paused and Julie braced herself for the proverbial foot-drop. "Any word from…Patrick?" her mom asked, tiptoeing lightly.

Though not light enough. *Good going, Mom.*

"You know, regret is a funny thing," her mom said all cryptic, as if Julie was supposed to know what that meant.

It may have been the hour, or the mention of his name, but even saying it in a sweet mom voice wouldn't make it palatable. Julie was tempted to keep the peace, but this was getting to be too much. Something had to give.

"Seriously, Mom? This is why I haven't called you. Can't you just see how I'm doing and not ask about him? It's hard enough as it is, but when you keep bringing it up, I'm back at square one. And maybe I've got more things going on in my life that have nothing to do with him."

"Lord have mercy, Julie. What's gotten into you? Is it that time of the month? Everything going all right at work?" her mom deflected. For her, nothing had ever been about Julie, per se. Maternal rights outweighed privacy and, apparently, the ability to feel emotions or desires that weren't hinged upon a man.

Julie wasn't her mother. She wanted someone to spend her life with, but she could be without a man.

"Look, I just wanted to tell you that I love you. I don't want anything. And I'm fine, so you can stop worrying about me. I'm fine. I'm always fine."

"Don't hang up." A breathless desperation laced her mother's words.

"Why, Mom? What else could you possibly say that you haven't already said?" She hadn't meant to sound so irritated and detached, but her mom had a way of picking at old wounds.

"I...I just wanted to see if you'd stop by this weekend, that's all. But I can tell you've got a lot on your plate right now. It's okay, honey. Call me when you can."

The sadness in her mother's voice killed her. Julie hated that her mother was alone. She worried about her all the time since her dad passed away. Why couldn't her mother try again? Why wasn't she enough? Her mother had given up her dreams for their marriage, but she was still alive. Why not pick up where she left off?

Her mother sounded fragile and desolate, and it pierced Julie's heart. She'd only wanted to talk for a few minutes and tell her mom how much she missed and loved her. As much as she hated it, Patrick had become her trigger point. A button her mother had become an expert at pushing.

"I'm sorry, Mom. I'll be there. Just let me know what time and if you want me to bring anything."

Julie could almost hear the smile in her mother's voice. "I'll make that taco soup you love so much with the jalapenos and yellow onions. I was just down at the farmer's market and picked up a good batch. Ooh and I'll even do that cucumber-tomato salad for a starter." Just like that, her mom was jubilant.

As she inched past a fender-bender on the side of the road, rubber-necking nostalgically about Nico as the traffic let up, she found that she felt good, too. "That's awesome. I can bring the wine. Want anything special, Mom?"

"Surprise me. You pick. You kids always seem to know the good stuff. I think there's a love movie marathon on, too. It'll be just like old times. The Laurich girls back together again!"

"Sounds fun," Julie said. It surprised her more than anything that she actually meant it. "I'm pulling up at the gym. Can't wait for this weekend."

"All right, honey. I love you."

"Love you, too." Julie ended the call. She had braced herself for the worst, but somehow things had turned around.

As she parked her car, checking the time on the dash, Julie was pleased to be five minutes early for once in her life. She glanced at her reflection in the rearview mirror. Not only had her complexion cleared to the rosy blush the receptionist had promised, but she was in a much better mood. This workout was going to be epic.

CHAPTER 13

An hour later, Julie dragged her lifeless body into the women's locker room. As she removed her drenched sweats and T-shirt, she had a good mind to march back out there and stuff one of her sweaty socks into Dane's foul mouth.

At the rate he was going, maybe two socks would be better.

She'd come in today motivated and ready to show what she could do. She was going to change the outlook of her day and beat her results from yesterday. If he wanted three reps on weights, she'd give him four. Twenty-five lunges on each leg? It was going to be thirty today.

He didn't even hesitate or consider her feelings. The second he turned around, it was all "Big Red" and "Gingy" and "Tomato." Every other exercise, he had jokes. "Is it too much blood rushing to your head? No, wait. It's just your face."

There was a point when he moved her over to the mats to work on core and Julie had a genuine moment of satisfaction and excitement. All week he had been drilling her to work on her center, but she hadn't felt a thing. Then, today of all days, she got the first whiff of her abs. With each second of her minute-long plank, she could feel the tightening of her abdomen.

They should have been celebrating her progress. Dane should have congratulated her or given her a pat on the back, or something. Instead, this fool, couldn't get past a little skin irritation without acting like a tool.

But then, he started in on her about Nico.

He teased her like they were back in middle school. Things got to be so childish, he actually texted Nico. Julie wanted to grab his phone and delete the message, but he'd jerked it away too fast.

For the rest of the session, Julie stone-faced him. She ignored his taunts about her going all emo on him. His empty apologies were lost on her. He gave the rep counts and she did them. And the instant she finished her cool-down stretches, she waltzed right past him without so much as a goodbye or a flip of the middle finger.

So, by the time she finished showering and dressed for work, Julie just wanted to make it through the rest of her day before some innocent bystander caught the wrath of her wretched morning.

She beelined through the gym with her chin down, eyes fixed on her phone. Liz had her calendar lined up for the rest of the week. At least she was finished with chemical peels. Tomorrow she'd be pampered—hair, brows, and lashes after work. Basically, her do-over appointment.

With all that, she didn't have time for Dane and his taunting, or Nico freaking Farfalla. Really, what kind of name was that anyway?

As she weaved past the juice bar near the spin and yoga rooms, she added a reminder for one hour prior to the do-over appointment. She steadied her finger to press the save button as her shoulder collided with another person. Her phone went flying in the air and slapped down on the floor.

"Shit," Julie yelled. Her face twisted into a squint-eyed, clenched-teeth grimace. "Damn it. Please don't be broken. Please don't broken," she chanted. That's all she needed was to lose all the stuff she had saved on her phone. She hadn't backed it up to her computer in weeks.

"Watch where the hell you're going," the other person warned.

Julie crouched down with her hands outstretched and tenderly reached for her precious phone. "Oh my gosh. Thank goodness. It works," she said as the screen illuminated. Miraculously, it hadn't cracked into a kaleidoscope of tempered glass.

"Julie? I can't believe we keep running into each other like this."

She'd had yet to look up, but at the familiar nasal-hacking pronunciation of her name, she tilted her head up, and immediately regretted it.

"Hey...Celeste."

How? How had Julie avoided Celeste for years and now here she was again?

Julie's gaze trailed downward and her eyes felt pried open. It was literally two days ago that Julie had run into Celeste in Walmart, and somehow in those forty-eight hours, Celeste's stomach had popped out.

Julie was no expert on maternal gestation periods or how many months a belly sticking out that far equated to, but this was outlandish. It could have been the skin-tight yoga pants. Maybe she had a vampire-hybrid baby growing in there at an exponential rate, or she owned some really good Spanx to keep her flat in that white dress the other day.

To make matters worse, it happened that the inflated navel stuck out just right at Julie's eye level, as if to ensure the topic remained front and center.

Attention everyone: Julie Laurich is still single without a prospect and no baby on the way, but everyone around her is apparently a Fertile Myrtle.

Julie staggered to her feet. "Wow! Really coming along there, aren't you?"

"Yeah, I'm fourteen weeks on Friday," Celeste bubbled. "Mommy Bliss has the best yogalates, have you tried it?"

The right words did not come to Julie. She still hadn't decided whether she should even be happy for Celeste. "Wow. Um, wow! Congrats. Congratulations," Julie fumbled, struggling to get upright.

"Listen, Julie. I've been meaning to call you ever since I saw you the other day. Sophia called me about a week ago to invite me to her shower. I told her I would make sure it was okay with you first." Celeste's shoulders hunched and she threw up her hands, waiting for Julie's response, as if to say, *the ball's in your court.*

Julie shrugged, mirroring Celeste, her lips set in a tight line.

This was just great. If she told Celeste she didn't want her there, she'd have to give her cousin a reason and put her relationship with Patrick out as fair game for Sophia and Aunt Helen. And if she said yes, there was always the super-awkward chance that she'd show up with Patrick in tow. *A real win-win situation.*

When Julie resurfaced from her internal debate, Celeste's gaze had taken a downward turn. As Julie followed her line of vision, her own eyes grew larger by the second when they landed on her phone. In the midst of all the collision and baby-shower talk, she'd forgotten that she'd yet to change her screensaver.

Which, at the moment, displayed a beautifully staged photo of Julie and Patrick, cheek to rosy cheek, on the day he proposed.

CHAPTER 14

"What type of document have you got with you today, Mr. Goronowski?" Julie unlocked her top drawer and pulled out her notary journal.

"It's the same one I get every year for my pension," he muttered, his voice scratchy and worn. He'd been coming to Julie since her first week at Regions—the loyal type she knew would stay with her as long as he was a customer.

"Ah. The life certificate. Has it been that long since we did the last one?" Julie shot him a disbelieving smile.

Mr. Goronowski came into the bank just about every other day. He would make a withdrawal, count his one hundred and twenty-five dollars in the same increments of fives, tens, and twenties, and then he'd dart over to Julie's cubicle for an afternoon wink and wave.

He was the kind of customer she loved. Nothing flashy about him, but he was honest and friendly, and he knew the difference between service and servitude. Good people like Mr. Goronowski were the reason she wanted to be a manager. She wanted to cultivate that type of banking relationship where the staff and customers were more like family and friends rather than order-takers and dollar-counters.

"I'll just need to borrow your ID, please. I've got to make sure you're old enough to be receiving a pension." She scrunched her nose at him as he handed it over, and she began filling in the log.

Out of the corner of her eye, she felt the weight of Elise's stare. From her office, there was a direct view, at a diagonal angle, of Elise's glassed-in fortress.

Before she'd mentioned her aspirations of being a manager, this was a good thing. They had their own code language of signals and facial expressions which they'd use to let each other in on possible fraud or irate customers who might affect their service scores. Now, the focus of those steel-framed specs felt more like a magnifying glass in the sun and she was the beady ant on Elise's hill.

Her boss always flicked her pen when she was irritated, a teensy baton that she teetered between her fingers because throwing it at people was frowned upon. That told Julie that the minute her customer left, Elise would bring down her latest hammer on her.

Hence, she took her slow sweet time shooting the breeze with Mr. Goronowski. By now, she already knew that all he had left was a son on the other side of the world living in London, and a scraggly dog named Bob. He'd just turned ninety the month before, but the spring in his step was much closer to an agile seventy-something. And the mouth? Definitely somewhere around the early thirties.

When Elise stood up and glared over at her impatiently with those bugged eyes that basically warned her to hurry up, Julie made a point of opening that particular can of worms.

"And how is Bob these days?"

This was exactly the kind of thing Elise hated. She was more of a "do-the-job-and-get-on-with-it" type of person—cut all the chitchat, smile, and send them on their way.

In Elise's experience, rapport was the enemy of profit. You didn't fatten your pockets by schmoozing anyone other than the affluent, she once told Julie.

What an asshat.

Julie liked money just as much as the next person, but that just seemed ass-backward. Happy, loyal customers who believed their banker had their best interests in mind were less likely to attrite. It all seemed logical, clear as ever in Julie's mind, and the fact that Elise didn't see it the same way made her question why she ever considered her any type of role model.

Ten minutes into her customer's K-9 update, he finally signed her notary book and the life certificate. At the right angle, Julie could see Elise and she would have sworn up and down that her boss had blown a gasket and fumes billowed from her ears. Julie figured the sooner she met with her, the sooner she'd find someone else to bug.

Julie signed the document and eyed the area at the bottom right of the page designated for her stamp. With both hands, she pressed it down and met Elise's stare.

"You're all set. I'll see you Friday." Julie rose from her chair with her client. "Have a great day, and give Bob a good scratch behind the ears for me."

"Will do now, Julie. I'll be seeing you." He tipped his tattered baseball cap at her and shuffled toward the exit.

Julie remained standing as Elise practically stomped her way over in sort of an overgrown childish tantrum. Only when Elise sat in the chair across from her did Julie take her seat. For a beat, they played the staring game, but Elise blinked first. She clearly had something boiling her blood.

Elise leaned against the back of the chair and crossed her legs, so that her foot dangled. The way her chin rested on her thumb with her index finger bobbing over the fuzz on her top lip, Julie could tell the wheels were turning in Elise's head—like she had something of high importance to discuss.

"I've given what you said some thought...and, I think I've found a way to make us both happy," Elise finally said, her brows lifting in a hopeful bounce.

"Okay, great. I'm listening." Julie perked up, eager to hear this grand compromise that Elise had come up with on her own.

"The way I see it, *you* want to be a manager, and *I* believe you'll be best served here as a personal banker—"

A tiny sigh escaped Julie's mouth and immediately she wished she could take it back. "Sorry. I um...didn't get much sleep last night. Please. Please go on," she urged.

Elise's skinny lips pressed together into a fine red line. "As I was saying, every manager needs to be well-rounded. You have to keep up your sales and operations, but also you have to adhere to your commitment to the community."

Elise adjusted herself in the chair and folded her arms. The crow's feet at the outer corners of her eyes sunk into pulsing gorges at the temples. Julie steeled herself in anticipation, still confused as to where this was going.

"So...I've taken the liberty of signing you up," Elise stated. A glint of amusement settled in her eyes.

"What? For what? What did you sign me up for?" Julie questioned in a knee-jerk reaction.

Apparently, this was the reaction Elise was banking on. Color rushed to her cheeks and she sat up on the edge of the chair. Her arms dropped over to her sides and she leaned in to make sure Julie could hear her.

"Kid Savers," she said plainly, as if it was a household name. When the name failed to register with Julie, she clarified to really seal it in deep. "As part of this branch's commitment to the community, you are going to represent us. I just got off of a division conference call and every branch is being required to participate next week."

She stood up completely erect like her back was against the wall. With Julie seated before her, she loomed over her like a shaky tower in a tornado. "I figured this was as good a time as any for you to build up that resume of yours for management. And, since I really don't care to spend a week with rooms full of ankle-biters putting their grubby little hands all over my Dior, we can kill two birds with one stone."

Julie looked up, her mouth agape, but nothing came out. Elise was vindictive, but this was on a whole different level of evil. Julie didn't mind spending a week doing community service; she actually enjoyed kids, and teaching happened to be something she was good at. But building Julie's resume wasn't something high on Elise's list. As a matter of fact, it was probably dead-last on principle alone, seeing as how Elise viewed Julie's career aspirations as abandonment.

Still, it took an insidious, truly narcissistic person to schedule community service for her when Elise was well aware that the interviews for the manager opening at the Northwest Branch were taking place that very same week.

"Which day next week?" Julie panicked.

Her manager stared at her, deadpan. "The full week."

"Elise, the interviews are next week," Julie said incredulously.

Her boss turned, doing her best impression of a decent manager hurt by such an insinuation that she'd done it on purpose. "Oh, are they?" she muttered.

"Yes."

And just when Julie thought there might be an ounce of humanity left in her, Elise quelled that suspicion. It only made sense that the newly crowned Ice Queen be cold-blooded.

"It's such a shame that you'll miss them," she said. Then she turned on the heels of her black leather pumps and sashayed back to her icy fortress.

The rest of the day, Julie's capacity to give a damn flew right out the window. Every client was met with a blank stare and absent-minded rapport. The ones who really knew her well asked her multiple times about her day, and whether or not she was feeling all right, to which she responded with a flippant, "sure."

They weren't stupid. Anyone with a kindergarten education could see the traces of disappointment lingering on her face. She'd tried to buck up and put on a good face for her clients. And when the traffic died down, she pulled up a new browser on her computer and typed in the words, "bank manager positions Las Vegas Nevada."

Armed with her search results—the especially good ones with a starburst asterisk in the left-hand column—Julie managed to escape after closing without further exchange with Elise.

By the time she reached the salon a few hours later, tears welled up at the sight of Liz.

"Seriously, Jules? You're so dramatic. Threading doesn't hurt that bad," she teased.

Julie latched on to Liz and held her for a moment too long, pulling her in tight. "I know. I've just really had a crappy day."

"Okay because, really, I was going to be so over you if you were crying over hair, lashes, and brows." Liz laughed and squeezed a little tighter. "Hashtag, first world problems."

This was what Julie needed—more time with her best friend and none of the worries from work.

When Jules failed to release Liz from her embrace, Liz stiffened. "Um…my brows are straight-up sketchy right now, so if you could just let me go, that would be great."

In just under three hours, the pair stumbled onto the sidewalk giddy with laughter and about half of the boxed Moscato Liz had hidden in her purse. Both of their brows and lashes were on point, but it was the hair that stood out the most.

On a whim, Liz decided she needed a break from her curls and got a Brazilian Blowout. Her chestnut mane trailed the length of her torso in slick sheets and stopped just short of her maximal glutes.

Julie was no modern-day Rapunzel, but under the pressure of the chair, she went rogue. For one: she hacked off ten inches; And two: she closed her eyes and pointed on impulse at the jet-black dye with an undertone of Wonder Woman blue. A bouncy asymmetrical bob framed her round face now, and she rather liked it.

Liz nearly freaked out at the insane choice, but once she'd

confirmed with Julie that she was really going to go through with it, all bets were off.

When they both finished, Julie spun in her chair and raised a brow at Liz. "Go bold or go home, right?"

She'd been back at the gym in full force for less than a week and already she saw hints at the new Julie taking shape. Small indentations in her aching arms and legs. Pressure as she contracted her abs. When she looked close enough, she swore she saw the curve of an actual waistline. And now this.

She was practically unrecognizable.

They stood in the blinking neon light of the bar next door to the salon and an idea too good to pass up came to Julie.

"This hair is too amazing for these clothes. Why don't we hit up the outlets for something as fierce as my new look and then go for drinks?"

"You know it's Wednesday, right? Everything is closing in like an hour." Liz pointed out.

"Okay, so how about we shop for half an hour, then go out for *a* drink?" Julie pressed. "After what that heifer did today, I'm going to need more than one."

Two pairs of black skinny jeans, one new vixen-red skirt suit, four loose-fit T-shirts in multiple shades of blush, two pairs of pumps, one pair of fluorescent orange sneakers, three maxi dresses, and one slick black leather jacket, all two sizes too small later, Julie steered her car toward downtown.

She took the long way around, winding down the one-way streets and creeping through the tourist crowds. With Liz following behind, it wouldn't take her long to know exactly where they were headed.

If they were going to be stubborn asses, Julie was going to let the reality kick them in theirs.

The second they pulled into the two spaces lining the sidewalk a block down from the Skyline Cafe, she braced herself for Liz's wrath. Sure enough, she heard a car door slam and Liz was in her face in two seconds flat.

"What the fuck are you doing?" she spat.

Julie gave her a dumbfounded shrug. "Uh...we said we were going to have a drink?" She dodged the obvious, but she needed to buy herself some time.

"Oh, okay. You must think I'm a fucking idiot. Don't play dumb with me, Jules. I don't need you meddling in my life. I told you we'd be fine, so let me handle it."

Julie smirked. "Is that what you call handling it? Ghosting him and sulking every day? Trolling his Instagram and Snapchat? Please. At least be a woman and face him."

"That's rich, coming from you." Liz expelled a haughty breath. "Have you called Nico? Better yet, have you even talked to another guy since Patrick? No. So don't talk to me about what I should and shouldn't be doing."

Julie skulked off in the direction of the cafe, hoping to high hell Derrick would materialize before she lost the only friendship that mattered to her.

Liz, tight on her heels, followed her, still going off on her. "If we're doing this, let's talk about why you're such a coward. Now, not only are you still holding out for a tool who's already moved on, but now you're letting that whore go to your cousin's baby shower? Talk about no backbone. Really, Jules?"

At that point, the two were directly in front of the cafe, but Liz was so busy reaming Julie that she failed to notice. Julie stood there and took it as Liz unleashed on her.

Truthfully, she hoped that Liz would yell a little louder, so Derrick would hear and come out.

"And another thing. Give me your phone," Liz demanded.

"What? Why?" Julie stared, paying attention for the first time since they came to a stop.

Without a word, Liz yanked it from her hand. Due to many drunken nights and drunk dials, she already knew the passcode. She jabbed her finger at the screen and it lit up with the same engagement night photo of Julie and Patrick that Celeste had scoped out before stomping off.

Liz held the phone out to Julie. Her brows raised and the left corner of her mouth curved upward. "Erase it." She dared Julie. It was a challenge. A bold-faced, verbal equivalent of a shove. She was effectively calling Julie's bluff and exposing her double standard.

But, Patrick was an asshole. Derrick was a frigging unicorn. Good guys like him simply didn't exist anymore. He just wanted to love on Liz and build a family together. He was fighting for a life with her. Derrick wanted the best for Liz.

Julie's gaze met Liz's, and then another piece fell into place. It wasn't that Derrick was such a bad guy for wanting the best for Liz. It was the fact that he *didn't* know what was best for her. Just like Liz seemed to be, Julie was also *sick* and *tired* of people thinking they knew better than she did what was best for her.

Slowly, reluctantly, Julie took the phone. In the bottom right-hand corner, a small blue and white trashcan glared back at her. This was the last piece of him. In an angry rage a few weeks earlier, she deleted every picture and video of him. She'd shut down every story on her social media apps in which he'd been included. Though she knew his number by heart, she deleted it, too, as a show of will.

This was all that was left.

Why *hadn't* she called Nico yet? She didn't have his phone number for one, but it wouldn't be hard to get it from Derrick. What was she still holding on to?

She took a deep breath and placed her finger on it. And just like that, she erased Patrick from her life.

While Julie weighed the finality in such a small gesture, Liz laid her head on Julie's shoulder, just as Derrick walked up with a banged-up Dane on crutches.

CHAPTER 15

The following morning, Julie arrived at the gym fifteen minutes early and ordered a green protein smoothie. Liz said it would help get her through the workout. Some sock juice concoction that consisted of spinach, bananas, mangoes, and flax seeds.

While she waited for the attendant behind the counter to throw in everything and the kitchen sink, she scanned the perimeter to see which trainers were on duty.

Dane said he was sending one of his good buddies to take over while he healed.

Again Julie searched the gym, keeping an eye on the trainers who usually worked with Dane to see if she'd previously met the person. This "good buddy" who he'd tasked with taking over her training during his recovery.

In the back by the Smith machine, Penny and her rock-solid thighs stood with her clipboard at the ready. The bony-legged guy she was training struggled under the weight to lower himself into a squat.

The other trainers, Doug and Sarah, were up front by the bench press, spotting, and Jeff wasn't doing much of anything, unless you counted playing on his phone probably for the past hour.

In just the amount of time she was sitting there, he'd already taken two selfies. Neither of which showcased anything noteworthy other than his overinflated injectable lips.

Jeff lifted his beady eyes toward Julie and she jerked her head back toward the girl behind the counter. She prayed he wasn't the one she'd be stuck with for whatever length of time Dane's bone needed to weld itself back together. He was nice enough, in a pocket-sized brain kind of way, but she couldn't imagine him barking orders and motivating her through her goals.

She wasn't in a position to judge, but in the week since she'd become a member, she had yet to see him with a client who wasn't his friend, or someone who he had talked about behind their back.

Plus, it didn't help that he had a serious case of dad bod.

Come on; if he was going to train for a living, he needed to be his own walking advertisement. No one wanted someone with ugly hair to style theirs, the same way a sickly doctor wouldn't exactly inspire healthy habits from his patients. That's just a given.

Probably not the best way to coach someone for results, she mused.

When Julie's smoothie was ready, she slurped it down so fast that her brain twisted into a frozen vise grip and she was rendered paralyzed until the freeze waned.

She was hungry and a little bit sick of green veggies and egg whites. What she wanted was a full stack of buttery pancakes with globs of syrup pouring over the edges. She wanted real bacon, not that rubber turkey that Dane and Liz swore by. Real, crunchy, fatty, oily bacon hot off the grill.

Her mouth watered at the thought.

There were plenty of things that tasted better than skinny felt. Not that she knew what skin and bones felt like over the last decade. She'd always been a foodie, long before loving food had a name. Julie could throw down in the kitchen and eat most men under the table.

She used her straw to scrape the sides of the cup and sucked down as much as she could. What she couldn't reach with the straw, she tried to get by taking the plastic top off and slurping it down. A slushy green avalanche skidded down the inside of the cup and dripped down onto her face and shirt.

"Damn it!" She cursed the stupid straw.

Julie grabbed a napkin from the counter and patted her shirt, but she only made it worse. Now, instead of one small green spot, she'd rubbed it around so much, the wet spot had travelled down to her boob.

"Great, a green boob!" she hissed.

"Uh oh. Do you need to reschedule?" a deep voice said from behind her. "That's going to stain. Nice hair by the way, I barely recognized you."

Julie turned, prepared to see anyone else, but who she hadn't been expecting to see was *him*. Nico.

She stiffened on impulse. Her mouth fell open and she could feel her face screw into a blend of flattery, annoyance, and pure unsaturated attitude. Heat ignited low in her belly and traveled up to her cheeks.

As much as she wanted to deny it, she couldn't. Her body wouldn't let her lie. Nico had striking good looks. The guy was blazing hot and every inch of her skin pulsed, just being near him.

Since she last saw him, he'd tapered his close-cut beard, further defining the strong lines of his jaw. He'd also gotten some sun, his usual tawny coloring bronzed with undertones of warm earth. Then, there was those deep-set honey eyes with sweeping lashes.

Julie didn't dare stare into them or allow her gaze to linger over the rest of his body, for his lean torso and strong arms might send her into a frenzy imagining him pressed up against her.

She was at a loss for words, but he and his untimely sense of humor, unfortunately was not.

He gave Julie a considerable once-over before starting in on her nerves. "This makes two stained shirts and one ripped skirt. Pretty soon you're going to be out of clothes at the rate you're going."

Tragically, the guy was standing there making fun of her and she was still stuck on the words, "out of clothes." *Ugh Pink buds.*

It was clear by the exaggerated way his brows raised and a laugh pulled at the corners of his full lips that he was joking, but Julie wasn't in any mood to joke. She was wound up tighter than a mattress coil.

Even the sight of his adorable dimple couldn't reverse the onset of her mood swing.

"Wow, no shit Sherlock. Nothing gets by you," she said. It could have been the shower fantasy still running through her mind inspired by the impression of his washboard abs against the cotton shirt fabric, but she sounded strained to her own ears.

About the only thing she could do, was look anywhere but at him.

With her attention fully focused on her dry hands and cuticles, she made a mental note to check her calendar for the mani-pedi Liz had set up.

Nico cleared his throat. Before he could get a word in edgewise, Julie continued snapping at him. "As much fun as this little reunion is that we're having, I don't have time for you right now. I have an appointment."

Refusing to look him in the eye, Julie stood up and made grand work of searching the room. She checked her watch. Already six o'five.

"That's funny. I have an appointment, too. Mine is at six. What time is yours?" He stood beside her, his arm lightly brushing hers as he searched the room, too. His hand propped over his eyes, as if he needed to look out ashore.

"Mine is at six, too." She narrowed her gaze on him as an unwanted thought popped into her head. "Wait a minute. You said 'reschedule'?"

"Yeah. You're my appointment. Didn't Dane tell you?" That megawatt panty-dropper smile spread across his face and out popped a mind-numbing dimple that she'd somehow missed before.

Julie leaned on the bar to keep her knees from buckling. "Uh, no." She rolled her eyes and her mouth hung open at the blatant conspiracy these two had worked out behind her back.

"Dane thinks this shit is funny, but it's not." She pouted. Not only because she could image her trainer getting a good kick out of this, but also because she could not be stuck with Nico. She'd already done the cheating, lying type. Adding a player to her list of mistakes probably wasn't the best idea.

"Look, Nico. No offense, but I think I'll just keep doing the things Dane taught me until he comes back. I don't need your help." At the same time, Julie's brows lifted as she shrugged.

Dane had said he needed five to six weeks to heal from his lower leg fracture. With Nico and that dimple, she'd give herself a week tops before her willpower gave out. She didn't stand a chance against her raging libido.

She walked over to the mats and began her stretches, but he was hot on her tail.

"Why are you so stubborn? I'm only trying to help you." He squatted down in front of her so that her eyes were level with the most perfect dimple she'd ever seen in her life. "I don't want anything from you, so chill. It'll be totally professional and when we're done, we can just go our separate ways, no harm no foul," he offered.

"What's in it for you, Mr. Nice Guy? Are you getting paid for this —is that it?" she accused him as she lowered her chest flat between her spread legs. She arched her left arm over to her right leg. "Tell you what. I'll tell Dane you trained me and you can still get paid and leave me alone. Deal?"

"No deal. I'm not in this for the money, Girl Boss. I'm not about that life. Why do you always have to be touchy about everything? He's not even paying me. He's just a good friend of the family and I told him I'd help out, that's all. Seriously, is it so hard for you believe that people can be good to each other without some ulterior motive?"

"Yes," she said flatly.

Nico raised his brows at her. "Well, believe it. Are we going to do this, or what?"

At her narrowed side-eye and the "fuck off" sign she projected on her forehead, Nico stood up and skulked over to the barbells.

She was right to be mad. Right to avoid this guy. If she didn't want to keep repeating the same insane cycle with men only to end up regretting it, she had to. Every hot-headed word she had said was right. Except she had directed them at the wrong person. Patrick? Yes. Celeste or Elise? Absolutely. But not Nico.

Shame washed over her. What had he really done to her? He'd run out in the rain to return her shirt. They shared a nice dinner and he made sure she got home safe. What was so wrong with that?

Nothing, if she didn't mind the fact that he was a self-confessed manwhore.

Damn it, why am I always drawn to the ones with the matching dangerous good looks and sketchy past?

Julie studied his reflection in the mirror. He double-fisted a pair of fifty or sixty pounders, she guessed by where he stood in front of the racks with weights from five to a hundred pounds. From across the room, she stared as he alternated them in butterfly tricep lifts with such ease and natural strength. His muscles rippled beneath his taut brown skin.

Where she was sitting, the muscles in his back flexed through his shirt and she couldn't help wondering what he'd look like without it.

To anyone else, he looked like he was just concentrating, focusing on his set. But, she'd gotten a glimpse of his anger that night in his truck. That clenched jaw. The throbbing vein at his temple. The way his long lashes seemed to flutter when he squinted.

God, he was cute when he was angry.

Feeling loose and stretchy, Julie made her way over to the tread-mill to warm up. Usually, she'd go four and a half or five miles an hour, comfortably. Today, though, at this angle? With Nico dead-center in front of her and her libido shooting off flares? She sprinted at nine miles an hour.

Bass from her "Sweat" playlist pounded in her ears, inciting her heart. Her new fluorescent running shoes barely touched the belt. Every ounce of fat on her body cried a salty river.

She could almost reach him.

Images of her fingers wrapped around his neck warred with the flashes of her legs straddling his waist. Why couldn't she take Liz's advice, and just sleep with him? What was she so afraid of?

Her breath billowed from her in a curtain of fog, but Julie couldn't stop running. Her legs weren't listening to her anymore. Her arms cranked in blazing circles the way train wheels kept wind-ing. The way her mind kept winding.

Concentrate on something else. Anything else. You have muffin top and Patrick called you boring. He left you. He clearly cheated on you with Celeste the wannabe. The whore. Sophia is a two-faced bitch.

Julie ran faster, but Nico's face was still there.

You're mad at Elise. Work. Yes, work. She fucking cockblocked you.

Something didn't make sense. Who was this guy? He said he was a player. But, he was sweet, too. Thoughtful. Funny. It just didn't add up. Why couldn't she get a good read on him?

Don't think about him. Think of something else. Anything else. Choco-late. Yes, chocolate is better than sex. Sex. No!

In the mirror, Julie found his eyes and for some reason she couldn't explain, she couldn't look away. For what seemed like forever, the portal between them flooded with every conflicting emotion she had about him. She almost didn't mind, until she real-ized he was walking toward her now.

Her stride widened and when he neared close enough to touch her, in the most graceless and uncoordinated fumble ever, those legs with the mind of their own wiped out from beneath her.

In a whirling blur, Julie grabbed the red emergency stop key and the treadmill screeched to a jarring halt. Her body floated in the air. Smeared faces and black rubber faded into a wave of red as her head hit the mat.

"Julie? Are you okay? Julie, can you hear me?" A muffled voice sounded like it came from under water, calling to her. "Do you need me to call the paramedics?"

Julie managed a pained grunt.

"Get me some clean towels for her head and call the paramedics," the voice yelled to no one in particular.

She shifted on the floor and cracked her eyes. Nico sat beside her, his handsome face etched with worry. Touching lightly, he parted her hair. "Looks like she's got a pretty good gash here."

"Don't touch her, man," another guy's voice warned. "Let the paramedics do it. If anything happens, you'll make the club liable."

Julie lifted her head toward the voice. *Jeff.* She hated him for good reason. Wasn't there something on his phone he should be looking at? He'd let her die if it were up to him.

"Just get me the towels and shut the fuck up, Jeff." Nico's lashes fluttered.

If she could move more than an inch, she'd like to kiss Nico for that one. Her head was cradled in his palm as his splayed fingers raked through Julie's hair. He was so close and he smelled so good. Deeply, she inhaled, trying to discern his scent.

Was that lemon? Cotton?

She blinked back the urge to sleep.

His eyes fell on her and she looked up at him. "No, don't call the paramedics." Julie placed her hand on Nico's arm.

He lowered his face to hers. A pink flush colored his cheeks. "Julie, I'm here for you. Don't move."

"I'm fine. It's just my head. It hurts a little right here." She touched the spot off the center of her forehead where Nico parted her hair. Her fingers dabbed at the sticky wetness and she brought them to her eyes.

"I'm bleeding," she said through shallow breaths.

"Not too bad, but we do need to get you cleaned up. Think you can sit up?"

She rolled to her side and pushed off of her hand.

"Slowly. Don't try to move too fast, Julie. I've got you." From behind her, Nico laced his hands around her waist and helped her to her feet.

The room spun as Julie struggled to find her footing.

"She's all right. Let's give her some room," Nico commanded. Fifteen or so people lined the mat, staring at her, horror and worry written on their faces. And while her head hurt, at that moment, Julie was more embarrassed than anything. Blood rushed to her head and she held Nico's arm tighten around her.

As hazy as her mind was at the moment, Julie reveled in the strength of Nico's capable hands.

"Whoa, there. I've got you." Nico swept Julie off her wobbly feet into his arms. "Oh, no you don't," he said as Julie's head fell back over his arm.

He shook her. "Wake up now. No sleeping. Not for at least two or three hours." He nuzzled her chin with his nose. "Where were you running to? We're not giving out any Olympic gold medals today."

CHAPTER 16

Nearly an hour later, Julie's graceless brush with death was old news. Nico had cleaned her head—which looked worse than it actually was—and propped her up on a window seat at the half-lap mark around the track. The two eased into the groove of comfortable conversation, while Julie sipped on her second bottle of water from a straw.

To keep her awake, he playfully harped on her to rehash her obsession with clothing stains. That playfulness moved to the conversation from the gym and back to their double date and Derrick's bombed proposal. Finally, as if there weren't any other topic worth talking about, he finagled his way into Julie's relationship history.

"I'm boring," Julie conceded. *Boring.*

"Wow, that's how he said it? He didn't even have the decency to lie."

"Nope. No sugar-coating. Just *boring.* That's what he said...and I'm kind of starting to believe him."

Nico took one look at her and refused to accept the invite to her pity party. "Me too," he teased.

"Jerk." She slapped his shoulder and immediately regretted it. "Ouch, damn. My hand."

"I'm made of steel. That ought to teach you to keep your hands to yourself."

"Okay, Iron Man. Then, what's *your* story, and what does Farfalla mean?" she asked.

Nico cracked his neck on both sides. "Another day. Today, it's about you. We've got to keep you talking, to keep you from sleeping…and Farfalla is Italian for butterfly." He leaned in and checked the bandage on Julie's forehead, his fingers warm on her skin. "This is looking much better. Finally got the bleeding to let up."

"Thanks," she whispered. Her mind lingered on the duality of this rough, muscular man and the gentility in his name. When she thought of butterflies, hope, change, and life came to mind. Could he be the change she needed? Was she crazy for even thinking of Nico in terms of a future?

He stared at her for a beat too long, that devastating smile flashing at her. She looked away.

"I like this new look. It's a drastic change, though. So, what brought it on?" he asked.

She refused to meet his gaze. "Thanks. I just…needed a change, you know? I wanted to do something different, if I'm going to make myself over."

"I like it, but I liked it the other way, too. Why do you need to change?"

Because staying the same isn't an option. Julie contemplated unloading everything about Patrick on him, but decided against it. "Why do *you* ask so many questions?" she retorted.

They laughed, but it didn't deter him. He had to keep her talking, so everything was fair game. The strangest thing was, she didn't mind talking to him. As much as she didn't want to admit it, she even *liked* the familiarity she felt just being with him. But, she couldn't let him know that.

"Ok, so then if that's off-limits, what about work? You said you had issues with your boss?"

"Shit, work." Julie patted her arm for her phone, but it wasn't there. "My phone." She jolted upright, her eyes widening.

Nico held his palms up to her. "Relax. I held onto it for you," he said, and slipped it from his pocket. "I wasn't sure what her name was, or else, I would've texted her for you."

Julie's eyes shot up at him. This was exactly what bothered her most about him. This concerned, thoughtful guy who put so much care into everything he did—he couldn't be a player.

She took the phone and sent Elise a quick text to let her know what happened and that she'd be back in tomorrow. "Thanks again." Her gaze fell on her fidgeting hands as she tried to answer his earlier question.

"I don't even know where to start. I've just got to get out of there," she confessed.

"This is your boss you're talking about? What's her deal? Was she always like this, or did something happen to set her off?" Nico asked.

"She used to be great. I really liked her…respected her, you know? We got along fine." Julie adjusted the towel behind her head and shifted into a more agreeable position for her achy back.

Nico's face twisted into a bold question mark. "And then?"

Julie took another sip of water before she answered. "I told her I wanted to apply for an open management position at this branch right by my condo."

"That'll do it every time." He threw his hands up and rested his case.

"Now she's got me signed up for this community thing next week at the same time the interviews are going on. Kid Savers is great, but I'm thinking about skipping out early one day to interview."

Nico sat up. "Wait, which bank are you with again?"

"Regions West, why?"

Excitement seemed to buzz over him. "Next week, you said?"

Julie nodded and winced as a sharp pain gripped her head.

He leaned back against the wall, lowering his lids as a satisfied grin crept at the corners of his mouth.

Ever since she'd met Nico, he had found a way to keep showing up in her life. At the rate things were going, Julie wondered whether she ought to keep fighting it, or go along with the plan the universe seemed content to unleash on her.

THE NEXT DAY, Julie's phone pinged beneath her desk and she rushed to put it on vibrate. She didn't want to give Elise any more ammunition by breaking the cell phone policy.

She held the phone low under her desk as she scanned the branch for customers. Surprisingly, for a Thursday before the Memorial holiday, it was slow, save for the regulars and a few non-customers cashing checks at the teller line.

By lunchtime, Julie had submitted her resume to five local banks, cleared all of her pending work, doodled her way through the Kid Saver conference call, and still had enough spare time to clean out her in-box.

When the main phone line rang two times, Julie watched as Elise eyed the caller ID, picked it up, and stealthily shut her door. She'd almost gone unnoticed as she strutted back to her desk, flitting her gaze over to Julie. But, Julie had long mastered the facade of looking busy even when she wasn't. She feigned intense concentration on her locked monitor until Elise rolled her chair backward into the corner of her office.

She must have figured that she was out of Julie's view because her body seemed to loosen up, her right leg draped over her left, exposing her upper thigh in a suit skirt.

You're not slick.

As Elise nestled the receiver between her ear and shoulder and settled into the seat of the chair with parted knees, Julie acted on her suspicion. Just to make sure the caller was who she thought it was, she glided her hand over to the phone keypad and pressed the call history button. Sure enough, the name Avery Beckstand flashed across the screen—Elise's guilty pleasure.

Increasingly, over the past month, she'd noticed a direct correlation between the number of times his name showed up and the growing frequency of Elise's alleged conference calls.

After each one, she'd come out short on breath and fanning herself, asking if anyone had moved the thermostat. Somehow, Julie couldn't acquaint P&Ls with the flushed, sated expressions Elise made behind her closed glass door. Banking was many things, but steamy and sexy didn't quite make the cut.

This particular conference looked as if it was going to be an epic one. Elise had already scooted low to the edge of the chair and though it might have been hard for anyone else to tell five minutes in, Julie had a prime view of what appeared to be a tremor of untamed pleasure. On that note, Julie estimated she had at least a good thirty minutes to an hour of uninterrupted time before Elise emerged. She slid her finger to the left to unlock the recent message from Liz.

Liz: Did you make it?
Julie: With five minutes to spare. btw the troll is at it with the phone sex again

To really emphasize their running joke, Julie texted a line of phallic eggplant emojis. The moment Julie had realized what Elise had been up to, she filled Liz on all the gritty details. They had laughed until it hurt thinking about how Elise tried her hardest to come off poised and put together, but failed miserably when it came to a good run of phone sex.

Liz: Nymph! Ew! Busted basic bitch. She's so tragic. And um…I know ur at work. Did you make it to see Rita?

Julie: Oh you mean the woman who nearly ripped off my vag? Yes.

Liz: You needed to clear that bush. No man is going to wade through that forest just to get to your sweet spot.

Julie: For real, I'm hurt. We're talking a whole other level painful. I could barely walk. This morning, Nico laughed at me…

Julie: Any word from D? Did he stop by?

Liz: Nico?

Julie: Dane's backup. Can you believe him? Those assholes were conspiring behind my back.

Liz: And you just got that fresh Brazilian? Oh shit…

Heaven forbid Liz miss an opportunity to drag the conversation there. Almost immediately after her text, she sent a line of purple eggplants of her own. Julie couldn't move her thumbs fast enough. Aside from the redness and sensitivity to the touch, Julie's mind had wondered to how good it would feel to have Nico's hands down there, blazing over her bare skin. She was crying laughing now, but had to call Liz on her shit.

Julie: Don't oh shit me. You're such a horn dog. So extra. And don't overuse the eggplant.

Julie: I don't even think he knows what a Brazilian wax is

Liz: Oh he knows what it is

Emojis popped up on Julie's screen. Winking, wagging tongues. Another eggplant with a peach that looked alarmingly like an orange ass. And then, the three eclipses bubbled up on the left.

Naturally, as soon as Julie got to the good stuff, a clueless client needed help with the ATM. Despite the fact that the words "insert card here" and "please enter PIN number" were scrawled in English on the glowing screen, people continued to be confused by the options at the bottom of the screen, prompting users to change the language.

After Julie had explained that the default language *was* English, the slick-tongued silver-haired ballbuster cooled her heels and withdrew her forty dollars. All the way out the door, the lady cursed the complications of technology and a bank which, for some inexplicable reason, decided to meet the needs of its clients on a global level. Craziness.

Julie huffed in frustration and painfully waddled her way back to her desk, careful not to let her thighs and pants fabric rub hard against her newly raw flesh. On the way, she passed Elise's office where she was still hot and heavy on her "conference call." When she pulled her phone from her desk again, she about fell off her chair when she saw the two messages awaiting her.

Though she desperately wanted to read the second one first, she'd never been able to resist one of Liz's gifs—a compulsion she deeply regretted the instant she opened it. Apparently, Liz had met with Rita, too, and Julie now had disturbing visual proof that she wished she could un-see.

With a renewed sense of urgency, Julie closed the picture of Liz's hairless kitty, brushing off the temptation to send a pic of her own mewing red Sphynx cat. God she wished she could forego pants and panties altogether today. The fit was a tad looser, but more than anything, what she craved was ventilation.

Her finger hovered over the next message as she weighed her options.

On one hand, at what point had Nico managed to get his number into her phone? It could've been at Nona's, or when she'd fallen at the gym and she was unconscious for however long after his chocolate eyes had hypnotized her. On the other, beside that minor mysterious detail, Julie hated her growing comfort level with Nico.

It was as if every minute she shared with him, she'd become increasingly aware of herself—aware of his proximity to her. The touch of his gentle rough hands on her arm. That adorable way his fluttery lashes seemed to take flight when he got angry. And oh, by the grace of the Lord of the heavens and seas, the way he smelled like an intoxicating combustion of lemons, soap, cotton, and earth.

There she had been practically dying on the dirty gym floor and all she could think of was how to maintain even a small semblance of dignity, enough not to rip off the man's shirt and take him right there.

Julie opened the message.

Nico: Drinks tonight?

CHAPTER 17

J ulie typed, then erased. She typed a few more words that felt flat and cliche and quickly erased them, too. What the hell was she going to say? She had no idea what drinks meant. Shit. What kind of vague question was that? Drinks? The only safe thing to do was wait for him to say something else. *Anything* else.

Nico: This is not a hard one. Yes, will do.

Gah! I'm such an idiot. He had to see me typing.

It was two words. *Drinks tonight?* Simple words at that, but Julie couldn't help herself. It was in her bones to analyze, overanalyze, and analyze it some more.

Drinks tonight? Practically a loaded question, if she imagined all the ways to read into his text. Was he asking her to join *him* for drinks tonight? Or, was he asking if *she* was having drinks tonight—not including him?

Why is it so hard to tell?

She hated that she wasn't as carefree and confident as Liz. Miss Puerto Rican Princess would say something flippant and cute, like "sure" with a Pantene hair flip and guys would fall all over themselves for the simple fact that she had responded at all.

But this was Nico. The guy who had done everything in his power to disprove her opinion of him. The guy who literally and figuratively saw her fall flat on her face.

Kind of hard to live down.

Julie sat up taller and squared her shoulders, figuring what to say next. She wanted to sound confident and sexy, flirtatious without being awkward. Somehow in a text message, be someone worthy of the compliments and kindness he'd shown her.

This could take a while.

Her phone pinged again. Another message.

A notification alert dropped down from the top of the screen. This time, it wasn't from Nico. It was only a phone number. No name, but those ten digits were ingrained in her memory, along with the face of the man she'd once hoped to marry.

With a quick swipe upward, she pushed it from her sight. Then, another one popped in.

+1 (702) 555-0348: Are you working today?
+1 (702) 555-0348: I'm here.

Julie's eyes shot up. They darted through a crowd that now trailed out the front door. How could they be busy *now*? For seven hours the place had been as empty as a politician's promise, now, all of sudden, a quarter 'til close, the masses arrive in time to block her view.

She glanced over to Elise to make sure she was still waist-deep in Beckstand's call. The phone remained glued to her ear, but her squinted eyes threw daggers at Julie. Once Elise had Julie's attention, those sharp daggers flickered toward the main door.

Out of the corner of her eye, movement captured Julie's gaze. She lifted herself slightly off the chair in hopes of a better view and the sea of people parted. All the blood rushed from her feet and her brain and lodged in her throat.

Being strong was one thing when Patrick wasn't around, or when she was sparring with her trainer and only saw his face. It was a completely different story though, when he was moving steadfast in her direction.

Patrick's gaze landed on Julie, and she wished she was invisible.

She wanted to remember all the times he'd disappointed her. It should have been easy to focus on how he had deserted her when she'd lost her grandmother, or when he made it clear that she wasn't good enough to be a part of his family. But as he veered in her direction, images of the nights they'd played strip Scrabble, and the way she'd catch him looking at her appraisingly in the bathroom mirror as she brushed her teeth, shot pangs of yearning through her spine.

It was his weird idiosyncrasies that left her drawn to him. Not many guys would admit that watching her cook made him horny as hell, or that he had an insane aversion to Starbucks for the mere fact that some of the patrons curled up with bare feet on the chairs that others had to sit on.

She cursed her traitorous mind.

The right thing to be was pissed.

He was engaged and expecting a baby, so why was he here?

Her mind raced through a mental image of her apartment. He hadn't left anything at her place. She'd made sure of it, and he wouldn't have dared let her leave even a hairpin—or heaven forbid, a hair—at his place.

Julie had seen him less than a week ago, and he just stood there holding hands with Celeste without even a mere blink in Julie's direction. Everything that needed to be said had been said. What could he possibly want?

And why would she even be inclined to listen to *anything* the lying, cheating asshole had to say?

"Jules." All six foot five inches of confidence and cologne towered over her with only the desk between them.

When speech evaded her, he filled in the silence. "It's good to see you, too. You're looking well. I like this new hairdo on you."

Absentmindedly, Julie ran her fingers over the strands of her short asymmetrical bob.

Despite the burn of her Brazilian, she thanked the lucky stars now that she'd worn a low-cut blouse and fitted pants to show off the inches she'd lost already. With his eyes on her, she felt sexy against her will.

Her brain still juggled with the possibilities she could attribute to his visit.

"It suits you. Gives you a hint of mystery. You look...*interesting* and thinner."

Typical, he went straight for the jugular. He hadn't said boring, but his backhanded compliment failed to slip under Julie's radar.

"What can I do for you?" She deadpanned. "Are you looking for a new account, or can I interest you in a loan? We have some great rates right now," she said in her sweetest voice.

He seated himself without invitation or a glance backward to see if anyone else waited to be helped. As always that air of entitlement he carried was worn like an overcoat. "I was in the neighborhood and I thought to myself, it's been a while now since we ended things, Julie and I should be able to be adults about this. After all, you and Celeste are friends, so why should we not be?"

Seriously? We?

She knew how the wheels turned in his head. Somewhere in the back of his warped mind, this actually made sense to him. The three of them cheerfully attending one of his parents' dinner parties or frequenting a fundraiser, taking in tea as a chummy threesome. That sort of shared existence was doable to him. She refused to feed into his ego.

Julie grinned and folded her hands on the desk. On the inside she wanted to deck him in his smug face. On the outside, she was cool as ice. "Perhaps, an appointment with our wealth advisor?"

"Jules, you and I both know that I'm not here about finances. I'm here to talk about us."

"Us." *Us? You have got to be kidding me.*

Calm and collected, she opened her mouth, then closed it again before answering him. She exhaled. "Maybe you missed it, but there is no longer an us. That ship sailed about two months ago when I became so 'boring.' Or, should I say, when you got 'sick and tired' of me?"

At her short measured words, he sat up straighter now and leaned forward, forming his hands into a steeple on the desk. He inhaled deeply through his nose, then exhaled through his mouth. "Well, I know you're about to close, so how about we have lunch together tomorrow?" He completely ignored everything that she had just said. "We can talk about everything then," he suggested.

Without waiting for her response, he continued, "Seeing you the other day brought everything to the surface. I miss you. I miss us," he said, as if it had just dawned on him.

Almost every single day for two months, she'd been on her knees begging for those words to come from his mouth. She had made bargains with God. Today, her unanswered prayers made sense.

In that moment, she felt weightless, breathless. She had been waiting for this. She'd been waiting to be completely and totally over him. *Damn, it feels good.*

Julie shuffled her papers into a pile and tapped them on the table to straighten them. Finally, Patrick didn't matter.

When she looked back to him, he'd gone silent, his face turned an unattractive shade of tomato red. Apparently, her lack of anger was a surprise to him. The funny thing about it, she didn't give a rat's ass about his feelings, or his surprise, *or* his regrets.

Across the room, Elise stood at the frame of her door with her fists planted on her straight hips. Patrick had been in the bank many times when they were dating, and it was apparent that Julie's conversation with Patrick was anything other than business. By the grimace plastered on Elise's face, she'd found yet another reason to add to her ever-growing list of reasons why Julie wasn't ready for management.

"You have to go," Julie whispered to Patrick. She stood with her arms folded across her chest at the edge of Patrick's chair and waited for him to stand.

When he did, a lost look of disbelief washed over him as he took a final glance at Julie and tugged at the bottom of his pressed jacket. She had spoken—rather, dismissed him without even raising her voice—the way no one likely had before.

"Please don't come back here again," she said.

And as his brow lifted into an unmistakable question mark, somehow, it felt like a challenge had been offered.

When the door closed behind him with a stuttered bang, Julie picked up her phone and responded to Nico.

Julie: Yes.

She slipped her cell phone back under the desk and walked with steel nerves to Elise's office to await her scolding.

CHAPTER 18

I t's just drinks.

Julie took another look at herself in the rearview mirror now. She was still wearing her suit, sitting in her car parked outside Frankie's Tiki Room. She'd spent the last fifteen minutes debating and trying to conjure up the gall to get out and go find Nico by the bar.

She could do drinks, but the hell with liquid courage. Julie didn't need it after the day she'd had. Searing hot adrenaline piped through her veins.

Damn it felt good to send Patrick and his bullshit lies packing.

Today, stuffy suit and all, she planned to walk right up to Nico, and let her lips tell him what her body wanted to do to him. And if he was game, Julie would let her player take her wherever he wanted, and gladly treat him to the happiest of happy hours.

She supposed that was why she'd agreed to drinks in the first place. There was no long time commitment, like with dinner. No sitting across from each other awkwardly searching for something meaningful or profound to talk about that wouldn't bore the other person, or send them running in the other direction.

Plus, she wasn't trying to impress him. Going out with him was simply a means to an end. If she were out with Nico, she wouldn't be home analyzing and overanalyzing every second of Patrick's visit to the bank. More importantly, she wouldn't need more batteries.

So really, she'd agreed to see Nico because of what he could do for her. As opposed to some therapeutic step forward toward healing and rebuilding her life the way Liz had read into.

Basically, Julie's inner self begging for Nico to kiss her, make love to her, and make her laugh. *Ha!* Her superego could go screw itself.

Who cared whether he could make her laugh or not? With the right drink, everything would be funny. They could skip all of the pretenses and protocols of the man's role and the woman's role. If need be, she could pay for her own Midori sour or vodka cranberry, and it wouldn't be a big deal because throwing back a few swigs of liquor and lust together wasn't that serious.

That was the point. It was just drinks, no matter what Liz said.

It's an, *"I might like you, so I'll agree to meet up, but I won't commit as much time as dinner requires."* Basically, it was a maybe. A digestible liquid form of *"okay for now."*

And she was, for now.

She was better than okay. Her chest puffed up with the steam of a person who just put a deserving asshole in his place. In the rearview mirror, she pinched her cheeks to give them that flush, blushed look and swiped on a fresh coat of lip gloss.

With that, she clicked a button and armed her car, almost in sync with the pink neon lights of Frankie's.

"Hi there," some slimy guy ran his sweaty palm over her back as she entered.

She did her best to slither away from his hand and offered a quick, "hey," as she weaved into the crowd.

Besides the thick smoke, she liked the atmosphere. Any bar that could expand on Disney's Enchanted Tiki Room and make it an adult playground in the middle of Las Vegas was her kind of place. Just beyond the neon lights and the arched doorway were carved posts of monstrous island warriors, raffia grass-wrapped awnings above the bar, and a bamboo explosion on the walls and furniture. The whole place was shrouded in a red and blue glare from the hanging roped sea-glass lights.

It really was a liquid vacation, and in her state of mind, she could think of nothing else she needed more.

As the waning outside light faded behind the weighted red door, Julie caught a glimpse of Nico at the end of the bar. It didn't appear he saw her, which was fine because it gave her a second to find her footing and enjoy the view.

He looked good. Better than good. He looked delicious and sexy in black pants and a rolled-sleeve chambray button-down. Even from where she stood at the front of the bar, she could etch the strong lines of his jaw and the sweet pucker of his full lips.

Without a moment's hesitation, she marched toward him.

When she came within a few feet of him, a tall burly man with a bulbous gut and a creepy lopsided grin rose from a chair two seats over from Nico. She tried to inch past him, but he wouldn't budge and she couldn't imagine letting his sweaty belly hair creeping out from beneath his shirt touch her skin.

"Ah...excuse me? I'm just trying to get to the seat on the other side of you. My, uh, friend is waiting for me," she explained. Her eyes flickered upward to meet his, but she wasn't sure this guy could get past the look of distaste she was sure she had plastered across her face.

"Can I buy you a drink there, Brown Sugar?" Everything about him was slimy. Pervy. The man's tongue slurped against his bottom lip as he rubbed the side of his bent index finger along Julie's arm.

"Ugh, uh, no. No thanks," she managed.

For a split second, she contemplated turning back toward the door or going around the full block of three or four tables to get to Nico, then the guy shifted on his feet as if he was going to move. But, he didn't. He only closed the distance between them and now his hot breath fogged down into Julie's ear.

She thought she might gag, or at least let out a dry heave at the smell of the rum-and-cigarette cocktail that billowed from him like a blow-dryer in a menthol tobacco factory.

"I'd really like to get by, so if you would excuse me..." She inched to one side, then the other, but the perv did the same, matching her moves on a dime.

"What's the problem? I'm not good enough for you?" His volume raised a few octaves, the stench of saturated liquor permeating from him. He eyed her suspiciously for a beat too long as he took in her full profile from head to toe.

Julie's eyes pleaded with the woman seated at the table on her left, but there was nowhere for her to move the chair. The space was cramped and the bar was packed. What's worse, the giant douchebag was blocking her view of Nico, who might have offered assistance had he been able to see that she was there.

When the guy's gaze reached hers again, he seemed to have drawn his conclusion. "Ah...I get it. You, uh, go the other way. You fish in the lady pond." He announced these words to the room, which had been buzzing with conversations and music, and now seemed to be on mute as he called Julie out as a lesbian.

"That's enough, Carl. I'm cutting you off." A man with a handlebar mustache and slicked-back gray hair yelled to the man before her. "Want me to call Stella?"

From what she gathered, this was likely an everyday occurrence with this guy. Carl probably spent half of his days and all of his nights at the bar. The way the bartender spoke to him was more like how people speak to crazy aunts or frisky uncles. Mr. Mustache dealt with old Carl because he was one of them, even if he got out of hand nightly. He was tolerated by everyone, it seemed—except for her.

Julie steadied herself on her feet and sized the husky man up with a gaze holding a pinch of pissed-off and a full serving of fed-up.

"Carl, is it? I'm going to need you to get the hell out of my way.

I've asked you nicely two times and now, you can either move or—"

At the same time that Nico caught Julie's enraged eyes, Carl grabbed her by both arms, as if to rein her in, and received a blunt-force knee to the balls for his trouble.

Seeing a rather large grown man reduced to a hunched sack of mush—holding his junk no less—she would normally feel remorseful for putting him there, but not today. Not when just about every interaction she'd had with a man in the past twenty-four hours had gone south.

Julie tugged at the hem of her coat and adjusted her neck. "Next time, step aside when a lady says excuse me." She shimmied past the guy, who was doubled over on the floor while his host of friends guffawed on his behalf.

When she finally took the seat next to Nico, she exhaled a chestful of air and turned to him. She rested her eyes on him as she sat up straight, her back rigid against the chair and legs crossed at the ankles.

"That was...kind of amazing," Nico admitted. An approving smirk tugged the corners of his mouth, bringing out the thigh-clenching reflex in Julie. "You really handled that guy. I was just about to get up, and turns out you didn't even need me."

She sighed. "I'm so over this day."

"Another article of clothing?" At Julie's side-eye, his brows lifted. "What? Was it work again? The dictator?"

Julie centered her attention on the wall behind the bar lined with liquor bottles. If this night was going to be better than the day she had, it was definitely going to take a lot of alcohol. "I don't want to talk about it." She slouched in the chair, with her arms resting on the sticky lacquered wooden bar.

"Okay, so...Julie Laurich, are you going to loosen up, or are you going to try to sell me a checking and a savings account? I don't think I have enough money on me to fund the account right now though."

His face was dead serious, but she had learned the hard way that

Nico liked to joke around. With his beautiful eyes fixed on her, she caved. "What? What are you talking about? And why are you staring at me and using my whole name?"

"Well, you're obviously still in business mode since you still have your name tag pinned to your jacket." He nodded toward her lapel.

Her eyes dropped to the name tag, and whether she wanted to or not, she laughed at herself.

Julie knew he was poking fun at her and she secretly loved that about him. How he could take a totally tense moment and make her laugh in spite of it all. But she didn't want him to know that just yet, so she punched him in the shoulder playfully and held up a flexed bicep. "There's more where that came from, so watch your step there, wise guy." She squinted her eyes at him.

"Okay, okay. I won't bring up your crappy day, or the fact that I think you might need anger management. You roughed up poor Carl pretty bad." He gestured toward the big guy still picking his ego up off the floor.

When the moment passed with a beat of silence, he looked to Julie again. "In all seriousness, though. What made you agree to meet up with me tonight?" he asked.

She pinched the bridge of her nose between her index finger and thumb as if it pained her to admit it. "I kind of like you. You're kind of cute." Her gaze washed over him quickly and her heart began pounding against her chest again as she bit her bottom lip. "There, I said it. What's it going to take to get a drink around here?" She deflected, blushing the whole time.

Nico cocked his head to the side with feigned concern. "So...you think I'm kind of cute?" His cheeks reddened as his lips parted just slightly.

It might have been the adrenaline talking, but Julie was feeling more than a little bit frisky. *Oh my goodness, I want to take you home now.*

"You're not so bad, compared to old Carl over there," she said, stifling a fresh batch of giggles.

CHAPTER 19

Nico hailed the gray-haired bartender over. "Have you got a menu? I don't know if you've decided to cut her off before she even gets started, but I'd like to buy this here ballbuster a drink." He winked at her.

"Seems to me, it's only fair that you buy her *two* drinks to make up for the shortage I'm taking on Carl's tab," the bartender said, leaning against the bar.

His voice was raspy, likely from years working in the smoky establishment. He smiled the whole time like he rather enjoyed the banter and giving Julie a hard time. It was the kind of thing that happened back in the day, when you'd work off a dinner tab by cleaning dishes.

"Give me one of whatever you know how to make real fast," Julie raised her voice to be heard over the music which began playing again. "I need to calm down first, so I can think."

He poured a double shot of Patron Silver and she gulped it down just as fast. Her face screwed into a twisted scowl before she let out a throat-burning howl and shook her head. As the heat from the tequila warmed her insides, Julie slipped out of her jacket and angled herself in the chair so that her knees were positioned between Nico's.

"That's what *I'm* talking about." She closed her eyes and let her head hang back with a deep cleansing breath. When she came up for air, the bartender and Nico were both watching her intently. Specifically, she supposed they were watching her cleavage as it threatened to break free from her low-cut blouse.

Nico made no apologies for ogling her, but the bartender who reminded her of Sam Elliott turned his eyes respectfully. He was all smiles and charisma as he chatted them up while they reviewed the menu. Nico settled on a drink called a Bearded Clam, which only had three skulls next to it. Their new master of mixology explained that the menu was organized around alcohol level. Three skulls would get you happy and buzzed. Four or five skulls, on the other hand, should probably be banned in a bar that didn't serve any food.

Though her day improved with the minutes spent with Nico, Julie decided she *could* use some liquid courage. If she was going to act on the fantasies that reeled through her mind, a little boost was in order. Plus, she'd spied a bowl of peanuts next to Carl and some maraschino cherries in the drink garnish tray.

"Just give me anything with five skulls. You pick. And don't skimp on the alcohol," she instructed.

"You sure you don't want to start off slow?" Sam Elliott's twin asked tentatively.

"Nope." She shook her head. "And put it in one of those tiki mugs, too."

The bartender grabbed two bottles from the top shelf behind him and made easy work of throwing together some kind of complicated concoction. There was rum, and more rum, and juices. In less than a minute, he had mixed both of their drinks and poured them into tiki mugs which looked like pint-sized versions of Easter Island totem poles. No garnish and no frills.

He gently set Nico's Bearded Clam in front of him, then he sort of slapped Julie's cocktail on the bar with an audible clap. He wasn't being rude; Nico and Julie just didn't have his full attention anymore. His mind had drifted down the bar to a smoky-eyed brunette with vixen red lips. Still, he lingered, propped on his elbows with his focus teetering between the growing tab in front of him and the showstopper a few feet down the way.

"It's a Zombie." He winked. "Don't ask any questions, just drink it."

He beelined over to his lady in wait, leaving her and Nico alone. Julie picked up her drink and sniffed it.

"So, you're feeling kind of bold, then?" Nico asked.

Bold? Bold is way better than boring.

"Uh, like I said, I've had a really crappy day. Correction, a crappy few weeks, if you want to know the truth about it. So, I just want to take the edge off."

Nico gave her a once-over. "Sure you can handle that? You look like a lightweight to me."

Julie took a cautious sip. "It's actually pretty good," she said, following it with a long swig. "And thanks for the lightweight comment. I think the gym is finally starting to pay off."

"All right. Slow down there, punchy. I was hoping to have a coherent conversation tonight. You know, get to know you a little better."

"I'm fine." Julie kept drinking until she was just below the halfway point in the glass. "Let's talk about you. You've got a big family and you like to joke at the most awkward, inopportune times, but that's it. I hardly even know you and I've seen you almost every day for the past week."

"There isn't much to know. I have three older brothers: Anthony, Matt, and Lorenzo. One younger sister, Gabriella. All my brothers are married with kids, so I'm living back at home with my mom because she's been sick and needs help with the bills. My dad passed away five years ago." He swallowed hard and Julie could read the pain in the lines of his face. She knew that kind of pain that still felt fresh, no matter how long it had been.

"I'm sorry. I know it's hard. I lost my dad, too."

Nico shrugged. "So, anyway, I think she's lonely. My mom." He seemed to do his best to wrap up the topic neatly. "I can't blame her either. I'm right there with her."

"I'm so sorry, Nico."

"It's okay. I still miss him all the time, but he's in a better place now. He smoked like a chimney and it caught up with him, you know?"

Julie reached out and brushed her hand over his arm. "I didn't mean to bring all of this up, I'm really sorry." A nervous laugh crept into her voice. "I thought you were going to tell me about how you lived in some bachelor pad and why you became a gym rat, or something. Maybe, some goal you're grinding toward. Now I've dragged you into the raincloud."

"It's cool. I don't mind talking about real stuff, real life." He paused for a beat, like he was contemplating something. Then, his forehead and nose scrunched and he raised an eyebrow at Julie. "Wait, that's what you thought of me? You thought I was some kind of brainless meathead?"

"Verbatim."

Nico let out a thunderous laugh that vibrated through his body. "Damn, woman. There's no winning with you. Had me all summed up, huh? And exactly, what are your sources? Or *who* is your source?"

"Let's just say I heard it from the horse's mouth," Julie said.

"Oh that's right. You're basing this all on that one conversation you eavesdropped on at the gym—"

"Correction. Overheard. I was not eavesdropping."

He laughed it off and continued. "What's funny is, you still haven't asked the right question. And since I don't think your mind was functioning properly after you tapped out at the gym, I'll just lay it all out there for you. I'm a third-grade teacher at Evans Elementary school. My students are my only kids."

Nico sliced a line through the air with both hands. "I have not fathered any children that I'm aware of, or donated any sperm. The broken hearts that Dane teased me about were my mom and my sister, and a few friends when I left for college. Anything else you want to know?"

"So no girlfriend?" Julie tilted her head, searching his face for any signs of a lie.

Nico seemed to soften at the fact that after all he'd said, this is what she really wanted to know. "I'm sitting here with you, Julie. There's no one else," he muttered, more serious now.

Suddenly, Julie felt really stupid...and dizzy. Her eyelids lowered and she steadied herself against the edge of the bar. "Nico—" she slurred.

Before she could get another word out of her mouth, Nico closed the distance between them and brushed his soft lips against hers. Bubbles rose up in her stomach. Her heart raced and her hands pulsed with the need to touch him, cling to him.

Her mind circled in a whirlwind and Julie wasn't sure whether it was from the mind-blowing feeling of his full lips pressed into hers, or the alcohol, but she couldn't seem to steady herself.

Nico's strong hands slipped around Julie's waist as he pulled her closer between his legs, kissing her deeper. Behind her closed lids, she smelled his clean citrus scent cutting through the smoky room. He tasted of sweet rum with a hint of spice. And though the room was full of people, in that moment, it was only the two of them.

As the fluttering in her stomach began to rise upward, Julie tried to turn away, but it was too late. A burp escaped her mouth. A whiff of the meatless almond-slice salad with light vinaigrette that she'd eaten earlier for lunch, blew right in Nico's face.

"I think I'm going to be sick." Julie blurted out, just before she hurled into her hands.

CHAPTER 20

J ulie's eyes flitted about the room as a breeze rattled the window, not that she had been able to sleep much once she'd awakened in the strange bed. She lay there on the edge of the right side of the bed watching Nico sleep, wondering about the final events of the night—how she'd ended up in his bed, wearing his shirt.

With the slivers of light from the blinds, she studied him in the darkness until daylight danced on his cheekbones. The way his lashes rested on his face and his hair sort of splayed on the pillows in bunches of small springs, he could've been Julie's personal Calvin Klein ad. A beautiful mouth-breather who gifted her with glimpses of his dimples between snoring riffs.

He looked peaceful, unlike Julie, who feared her slightest movement would rouse him. Everything was perfect with him asleep. Her fuck-ups were limited then. Or, at least he wouldn't be conscious to witness yet another of the million and one she had in her arsenal.

She just *had* to raise the ante to five skulls, didn't she?

A monster headache pounded at her temples, payback for being a showoff. Surely a harbinger of an oncoming hangover, she stifled a groan. This was exactly what she deserved for consuming anything—liquid or solid—with a name like Zombie.

She combed through the staggered images of the night before. Mostly alcohol and loud singing and…kissing.

That kiss.

A soft, tender kiss. The kind that grew slowly in intensity while invisible fireworks went off in the distance. Shallow breathing. Nothing but sugar-spiced goodness. That is, until the unthinkable.

Julie cringed at the memory and gagged as the instant replay reeled in the back of her mind. She had burped. And not like a small ladylike breath slipping between smiling lips. No, that would have been far too much to ask. So typical; if she was going to screw up, she did it royally, and put some extra stank on it. No dainty shielded hiccup. She had unleashed a hearty rancid belch that came from deep down.

And to make matters worse—though at the time she'd thought it impossible—she'd managed to outdo herself. Because breathing fire wasn't bad enough, she had hurled on the man. Literally, upchucked on his Chucks.

On a mortification meter, she was off the charts. Julie grimaced at the thought of Nico waking up to endure any further antics from her. She scooted over the edge and slid out of the sheets onto the floor. Quietly, she tiptoed around his room, searching for her clothes and shoes.

Beneath the bed, she found her black pumps, wiped clean and neatly paired next to her purse and his slippers. And while her clothes were nowhere to be found, a whole closet full of *his* peeked out at her in the morning light. She glanced over her shoulder at Nico and slipped into another one of his shirts and a pair of his drawstring sweatpants, and rolled the waistband a third time to keep them from falling down.

She checked the clock on his nightstand. Six-thirty in the morning. Very ninja-secret agent like, she moved stealthily around corners, barefoot with her heels in hand. Based on self-preservation and what little she had left of her dignity, Julie should have snuck out and never looked back. But, at the sight of Nico, still lying peacefully asleep, she couldn't bear it. He didn't deserve it.

Her heart beat faster. She inched closer to the bed, careful not to wake him. Kissing her fingertips to her lips, Julie reached over Nico's shoulder to lay them on his cheek, and stubbed her toe on a weight below his bed.

"Shit," she whisper-yelled.

Julie cupped her hand over her mouth as tears stung at her eyes. She steadied herself on one leg and pulled her foot to her, and squeezed her throbbing pinky toe in her hand.

"Julie? You okay?" Nico asked, his voice groggy with sleep. He rolled over to face her, still halfway tangled in the sheets, and shirtless.

She bit her lip. Mostly because he was hot as all hell with a come-hither bedhead look set into the lines of his face. But, seeing as how she'd thrown up on the man and now ruined his sleep, she felt a little bit bad. "Damn it, I'm sorry. I was trying not to wake you, but I stubbed my toe on a weight."

Nico sat up and threw his legs over the side of the bed. "Let me take a look at it." He pulled Julie close to him and lifted her foot into his hand.

"I'm sorry. About everything. Really, I'm just going to go." She tried to loosen her foot from his grip.

Still holding her foot, Nico's eyes reached hers. "Would you stop apologizing? There's nothing to be sorry about. Why don't you just sit down for a second?"

Even though there were no traces of irritation in his voice, Julie still felt bad. There was only so much that a guy could take from a girl before he deemed her a lost cause. "I need to go. I don't know what it is about you, but every time I'm near you, I can't seem to act like a normal, functional person. Between my gag reflex and my motor skills, I don't know what's wrong with me lately."

"This is going to be fine." He rubbed her toe and gave it a firm press before releasing it.

As she flopped down on the bed beside Nico, he wrapped a hand around her waist and gave her a tender squeeze. She rested her head on his shoulder.

"I'm sorry." Before he could stop her, she explained, "I felt like I needed to say it at least one more time after all I've put you through."

After a few minutes, Nico turned to Julie, taking her in for the first time in the daylight. "This outfit looks good on you," he mused.

Even though she could hear his facetious tone, the way he stared at her was unmistakably appraising. "Just my size. You know, it's all about the fit." Fully equipped with her self-defense mechanisms and self-deprecation to keep her safe, she stood up and gave him a twirl before landing directly in front of him still seated on the bed.

Now, he stood and closed the distance between them, towering over a barefoot Julie. "I would kiss you right now...but, unfortunately, I know where your mouth has been." A wide smile settled across his face as he took her in his arms and pressed his lips to her forehead.

The man had a way with words, for sure, but he was right. She didn't want to kiss herself at that point. The vomit was one thing. But vomit *and* no toothbrush? She wouldn't *let* him kiss her...yet.

Julie tried to wriggle out of his embrace, but his fingers latched onto hers. She lifted her gaze to Nico in question, but he said nothing. Without releasing her hand, he slowly led her into his bathroom, shut the door, and locked it.

CHAPTER 21

J ulie searched Nico's eyes, but his expression gave nothing away. He was calm and collected, at ease in his mission, whatever it was he had planned. He stared at Julie deadpan. Then, his eyebrows pinched.

"I'm sorry about last night," Julie said, biting her bottom lip, finding it hard to really concentrate with him standing there in all of his shirtless glory. "Are you mad at me?" she asked, thinking about her antics the night before. She wouldn't blame him if he was, no one deserved to have someone else's bodily fluid on them.

"No," he said, plainly. She hoped he would say more, but in his cryptic way, he simply shook his head and left her with that one, unhelpful word.

"Did I say something to upset you?" She dropped her gaze to the sandstone tiled floor and sighed. "I can go."

Damn it. He is mad.

When he still said nothing, she pivoted slowly toward the door. Nico steeled her in place with that look again—a mix of irritation and hunger all smushed up together over his gorgeous face.

A mixture which apparently had something to do with unsettling Julie's insides. Every inch of her skin pulsed with yearning as she remembered the hot pressure of his lips on hers the night before. Now, she wanted those lips on her again. She wasn't going to screw this up twice. *Or was it three, no four times now?*

"What are you doing?" She tried again. He was simply staring. Not moving, or doing much of anything, which only left Julie feeling antsy and self-conscious under his gaze. With every second of his silence, Julie resisted the urge to say something, at least to break the tension. Still, he remained tight-lipped.

Then out of nowhere, he closed the narrow distance between them and gently tugged at the hem of the long t-shirt that landed at Julie's thighs. He lifted it over her head in one fail swoop.

"Okay, this works, too." Julie bit down on her bottom lip and stood there, her bare breast free, nipples rising to meet the brush of air flooding in from the vent above. Instinctively, she went to cover her chest with her arms, but he staid them in place by her sides.

"Don't. I want to see you," he said. "Every inch of you is beautiful." It was all Julie could do not to come undone on the spot, but she held her breath. How could she breathe? The glaring white lights were highlighting and contrasting every curve and ripple of her skin and he had said every inch of her was beautiful.

Her heartbeat stuttered and stopped before coming back fierce and erratic.

Nico bent at the waist and lightly covered her left breast with his lips, warm, wet, and hot. Julie inhaled a short, sharp intake of air as heat blazed her sensitive skin under his tongue. It grazed her stiff nipple and fire shot through her.

"When was the second time?" he asked, rattling Julie's trance.

Her back arched without her permission. Her hands flew up to his shoulders. Partly because she needed something to hold onto for balance and he was the closest hard structure, and in part she wanted to guide his motions with pressure to let him know how much she enjoyed his touch.

"What?" Julie dug her nails into Nico's back and he winced, a shiver trembling over his shoulders.

When Nico was finished working her body into a frenzy, he moved on to her right breast and repeated the dance of his magic tongue until her knees weakened and he was the only thing holding her upright. "You said twice. When we were at Nona's. You said we'd met twice?"

"Uh huh."

Slowly, his eyes lifted so that his gaze was aligned with hers. "There are so many places I want to kiss you right now," he whispered, and Julie's mouth parted. Under what circumstances Nico thought it was a good idea to rehash her horrifying night while her breast was in his mouth, Julie had no clue, but she followed along through her haze.

"Fourth street. We were stuck in traffic," she whispered, weary that he might think she was stalking him. "You were looking down at me from your truck."

Julie's chest rose and fell to a rapid staccato, sounding in her ears as a drumbeat. So loud and hard. She almost didn't hear Nico when he asked for permission to kiss her *anywhere*. A throbbing pressure squeezed at the meeting between her thighs and Julie nodded on a whispered consent.

She was lost somewhere between the tightness throbbing at her thighs and the questions, but the word was caught in her throat.

"Did you want me then?" he asked.

"Yes," Julie finally said aloud, just loud enough for him to hear. "Yes, please." It was a mix of labored breathing and beguiling begging. "Anywhere."

A heart-stopping smile pulled at the corners of his mouth, reaching up to his hooded eyes. Though it seemed impossible, his molten eyes darkened. Nico lowered himself onto his knees and unrolled the waistline of the large sweat pants Julie wore until they pooled around her ankles.

"Anywhere?" he asked again.

The yearning was torturing Julie. She wanted him to hurry up and free her of her panties. But then again, she wanted him to take his excruciatingly slow sweet time, teasing her and winding her up to her peak.

"What about the other time?"

Through her thinly laced pink cotton panties, Nico kissed her nether lips, softly, continuing to breath air into her most intimate spot.

Julie stumbled backward, reaching for something to hold her up. There was a catch in her throat. Her hands landed on the edge of the cold slick countertop and she gripped it with herculean strength. "I wanted you every time," she said, unable to catch her breath.

Please. Nico, please.

She arched her back as she allowed her head to fall backward in agonizing want. Just when she thought she couldn't want Nico any more, he used his teeth to slide the thin fabric to the side and began kissing her there. Just the heat of his full lips sent shivers down her spine only to boomerang back up again. He started slow with light pecks which grew harder and faster before he used his hot slick tongue to pry into her opening. He dipped inside and out to a steady, hurried rhythm while Julie lost all feeling in her legs. It was like her weight was teetering on his tongue.

"Oh my goodness." *Fuck. Oh my goodness.* "Nico," she breathed. "Oh, Nico. I want you so bad," she said, releasing the death grip of one of her hands on the beveled edge of the counter and working her splayed fingers into his hair. "Nico," she breathed his name again.

She couldn't stop saying his name.

Julie had had orgasms before, but she had probably faked them more often than she had real ones. Of the real ones she did have, none were on this level. This earth-shattering, mind-blowing level. Her body trembled and she could cry from want alone.

As if he could read her mind, Nico covered his lips over the hollow between her thighs. He licked and sucked ravenously until Julie's body quaked, releasing all the pent up rage and tension she'd harbored for too long. Though she bit her lip, muffled squeals and moans released into the air seemed to fuel Nico's magic tongue.

If she thought he was finished, Julie was mistaken. When her tremors began to subside, Nico slowed his pace, but continued kissing her between the thighs. He concentrated on the tender skin of the inner thigh, millimeters from her pulsing pink bud.

"Did you want me?" Julie asked, but he ignored her.

Then, without warning, he got to his feet, lifting her up with him so that her legs straddled his waist. His strong fingers gripped firmly on her ass, Nico took her into the shower with him—plaid pajama bottoms and all.

Loosening his grip, he freed one hand to turn on the shower. The shock of the cold water doused her blazing skin to a comfortable cool. As the water warmed and sprayed over them, neither Nico nor Julie moved. For a moment, they stared into each other's eyes, allowing the stream to pour over them. In his gaze, heat lingered, the way it had taken up dwelling between her legs. She was greedy with lust. Julie wanted more of him.

Then, she remembered, she hadn't pleasured him.

Julie wiggled free from his slippery grip beneath her bottom. On her feet again, she stood before him, shimmied out of her panties, and licked her wet lips as she ogled at him. As he raked the water from his hair, Julie couldn't believe that Nico had given her the shower fantasy. Just like that day in the rain outside her car, Nico was here.

This man was unnervingly handsome, lean and fit with washboard abs and the convenient superpower to tie everything inside her into knots. Only, with the added bonus of spraying, splashing, slippery wet goodness.

Between shallow breaths, she pulled the drawstring of his drenched pajama bottoms toward her and slowly worked them down to his feet.

"I wanted to ask for your number that day," he said out of nowhere. "In traffic," he clarified.

Julie took one look at the dripping length of him—the same tawny brown skin, though thick and veined with a soft tip—and she wanted to feel him inside her. Moving and rubbing and working himself against her raw flesh.

But it wasn't just his jutting erection, it was him. He was real. Nico stood there in front of her, a masterpiece in male anatomy. His chest alone was enough to make her want to cry. Flat pectorals, curved around the carved edges. He was muscular with chiseled abdominals that narrowed into a flashing arrow, pointing south.

"I'd just left the café that day. It was you who I was supposed to meet." His hard-on tightened as his gaze fell on her. "I wanted you."

She leaned into him with both hands on his chest, his thickness on her stomach. As she lifted herself up onto her tiptoes, she trailed kisses from the soft skin behind his ear down to his neck. Lightly, she whispered into his skin, the questions she needed answered before she could wholly let go.

After they'd both confirmed they'd been tested with negative results and Julie was on the pill, she took it as a green light to return the heavenly favor he'd given her.

"Pick me up again," she whispered.

When he did, Julie raised herself up in his arms to center Nico, then slid herself down onto the full hard length of his erection. Her insides were full. As she squeezed, he encircled her waist with his hands, lifting and gliding her up and down. He plunged himself in and out of her. Deep raw friction igniting between them with every thrust.

Water streamed over them, just loud enough to drown out her satisfied moans.

"You feel so good," he said into her neck as he kissed and licked every inch of Julie's wet skin, setting her body afire. Nico lowered his mouth to her breasts again and took in his fill of her. He suckled the nipple as he pulled and pushed his thick cock, grinding it in deep, until it could go no further. They were as connected as two people could physically be.

In that moment, Julie wished she could freeze time and forget about regrets and what would inevitably happen next. She didn't want to know whether or not Nico had perfected the lie. Whether she'd really end up another broken heart on his trail.

The way Nico fit her now—comfortably, interchangeably, body and mind—he was giving her all the feels. She might as well have been hooked up to machines pumping her heart, brain, and lungs for her. He was giving her life.

This man was life support.

With every gentle, careful touch of his flesh upon her flesh, he was awakening a dream she'd long since given up on. Just for now, she could live the lie, too. For this moment, Julie reveled in the primal pleasure Nico gifted her body, and for once she didn't wonder about all the things that could go wrong. For once, she was singularly focused on everything that was right about this perfect snapshot of her life. She didn't need to think.

This was better than any fantasy.

He held himself inside Julie as he pinned her against the wall, a waterfall pouring over them. Pulsating tremors shook his body inside her in violent jerks as he convulsed with a final tired thrust of satisfaction, and she held him tight.

He gripped Julie flush against the tiles until his breathing evened. "I'm so glad it was you," he said, his voice husky.

A laugh escaped Julie's mouth. "You're so fucking hot," she mused, kissing behind his ear as she fingered his wet hair.

Drawing his head back to face her, Nico gave Julie an incredulous smile. "Not just 'cute' anymore?"

"We just had amazing fantasy sex in the shower. I'd say we're way past the point of cute." Julie grinned. She didn't know what had gotten into her. All this open communication and blatant flirting, this was new for her.

Nico squinted his eyes. "Fantasy?"

"Um...yeah." Julie winced, heat rising to her cheeks. "I sort of have a thing about shower sex. And that day we were in the gym parking lot? When it was raining? I had a fantasy about you all wet and hot in the shower," she admitted, a glint of amusement in her eyes.

Nico's smile spanned the width of his face and all of his teeth were showing.

"What?" Julie asked. Despite the fact that they were still naked and he was still inside of her, she was self-conscious.

"So you had a shower fantasy about me?"

When he put it like that, it made her sound kind of weird and stalkerish, like she'd been plotting to have shower sex with him all along. "Maybe." She tilted her head toward him, clasping her fingers tighter around his neck to keep her from slipping.

He said nothing, but he lathered soap over their bodies, washing Julie gently and thoroughly before cleaning himself. The small space filled with the masculine clean citrusy scent of Irish Spring soap. The aroma, mixed with Nico's natural body oils, intoxicating. The urge to pull him to her again, flooded Julie's insides, inspiring her to touch her lips. The taste of him still lingered on her lips and on her fingertips.

She scooted to the corner. Mostly, to give Nico some elbow room to get all the hard to reach areas, but also, the undying craving she had for him was getting to be too much. Julie needed to put some distance between them, even if only inches. She eyed him hungrily, though that smug crooked grin remained etched into his profile.

As they rinsed away the soap and Nico turned off the water, Julie couldn't take it anymore. "Want to tell me what you're still over there beaming about?"

After grabbing two towels from the cabinet beneath the sink and handing one to Julie, Nico shrugged. "No. It feels like we're on the same page. I just...I kind of like the fact I can make your fantasies come true."

CHAPTER 22

A little while later, Julie was still finding it hard to live down Nico's words. Not that he wasn't right, but it made her nervous to admit it. Way too much had happened in twenty four hours and she needed to leave. She needed distance and time to let the fog clear. She couldn't think straight with Nico so close.

Plus, she had to get home and get changed for work, so she didn't *really* have the time to mull over the meaning of everything just yet.

Julie dressed in her freshly laundered shirt and pants that Nico had washed for her sometime while she was sleeping off her drunken stupor. She gave him a closed-mouth kiss goodbye, before traipsing down the stairs with a little extra bounce in her step.

As she turned the corner, hoping to find the front door—having only vaguely recalled entering the house in the first place—Julie bumped into a woman who only came up to her shoulders and wore a familiar amused expression on her face.

"Shit—"

"Dio Santo!" the woman exclaimed, holding a powdery floured hand to her chest.

At first glance, the woman could have easily been mistaken for a housekeeper, given her ruffled apron and the wooden spatula she had aimed at Julie in defense. Clearly, Julie hadn't been expecting to run into anyone either. But, as Julie's heart rate settled and she narrowed her gaze on a few of the minute details, the resemblance was indisputable.

The woman wore her hair in a tight bun behind her head, pulling the fine lines of her tawny skin taut. She had the same kind, warm chocolate brown eyes with sweeping lashes and thick arched brows, though her face was slightly more rounded and she had a teensy mole below her right eye.

Realization settled in and Julie knew this wasn't just any cute little old Italian lady.

Fuck. Nico's mom.

Immediately, Julie covered her mouth with her free hand. If her eyes opened any wider, surely they'd fall out of their sockets. Her heart began to pound again and her breath shallowed. Nico had said he'd moved back from the East Coast to take care of his mom. To *live* with his mom. This was Nico's mother's house.

Oh. My. God. Kill me. Kill me now.

Julie had just had the most amazing sex of her life in this house—with his mother in the next room. Sex, which involved loud wet body-clapping in the shower and orgasmic moans, from both of them. His mother had heard her son, her baby, fucking Julie's brains out. She cringed. *What must this woman think of me?* The words *whore* and *floozy* sprang to mind.

God she needed to get out, fast.

Her gaze darted around the homely living room in search of an exit, but her feet were leaden and she hadn't spotted the front door. The walls were closing in on her and suddenly the room was spinning.

Julie eyed Nico's mother, but couldn't bear the embarrassment and turned away again. She stared down at her heeled feet sinking into the long pile forest green carpet. *Focus.* As she lifted her gaze again, she took in the quaint space. The walls were muted in warm earth tones. A giant paisley sofa centered the matching antique wooden coffee table, end tables, and sideboard positioned around it.

Along the far wall, oval-shaped frames chronicled the highlights of Nico's family over the years. One in the middle, in particular, showcased a beautiful sepia-tinted image of a younger version of the woman before her. Strands of gray now streamed seamlessly with her dark locks, but in the picture, her hair flowed in shiny ebony waves and her pouty lips were painted a bright candy apple shade of red. She was facing a man who Julie assumed to be Nico's father based on the fact that he looked practically identical to Nico, but the photo paper itself had been tinged with the yellowing of a few decades of aging.

"Are you all right, Cara?" his mother asked.

Julie stared at her for a moment, confusion twisting her brow. "Cara? I, I'm Julie."

A smile pulled at the corners of the woman's eyes. "Si. Yes." She shook her head. Cara means "dear" in Italian," she explained, dusting her hands on her apron. "*Allora*, I know that you are Julie. You were asleep last night when my Nico brought you home. He said you weren't feeling so well, so I'm making you something to help. I already finished the gnocchi soup. Now, I'm making you ciabatta. You'll feel better."

"Oh, no. It's okay. I have to get going—"

Before Julie could finish her sentence, Nico's mother cut her off. "Then, you'll take it with you." The way she said it, there was no point arguing. She clapped her hands together and turned on her heels toward the warm, hearty scent of tomatoes and herbs and fresh bread, which Julie hadn't actually noticed until now. Although, now that she did, it explained why she was drifting, being dragged by her nose toward it.

She'd been so caught up in the awkward moment and the fact that she was meeting Nico's mother, but she supposed it was time to start acting like a big girl and start facing things head on. No matter how scary, or sweet.

Julie walked at a glacial pace in the direction of the delicious aroma wafting through the air. In the kitchen, the beautiful older woman pulled out plastic containers. She ladled a heaping serving of the colorful soup in the larger one, and a half loaf of bread in the smaller one. As she stacked them and stuffed them into a handled paper bag, Julie just about wanted to die. There was no way this astute, kind woman hadn't heard the intimate, practically porno-graphic sounds of Julie and her son this morning, but she was merciful enough not to mention it.

As Julie slinked out of Nico's mother's house, unhinged and frankly, a little bit edgy, she couldn't get a certain niggling question out of her mind. Nico had explained away the kids and trail of broken hearts he'd left behind to be his family, friends, and students. Although her judgment and lie detection skills had improved some, she couldn't help wondering whether Nico's mother was just being nice, or if she'd just become accustomed to meeting her son's endless line of women on their morning-after walk of shame.

CHAPTER 23

I f there was one thing Elise was a stickler for, it had to be time and attendance.

One day? Sure, take care of whatever you've got going on, and don't get the rest of her staff sick. Two days? Two consecutive days missed? You were really pushing it. Pressing your luck. Practically asking for Elise to micromanage you out of the place.

More than two unplanned, inconsiderate, flipping days? Unheard of.

No one had ever lived to see three or more days and tell about it.

On the books, it was always a voluntary resignation or some other legal designation that absolved Elise of fault. But anyone who had ever worked for her knew she had ways of helping people find the exit. Add in a banker asking for a promotion, and Julie might as well blackball herself from the whole industry.

The case of indigestion was one thing because Julie had shown up for work, but the dang treadmill debacle had put Julie on the radar. There was no time to haggle with a hangover and shot nerves over meeting Mrs. Farfalla. Especially, not when Julie was going to need to fake some kind of rare disease to be able to make the interviews for the branch manager opening.

Julie rushed home to shower, change clothes, and scrub her foul mouth clean. Thank goodness it was Friday. She needed a Friday in her life. Although Julie had just survived mind-blowing sex and body-breaking orgasms, she had had some uber-epic fails lately, and Nico had been around to witness all of them. Still, she didn't dare ask what else could go wrong. The universe would find a new way of answering her. It had made a believer out of her.

If she was going to do this—this whatever it was that was brewing between her and Nico—Julie had decided she was done with the pretenses and putting on a brave face. He'd have to take her, foot-in-mouth disease and all.

After nearly an hour of the brain-numbing *thud-swish* of windshield wipers, Julie pulled her car into a space facing the branch. She watched as Elise entered the building and inspected every inch before putting up the all-clear signal.

Elise had laid down the law yesterday in a novel-length text message. From the first few sentences, Julie was discovering that her days on easy street were a thing of the past. Next week, after the long Memorial Day holiday weekend, Julie would be at Kid Savers to fulfill Elise's community service requirement with the bank. The week after that, the shit would hit the fan.

Between her days filled with shadowing, coaching, cold calls, portfolio management, and the new progressive goals Elise had set for her, Julie had her work cut out for her. Really, what was she waiting on? Now, more than ever, it had become apparent that she ought to consider other employment options, and quickly.

Sometime after Elise had outlined the guidelines for Kid Savers and Julie had demonstrated how to reset an online-banking password for the umpteenth customer of the day, her cell phone vibrated against the inside of her desk drawer. A message from Nico.

On the outside, her face was blank. On the inside, slippery wet images of them in the shower scrolled through her mind, and she was all gooey and doing her happy dance.

She swiped at the message and touched her finger to the widget to unlock the screen.

Nico: Can I see you tomorrow?

They were the words Julie wanted to hear, but she'd hoped he wanted to see her tonight. Maybe for dinner or drinks. Better yet, there were at least three new movies at the theater she'd been dying to see.

Movies?

Julie remembered she'd promised to visit her mom. She'd sounded so excited about cooking together and getting the Laurich Girls back together for a good romance movie marathon.

But, she didn't have to stay the whole night.

Julie: What time are you thinking?

The three ellipses bounced onto the screen and settled there for a moment, then they disappeared. This was the root of all Julie's mixed emotions with texting. It was great if you wanted to get a quick message across, or if you didn't want to talk to a long-winded person. On the flip side, so much could be read into a series of letters, punctuations, and emojis.

Nico had read her message, but he was either crafting a two-page text, or he was hesitating. But why? He'd asked to see her tomorrow.

Julie's mother's voice rang in the back of her mind. Something about paying for the milk when he could have the cow for free.

Dammit.

As the ellipses disappeared a second time, Julie bit her lip and tried her hardest not to read so much into the message Nico had sent without sending a word. He could be doing anything. He could be using the bathroom, or eating. Maybe he had another call.

She cursed her need for instant gratification. Her patience, or lack there of. The waiting was killing her. Just as she was about to turn off the ringer and stuff the phone back in her desk, a chime pinged.

Nico: If you have plans, it's okay.
Was that doubt she heard? Now he sounded like her.
Julie: I just promised I'd hang out with my mom for a bit. How about 7:30?
Nico: It's a date.

Julie exhaled a breath she hadn't noticed she'd been holding and gave a small fist pump. *Yes.* She looked around the branch and no one seemed to notice her on her phone. Elise was still in her office being frigid and evil. The tellers each had clients at their windows, and no one was waiting in the lobby to be helped by her.

A smile tugged at her lips as she allowed herself to revel in the exciting premise of what they might do tomorrow night. As the image of the previous night flooded back to her, Julie panicked. *Shit.*

Julie: Mind if we stick with food this time?
Nico: Lol. Nope. I've got something planned. Something, fantasy worthy.
Julie: Want to share?
Nico: Nope, but I'm counting the minutes until I see you again.

With that, Julie put her phone away, hoping beyond hope that whatever he had planned involved his magic tongue.

That night when Julie got home, she took one look around her cluttered apartment and collapsed on the couch. As she kicked off her shoes, she took in the snapshot of her life on the go. She'd only been in the place for a few hours at a time in passing, what with Liz's appointments, her training sessions, and all the Nico run-ins. It was no wonder her life had unraveled on her. Sadly, her living space reflected that chaos.

It was Friday night and all she really wanted to do was throw her suit in the laundry bin and change into her extra-soft micro-fleece pajamas and a pair of fluffy socks. A little white noise in the background and a good book spelled bliss. Then, she could float back up to cloud nine, where she'd spent the rest of the day after Nico's text.

At work, she'd worn a goofy grin that wouldn't fade. And Julie could tell that it got under Elise's skin, too, which only made it that much more fun. But Nico was "counting the minutes" until he saw her again. What could have been better than that?

Julie dragged her bones off the couch and picked up the few scattered cups on the coffee table and set them in the sink. The place really was a mess. She leaned against the counter and cracked her neck at the job ahead. She'd do some light picking up tonight and save the deep cleaning for the morning. The sooner she started, the sooner she could get back to her daydream.

One floor up, someone turned on some music. It wasn't loud enough to hear the lyrics, but the melody floated into Julie's apartment, something light-hearted and upbeat. The kind of song that made her want to grab the broom and sing into the handle. It was what she needed, a little mood music. To add to the ambiance, she lit the mandarin pineapple candle on the entry table.

Under the sink, she unspooled a garbage bag off the roll and shuffled to the beat through the apartment, emptying trash cans. Her next go-around was with the laundry basket.

Julie could almost see the newly-cleaned shine on the tabletops and the floor when the doorbell rang. She flipped her wrist, checking her watch. It was nearly nine o'clock. She wasn't seeing her mom or Nico until tomorrow. Earlier, she had talked to Liz, though. Her friend and Derrick were working things out again, so maybe she wanted to talk.

"Who is it?" Julie called, lightly padding toward the door. She peeked through the peephole and jerked back almost as quickly. Her hand rested on the knob for a beat as she took in a deep breath before turning it.

"Sophia," she muttered, nonplussed.

"Well, hi to you, too, Jules." Her cousin gave her a once-over before she breezed past her in a brightly colored Lily and Jack frock. She made herself at home—basketball belly and all, sinking into the couch. "I'm not interrupting anything, am I?" she asked. Not that she cared.

As always, Sophia didn't wait for Julie to answer, she was always regimented and reeling. "I see you've made some changes. The hair is great on your bone structure." She twisted on the edge of the couch in Julie's direction. "And what did you lose...thirty or forty pounds? It's amazing, really."

Julie stood at the door with a white-knuckled grip locked around the knob. She closed her eyes and inhaled before she reluctantly shut the door and locked it with Sophia on the wrong side of it.

She sighed, fully prepared to ignore Sophia's backhanded compliments. *Thirty or forty pounds? Damn, how much did she think I weighed?*

"No. I was just straightening up a little. I'll be out most of the day tomorrow and I won't have time to clean."

"That's all right. I'm here now, and this won't take long. Austin's flight lands in about an hour and I need to be there to pick him up." Sophia pulled a planner from her sensible brown leather tote. She opened it up about halfway, where a blush-pink polka dot bookmark held her place. It read, "bless your heart" in dainty script.

A laugh bubbled up inside Julie. She could diminish Sophia to the size of a grain of salt if she wanted to—bring her right back down to planet earth. Thankfully, though, when she'd dropped the pounds, she'd held onto her tact and dignity. Of all the things that she admired about her cousin, her tendency to bend whichever way the wind blew wasn't one of them.

When they were young, Sophia had backbone. She was a brilliant firefly with convictions and righteousness and the best ringlets at Johnson elementary. It might have had something to do with

Aunt Helen kicking Uncle Charlie out when she caught him dipping his stick in someone else's hole. When he left, he took all of his money with him. Either way, Sophia had changed then. That was when Julie took note of Sophia's favor toward those who had nice things.

For them, she'd bend.

Like a weed, she swayed in the way of things and gifts. In the name of keeping up appearances, she only wore the best clothing and carried the best bags. Only certain name brands were allowed in their house. In the same token, only certain people fit the bill. Most importantly, no man measured up without a boost from his bank account.

The first time Julie met Austin Harman, she knew Sophia and Austin's was a match made in a luxury-loft heaven. He was rolling in dough; his sweet-tea trust fund made celebrity riches look like they were just scraping by. The way Sophia had looked at him, she couldn't get him down the aisle fast enough. She hadn't been with him a month and she was already finishing his sentences and taking on his Southern euphemisms, changing from a city girl to a Southern belle overnight. She hadn't ever *been* to the South, yet suddenly she was blessing everyone's hearts and "fixin' to do this" and "fixin' to do that."

Julie could have died when she heard Sophia tell Aunt Helen that she "reckoned Austin was madder than a wet hen." This was Sophia, who had cried at a petting zoo. Wouldn't come near an animal, now every reference she had included one.

Between wet hens and holding horses, it just didn't suit. She'd put on the mask and now it was stuck. Or rather, she was stuck in a sweet-tea world of pastel clothing and "bless your heart" bookmarks.

Sophia cleared her throat, all business now. On the page in front of her, she pulled her slender finger over a checklist that ran the length of the sheet and stopped at a section with an unchecked box. "We're just about forty days out from the shower now, and Mom and I were discussing what tasks we thought you could handle. We've got all the big stuff covered, but if you would be a sweet peach and take on the games, that'd be dandy. Give you something to do. You know, keep your hands busy, since you'll be stag."

Julie bit her tongue. Sophia and Aunt Helen never missed an opportunity to rub anything in her face. Stag? Since when had baby showers become the go-to couples event? Normal people gathered their best female friends and relatives for a quaint get together with light food, gifts, and games. Who in the hell knew this "shower" was going to get so out of hand she'd need a date?

She tuned Sophia out and wondered if it would be too weird to invite Nico. Would he think she was insinuating something by it?

When Julie met Sophia's gaze, her face screwed into an apologetic smile that failed to reach her eyes. "What? You don't have a husband." her cousin asked.

It wasn't what she said that annoyed Julie. It had more to do with the sneaky, unnecessary way she always managed to throw in the irrelevant fact that Julie wasn't married yet. Without saying it, Sophia was highlighting the fact that Julie and Patrick hadn't worked out. They never made it down the aisle. As if it just wasn't in the cards for Julie. She supposed in her cousin's mind, Julie's singleness was permanent.

"Really, Sophia? Can we try to focus on this *shower*? I've got other things to do, so if you could get to the point, that'd be great." Julie wound her finger in a circle a few times, indicating that she wanted Sophia to wrap it up.

"I'm just saying," she sang with an extra dose of Southern twang.

For the sake of Mom and Aunt Helen, Julie bit her tongue and stifled an urge to punch a pregnant woman in the throat. Her cousin could do petty better than anyone she knew. So Julie clenched her teeth and nodded her assent. "Sure. I'll do the games."

She had to pick her battles.

"I knew you wouldn't leave us hanging. I told Mom just the other day how you were sweet as pie and surely you'd do the dirty work. Now," Sophia skipped all the fake flattery and immediately put on her business cap, straightening her posture until it was ramrod straight. She checked the empty box and flipped to an empty page in her notebook. "What's the first thing that comes to mind when you think of shower games?"

Sophia's gaze narrowed and nodded like she was in serious focus-mode. The way she looked at Julie, anyone would think Julie was about to reveal the secret to the fountain of youth. It was *that* important.

If she was being honest, Julie hadn't given Sophia's baby shower a second thought. She knew her presence would be required, but she had no plans of being part of the planning. If anything, she was hoping to lurk in the back and slip out when the games started.

"Well...we could stick with the regular games like *who knows Mommy best, baby bingo,* and *baby predictions.*" Julie listed the first games that came to mind.

"No, no, no. That won't do at all. This is going to be an amazing event to remember. Think Southern chic. We've already hired the planners to turn the backyard into a garden extravaganza. We're talking cedar wood and gossamer silk. Stunning centerpieces filled with pink peonies and hydrangeas. Parisian macaroons. Only the best scalloped floral china and tea sets. I need you to think bigger." Sophia threw up her hands in exasperation. "Bigger," she echoed for effect.

Bigger? A *big* headache.

Julie's brows raised with Sophia's rising octave. This was getting out of hand. She'd have to talk to Mom. Worst come to worst, she might have talk to Nico about attending this "big" event.

CHAPTER 24

"Mom?" Julie called out, juggling a wine bottle in one hand and pulling her key from the door lock in the other. "I'm here."

"Come on back, honey. I'm in the kitchen." Her mom's voice rang high and honeyed as it echoed against the vaulted ceilings.

It almost felt like déjà vu, as many times as Julie had let herself into this same house. She had always announced her presence the same way, yelling at the top of her lungs for her mother. For so long, it had been only the two of them.

As she rounded the corner from the foyer into the living room, Julie slipped her key into her purse and brushed her free hand along the back of her dad's La-Z-Boy. Time had stood still in this house; the rustic wooden coffee table and sideboard with the beige club sofa. All shades of green accents and knickknacks made it feel earthy, fresh, and safe. Everything was the same, and still in pristine condition.

Better than anything, her mother knew how to preserve the things that mattered. For half of her adult life, she had loved hard and unconditionally. She had loved Dad through loss, through fair-weather friends, and torrential rainy days. Through the times when the two of them had come to terms with the possibility that their twosome might never grow to be a threesome—or any other number. And when God answered her mom's endless prayers and Julie was born, completing her family and her dream.

Up until Dad lost his battle with diabetes, she'd busied herself with the work of loving and taking care of her family—making the framed memories and hoarding the moments in between close to her heart.

Julie and her mother had watched thousands of movies and laughed a million laughs in that same room. When all else failed her, Julie knew she could always come home and heal her hurt, and her heart.

Julie followed the warming spices in the air into the kitchen.

"Stir that for me, would you JuJu Bean?" her mom asked without lifting her eyes.

On the stove, a saucepan brimmed with an explosion of seasonings for the taco soup—a tantalizing combination of earthy and robust flavors. Paprika, cumin, garlic, chili powder, and an array of peppers, blended and hearty.

"Hey, Mom." As Julie moved into the kitchen, she kissed her mother on the curve of her soft bare cheek and set the wine bottle on the counter next to the stove. She lowered the heat and stirred the soup. When it began to simmer, Julie turned on her heels toward her mom.

Julie watched her. Knife in hand, she cut thin yellow onion slices and pushed them toward the tomato and cucumber pile on the cutting board, the way she'd always done. Everything Julie's mother did was what she'd always done. She'd made no changes, never veering off course. No spontaneous detours or serendipitous missteps. She was just like this house: the same, and in pristine vintage condition.

She hadn't reinvented herself, and this was where it got her. Alone and wasting away.

Was this why Julie hadn't come to visit? Was she afraid of becoming her mother?

Fear of regret and passion jumbled together and lodged in Julie's throat. She didn't want a life of sameness any more than she was ready for the kind of love that broke people down. She wanted change and surprise, something to look forward to each day. Julie wanted more days full of shower fantasies, and ripped skirts, if that's what it took. But, she also wanted to know what she was getting into.

Anything other than routine, run of the mill.

As her gaze measured every detail of her mom's movements, Julie clenched her teeth and bit back the urge to beg her to do something, anything other than what she'd always done. Maybe a new friend, or a new man. It didn't have to be a man. A hobby would work, although a man would be nice, to be able to share her days.

"Oh, I'm so glad you came. We're going to have a blast." She chopped fast and precise, likely the same number of slices to yield the same number of diced chunks. A practical protest of change and variety in and of itself.

For Julie, It was almost like watching a time-warped mirror of herself in a couple of decades. A glimpse of what happens when your shine is dulled by life and loss.

Her beautiful mother's hair was pulled back in a smooth bun and she wore no makeup, clad in simple, unflattering colorless clothes. She was still as beautiful as she'd always been, but to look at her, no one else would see the traces of the vibrant, social butterfly teetering on the edge of her smile and in the creases of her eyes where laughter lines once lived.

"Wait until you taste that soup. Mmm, mmm, mmm, it is *good*," her mom proclaimed. "This might be my best batch yet." Her eyes welled to a glassy shine as she spoke.

It made Julie sick to her stomach that she almost hoped her mom would cry...and break, if only to have a chance to acknowledge the pieces of the mask she'd been wearing.

"Mom?" Julie scurried toward her. "What's wrong?"

She dropped the knife on the counter and wiped her eyes with the backsides of her hands. "It's those goddamned onions. Gets me every time," she laughed through her tears.

Julie was fueled to hear the sound of that joy dancing in the air. She pulled her petite mommy into a tight embrace and inhaled her familiar scent of home cooking and floral perfume. "I love you, Mom, but you scared the ship out of me. I thought something was really wrong." Giggles bubbled over as Julie kissed the top of her head.

"Oh, JuJu Bean. You still won't curse around your mom? Go on, give me a good shit, damn, fuck. That little 'ship' is not going to cut it."

Still doubled over, her mother pulled apart. Shock blurred the time-etched lines of her infallible face as she stared at Julie, shock emblazoned in her bright eyes.

"What?" Julie stepped backward.

"When did you…what…wow." Her mother covered her mouth. "I love it," she exclaimed, reaching for the ends of Julie's restyled hair. "You look beautiful." Emotion poured from her eyes as she took her daughter in from head to toe.

"Do you really like it?" Julie asked, biting her bottom lip, suddenly feeling shy and a bit self-conscious.

"JuJu, those ankle boots are right up my alley. Oh, and that little dress fits you so nice, honey."

Julie tucked her elbows in. "Even if it shows a little side boob?" she asked, raising her brows hesitantly on a wince. The casual black sheath dress fit loosely and laid on her body, revealing soft curves and a glimpse of the sensual woman beneath.

Hands planted on her hips, Julie's mom gave her a once over. "I'm much more concerned about those bones poking through, but how in the hell do you think you got here? Your mother was no prude. I showed a lot more than half of my breast, back in my day."

She pursed her lips and swallowed another wave of emotions.

"All right, all right. Turn. Let me have a look at this new *you* that you've got going on here. I want to know everything: the why, the when, the where, the how." As if realization set in, her eyes bugged impossibly further out. "The who? Is there a *who* involved?"

A mischievous grin tugged at Julie's mouth. "That's classified... but I think I might be able to get you clearance." She pulled another bottle of wine from the black crossbody purse wrapped around her. This was going to be a celebratory talk. "We're going to need more wine if we're going down that road."

The two made short work of plating the salads and ladling bowls of taco soup. Julie doused the salad with olive oil and parmesan cheese, while her mother added sharp cheddar, sour cream, and tortilla strips to the soup.

When they were ready, Julie raised the wine bottles. "I brought you two choices. A delicious Moscato. I've tried it a couple of times and it goes really well with fruit and cheese or pasta. Or, I have a Cabernet that you'll love, too. Pairs with savory stuff. So, what's it going to be, white or red?"

Quick to raise the ante, her mother pondered the best pairing, and gave her daughter a few options of her own from which to choose.

"Since we're doing the taco soup and the cucumber tomato salad, let's do the Moscato. And you have a choice to make, too. For the movies, I've got that Diane Keaton one with Mandy Moore, *Because I Said So*, and the new suspense one from M. Night Shyamalan. What kind of mood are you in? Do you want to laugh and swoon, or have a few jump-scares?"

In record time, the reunited Laurich girls took their places on the well-loved sofa with soup, salad, and wine, ready to enjoy the mother-daughter rom-com. For the first twenty minutes, there was only a cacophony of smacking, slurping, and utensils scraping against the dinnerware. Right around the time Diane Keaton overstepped her boundaries and decided to choose a mate for her single daughter who had a knack for choosing the wrong guys, another meddlesome mother turned to Julie with raised brows.

"Well, are we going to talk, or what?" she blurted out.

Julie had been content to let her mother stew in her impatient curiosity. "I'm thinking about leaving Regions."

"What? Why? I thought you were happy there. Elise seems so nice."

"Keyword, 'seems,'" Julie clarified. "She's pretty much a bitch. If she could have things the way she wants, I'll be a PB forever. Plus, I received an email yesterday requesting an interview with American Bank," she asserted proudly.

Her mom took a moment to process the new information. "Well, if you're going nowhere with this company, then you've got to go someplace else." Seemingly satisfied with her supportive response, she shrugged and hesitated. Julie knew she really wanted to talk about her favorite subject, but her mother was holding back on asking about Patrick for her daughter's sake.

"I saw Patrick," Julie asserted, diving in feet first.

Her sweet little nosy mom curled her feet up behind herself and scooted closer. "Oh?" It was all she said, but it was what she wasn't saying that let Julie know she had her undivided attention.

"He didn't come crawling back, if that's what you think. He strolled right through the crowd at the bank and sat his cocky self down at my desk." Julie reached over and sat her soup bowl down on the wooden coffee table. "And if you must know, I didn't beg him to come back. I don't want him anymore."

A smile that bubbled up from deep down in her stomach tugged at the corners of Julie's mouth. This was the first time she'd really said it aloud, and meant it. If she was being honest with herself, she had to admit that she liked the feeling. In fact, she hadn't realized that she'd apparently been holding out for the moment when she was truly over her ex.

"Your perfect Patrick is engaged and expecting a child

with....drumroll, please." Julie patted her thigh for sound effects. "Celeste. No big surprise there. Did you know that, Mom?"

It must have been all of the air in her lungs that dispelled from her chest because her mom held her heart and a chalky pallor discolored her face. "Well, I'll be. If that's not some Lifetime movie mess, I don't know what is. And that little jealous witch. She's had it in for you from day one. I told you she was jealous of you."

"Are you hearing yourself? You're missing the point, Mom. I could have gone off on him, but I didn't. That's what people do when they're still stuck on someone. I didn't do that. I simply acknowledged what he'd done and politely asked him to leave. In other words, I called his spade a spade and told him not to come back...ever."

Her mom blinked a few times and swallowed, appearing to process what she had just told her. Then, a smile spread over her face like the shadow of the sun, warm and bright.

"Honey, I don't know what's gotten into you, but I like it. Good for you." She patted at Julie's arm. "I was wondering when you were going to figure out that he wasn't good enough for you. It's damn well time for you to move on."

Julie had just sipped her Moscato, but at her mother's words, she sputtered and nearly spit it all out. "What?"

"He was never good enough for you. I just thought that's who you wanted and I tried to be supportive. Who am I to tell you who to choose?"

Only my mother. Now you want to mind your own business?

Flabbergasted, Julie shifted in her seat until she faced her mother. With disbelieving eyes, Julie stared for a beat with her mouth agape, shaking her head. This wasn't at all what she thought today was going to be like. Of all the things her mother had done and said lately, this was the one thing she hadn't expected: to be surprised.

"Mom? Why didn't you say anything? I can't believe you knew all this time?"

"Well, you asked me to stay out of it, so I did. I figured I had better start listening to you if I wanted to keep you around. You've been so distant and I've missed you, honey."

Julie shook her head. She wasn't hearing her right. "Wait. What happened to 'regret is a funny thing?'" She narrowed her gaze on her mother, waiting for her to make it all make sense.

"I was talking about *staying* with him. That would be the regret, JuJu. He was nothing but a learning lesson. A passing fancy. I never thought he was 'perfect' for you. That was all you, baby," she clarified.

Julie was only inches away from her and could have reached out to grab her as a bout of homesickness washed over her. She'd just assumed her mother was saying that she would regret *losing* Patrick. It never occurred to her that she meant, regret *staying*.

This was the mom she remembered. The pre-life-altering parent who worried and wished and loved so hard it hurt. The mom whose hugs felt like cotton candy clouds and sunshine all wrapped into one. This was the woman who dropped mind-blowing mom bombs like a DJ drops beats.

CHAPTER 25

J ulie inhaled, a breath caught in her throat. She washed it down with a swill from her wine glass. For a beat, she savored the sweetness on her tongue, feeling a sudden boldness surge through her veins. Without turning, she spoke matter-of-factly and met her mother's gaze.

"There is *someone* new. Or, at least the *possibility* of someone new," she said. Her tone was low and nonchalant, though the admission tugged at her mouth. Suddenly, she was invigorated. She felt damn good. Not an ounce of regret about Nico as she sat up straighter on the sofa.

Her mother stared at Julie with a pinched expression for a pregnant pause. "I knew it." The words came screeching out, fast and dangerous. "Lordy, I tell you I knew it the second I laid on you." The words coming out almost in a song of church-style testimony.

"You knew what?" Julie rolled her eyes.

Here we go. Back on the rollercoaster.

"Whenever you start to fall for someone, you go and do something drastic. With Patrick, you went through that whole red-lipstick phase. With whatever his name was before Patrick, you had that obsession with trying to get your breasts augmented." She ticked the men off on her fingers one by one. "The moment I saw you in the kitchen with your new short hair and this weight loss, I had a mind to tell you exactly what I thought, but I figured I had better let you tell me yourself."

As the third finger lifted, Julie flushed and she could feel her skin running hot. "For the record, I did all this in *spite* of Patrick, and *before* Nico came along."

Ugh. Julie's mother had a way of putting all the cards on the table at once and dealing people a hand of their own hang-ups. Ironic, since she never seemed to notice any of her own.

What could she say to that? It hadn't started out that way, but eventually it *was* true. She'd set out to carve a revenge body to help Patrick see the error in his ways, but somewhere along the way, she wanted it for herself. When Nico showed up with that look in his hypnotic chocolate eyes, it had only strengthened her conviction to reinvent herself. Albeit, she wasn't in the same age range as Stella, but nevertheless she wanted to get her groove back, too.

Julie hadn't realized she was doing it, but when her mother put it like that, it was sort of hard to deny.

Comfy and smug in her accusation, her crazy mom must have seen the wheels turning as Julie contemplated the truth in her statement because she waved it off. Her hands circled frantically, as if to wind the conversation back around to the good stuff. "Ah, so he has a name?" She chimed in, her brows raised in response to whatever expression was smeared across her daughter's face.

Julie wasn't sure what look that was exactly, but whatever it was, it was enough to keep the oil in this conversation burning. "Don't go spending all night trying to make sense of it. Just tell me about your new beau. I want to know everything about this...this, Nico character."

The way she said his name wasn't specifically with distaste. After years of her "perfect Patrick," it was almost like she needed to test Nico's name on tongue—see what kind of ring it had to it.

"Well, it's still pretty new," Julie said sheepishly. "So far, I've shown him the worst of me and he's still sticking around, so I guess that's a good sign." Julie cocked a brow at her sordid logic. "All we've really done is kiss, sort of," she said, biting her lip at the memory.

Slippery wet images of their shower fantasy flooded back to Julie. The searing heat. His lips blazing trails of fire over her skin.

There are so many places I want to kiss you right now, she heard him say near her ear.

She couldn't very well tell her mother the X-rated details. Kissing was safe.

Mirroring her thoughts, her mother said, "kissing is just the beginning." She inched closer to Julie and wound her hand in a circle again, impatiently urging her to continue.

Julie shifted into the cushions of the couch as her body tensed and tightened at the thought of Nico. *You have no idea, Mom.*

For the rest of the movie and about twenty more minutes following it, Julie recounted her Nico sightings and blunders leading up to their date tonight. Against her better judgment she even included her alcohol-enthused evening at Frankie's Tiki Room and waking up in Nico's bed, minus the adult activity and the run-in with Nico's mother.

Through it all, her mother remained quiet and only nodded here and there for Julie to continue. If she was judging, she hadn't let on, and Julie was grateful for it.

When she finished, Julie had expected the questions to pour forth, but her mother only squinted her eyes as if she was still chewing on the new information.

"Well?" Julie asked, the impatient one now.

Her mom finished the last swig of her wine and placed the glass on the end table beside her before pulling one last mom bomb in the span of a few hours. "Do I get to meet him?" Her big amber eyes batted innocently below her thick brows.

Out of all the things she could have asked—all of the things a mother *should* ask—Julie hadn't expected that.

She must have seen the confusion on Julie's face because she clarified. "It just seems like there's something different about this one. I like him already. A gentleman without being a doormat. He's got staying power, honey."

"What makes you say that?"

"This man has been yelled at by you, picked you up off the floor, and had the contents of your stomach on him"—she stressed the word *on*—"and he's still sticking around. Most men would be running for the hills by now, and he's asking to see you. Counting the minutes to see you." She pursed her lips and gave Julie a serious eye as if to let on that this was the advice she needed to heed. "I like him. He seems to be good for you."

Yes. He was *counting the minutes*. Julie was right there with him watching the clock.

The thought of Nico made Julie blush from the inside out. Her nerves buzzed and her skin tingled with the memory of his delicious weight on her. Without warning, he'd come from nowhere and now she was beginning to wonder what she'd do without him.

Julie checked her watch. She did need to know the time, but mostly she needed to look somewhere other than into her mother's knowing eyes if she was going to ask the question she'd been itching to ask. The two of them were the same that way—facades had no fighting chance with the intuitive bond they shared. Julie was counting on it.

"Mom?" It was almost a whisper.

Her mother didn't respond. She'd been looking at the television. Some unrealistic lovey-dovey ad for an online dating service. Julie caught the last few seconds of it filled with the membership marriage statistics, when her mother met her gaze.

There really wasn't a right time to ask.

"When do you think *you'll* be ready to find someone good for you again?" Julie asked, dropping an atom bomb of her own.

Later that night when Nico rang Julie's doorbell, she was surprised by how nervous she felt. He had asked her out and confirmed their plans just after she left her mother's house, so why couldn't she keep her clammy hands from fidgeting? Why on earth couldn't she just stand still, instead of shifting from one foot to the other like an antsy child on Christmas Eve? The man had seen and tasted every inch of her, there wasn't much else to be nervous about.

Before she opened the door, she checked herself once more. The dress fit well and there were no tears or stains. The heels on her booties were just the right height for her to reach his full lips without climbing. A final glance in the mirror above the entry table showed her makeup was neutral with a tinted hot pink lip.

Perfect for whatever he had planned.

Julie unlatched the lock and twisted the handle. Nico stood on the other side, gorgeous as ever in loose-fit jeans with a long sleeved two-tone blue and white baseball shirt and a light jacket wrapped around his waist. She wasn't sure what he had planned, but his outfit was a little more casual than what she had imagined. From his text, she figured maybe a meal and a movie, or a little blackjack and getting lost on The Strip. Instead, he was dressed for something that required breaking a sweat. And not the kind of sweat-breaking physical activity she had hoped for.

His large hands gripped two stuffed brown paper bags.

"Change of plans." He shrugged. When Julie failed to clear the entrance, he bit his lip. "These are kind of heavy, so are you going to let me in?"

As Julie stepped aside and waved her outstretched arm toward the kitchen, Nico hurried over to the counter and hoisted the bags up on it. She watched from the door as he began unloading the whole grocery store and the farmer's market onto every bare surface.

She finally decided she had better get on board and shut the door behind herself. "Mind if I ask, what prompted this change of heart, Top Chef?" She propped herself up on a barstool, sitting eye to eye, with only the counter between them.

"Uh...given our previous meetings, I kind of felt like it would be a safe bet to stay in tonight." He winked. "You know, if that's okay with you..." He raised a brow and smirked. In so many words, he hinted at Julie's countless fails since their first meeting. No way he'd let her off the hook that easy.

She returned a knowing grin at him and those gorgeous lashes. Hey body was crying and begging her to jump his bones. It was all she could do not to push everything to the floor and take him right there on the bar, and think about food later. And now he *cooks?*

Who could eat at a time like this?

Somehow, she managed to sit patiently and engage in mindless banter as Nico finished unpacking, only pausing between sentences here and there to guide him in the direction of the utensils and pots and pans. Before long, he was chopping and slicing and dicing and throwing it all into an oversized gumbo-like stew with ground beef and a colorful array of vegetables and spices. The smell perfumed the air, warm and flavorful like some kind of camp fireside adventure soup.

Within a few minutes, he turned the heat down to a simmer and assigned Julie the menial task of stirring while he relieved himself in the bathroom.

Dutifully, she stirred. And in the numbing movement, her mind also stirred.

A few weeks ago, she'd come to terms with the downward turn her life had taken. Both at home and at work she was failing. There was nowhere to turn for relief. Then, one day, it was like her prayers had been sent to processing. While things were nowhere near where she wanted them to be, she'd regained hope.

The stars were working their way into alignment. A change had found its way onto her horizon.

CHAPTER 26

J ulie's mind was lost in a flurry of emotions and hope.

The interview for the management position was coming up, but there wasn't an offer for employment on the table. Still, there was possibility on the work front. Just the prospect of other options had lifted her from her rut.

And there were new possibilities on the romantic front, too.

Julie's ex had left her and she couldn't see the trees for the forrest. But now? There was Nico. And while they hadn't had a normal, regular day together, there was possibility—the prospect of something more. The hint at something meaningful. Just the idea alone dug down deep in her heart and dragged an ear-to-ear smile onto her face.

Nothing noteworthy had happened, but the feelings she was feeling were magical. She wasn't even sure *what* was happening with them. Still, the possibilities made every minute worth it.

Julie was so busy grinning like a fool, that she didn't hear Nico leave the bathroom. In the time it took him to walk the short distance back to the kitchen, she noticed the sauce had begun to bake against the sides of the pot in hard crusted scales. She must've gotten lost in her thoughts. Slowly, she began to stir again.

"Care to share?" Nico asked, low enough to be a whisper.

Julie started, surprised by his presence. "Damn. You scared the shit out of me."

He stood directly behind her. So close she could feel his warm breath on the back of her neck. His hard chest on her back. Something harder on her butt.

"Based on the look on your face, it must be something good," he said.

She pressed her hand to her chest and shifted to turn toward Nico, but his hands latched onto her hips, stilling her in place. Nico's lips were inches from her face and she was afraid to breathe. Every inch of her skin reacted to his touch, pulsing and buzzing under the weight of his strong fingers. The beat of her heart, pounding so fast and hard…she thought surely it would betray her excitement.

"Looks ready." He leaned in over her shoulder. "Can I have a taste?"

Julie dipped the wooden spoon in the sauce and cradled her hand beneath it as she turned and lifted it toward Nico's mouth. He didn't give an inch. Instead, he pressed his body evenly against Julie's.

Slowly, he parted his lips and tasted the sauce. God she would have given anything to be that spoon. To have his full lips on her.

Julie tilted her head toward his, and released a low gasp. Their faces were a whisper apart. So close that she was dizzy with the fresh cottony smell of him—his scent. She searched his face and found the same longing in his eyes that she was sure lingered in hers. As much as she tried, she couldn't keep her eyes from traveling downward to his lips.

"It's delicious," he murmured, behind closed lids.

After a satisfying moan, Nico opened his eyes and grazed his wet tongue over his lips then turned the spoon toward Julie for a taste. At that point, the tightening low in her belly throbbed and she feared she might unravel from his proximity alone.

She wanted more than a taste. She'd already had a taste of him in the shower the other day and now she was craving him.

As she lowered her bottom lip, he slowly dragged the warm spoon across her lips, glazing them with red sauce. When he was finished, he placed the spoon on the counter and returned his gaze to her. "Don't move."

Before she could object or even determine his next move, he took her face in his hands and pressed his lips hard over hers, sucking and biting softly. Effectively winding her up. He looked at her with those eyes she loved so much and Julie exhaled only to take in a sharp intake of air. The catch in her throat intensified as his gaze darkened.

As if she *could* move. Her knees were losing strength and the handle to the oven behind her was digging into her back. She gripped it to keep her upright and a laugh bubbled up at the sense of deja vu. Was this how it was going to be every time, Nico ravishing her and Julie trying and failing at keeping her motor skills in order.

"What's so funny?" Nico smiled into Julie's lips.

"It's just…I'm falling," she said.

Nico's decadent chocolate eyes fluttered open, ablaze with questions.

Julie knew exactly how it sounded. Although, she was physically falling to the floor, the words struck a chord. Was she falling for Nico?

Her breath hitched and her mouth fell open. Before he could say a word, she turned her gaze. "To the floor," she quickly clarified. She couldn't look directly at him. It was too much.

Nico bit back a smile. Then, sweet and tender, he brushed his lips over hers once more. It was the kind of kiss that said more than any million words could communicate. It was soft and gentle. Without a word shared, it said I want you so bad. I've missed you. Maybe, I might be falling for you, too.

It was Julie's undoing.

"Say you want me," Nico whispered as he trailed light pecks

down her neck to her collarbone. He wrapped her hands around his own thick neck and moved her away from the stove.

Julie thought she might hyperventilate as he deepened the kiss, allowing his hands to dip under her dress to her bare back. With both hands, he pressed her into him where she could feel how much he wanted her, too. His erection pressed into her stomach and Julie released an agonizing groan.

"I want you..." she breathed. "To respect me."

The second the words were out of her mouth, Julie could have kicked herself. She wanted Nico. She deserved Nico. Her body deserved Nico. But, deep down, she knew this wasn't exactly the best route to go to keep him around.

Images of his beautifully thick, veined erection flashed in her mind and she wanted it again, needed it. Every wet inch of him. Julie was feening for this man and she hated how much she wanted him. One proper lay and she was practically a junkie going through withdrawals in need of her next hit.

As Nico let his tongue slink back into his mouth, replacing it with a sweet kiss, Julie hated herself. She hated her damn brain for getting in the way of what her body craved. Nico removed his hands from beneath her cute little black dress which would have been perfect for unobstructed counter sex and Julie could have cried. God she hated reality and knowing too much. Ignorance was so much more fun.

In the back of her mind, Julie knew another round of sex with Nico would be as amazing as it was the first time, but what was she doing? She was insane to keep doing this to herself and expecting different results. If she wanted Nico, and she did, *painfully* so, she knew what she had to do.

Willpower was one thing, but it took grit and a special kind of stubborn resolve to let Nico leave. Here was this beautiful man, who had cooked for her and kissed her properly like she deserved to be kissed, and she was letting him walk out.

Or, rather, pushing him out before she did something she'd regret in the morning.

In the back of her mind, she warred with herself. On her shoulder, a teensy angelic version of herself urged her not to go jumping in headfirst. And on the other, a devilish red version of Liz. Little Liz, persuasive as ever, begged Julie to bed Nico. Convincingly so, she argued that Julie could ask for forgiveness later, once she recovered from sex so good it put her to sleep.

Mostly, Julie fixated on the fact that nothing bad had happened.

They'd actually spent several sane, sober hours together and she hadn't ripped anything, hurt herself, or required any sort of medical attention, excluding minor heart palpitations.

What was worse than her fledgling emotions grasping for anything real to grab hold of was the white box. And not just any white box, but a small white box. The kind that often held an even smaller velvet box that likely displayed delicate jewelry, like...oh say, a ring.

They'd been standing in the doorway prolonging the inevitable, both recapping the evening. Julie was going back and forth in her mind a thousand times about letting him leave, and every time, Nico staying outweighed her worries of what they might do. She was on the verge of caving when the rain outside began spattering against the window.

At first, it was a light drizzle. Within a few minutes, it poured in sheets, blurred and heavy against the living room window pane. As clear a sign as any, Julie urged him to get home safely before the roads slicked too badly.

Nico nodded and untied his jacket from his waist. As he flipped his jacket over his shoulders, the pockets emptied on the floor.

Julie bent down to help him pick up his belongings on the floor and that's when she spotted it. Between the jingling coins and a black leather wallet was a small white box.

At that moment, about a million thoughts flew through her head.

CHAPTER 27

W as he going to propose to someone? *Is he planning to propose to me?*

She hadn't fully wrapped her mind around his plans for the ring she was sure was inside the box, and already the panic ensued. If he asked her, what would she say? Did he know her ring size? Mostly, did he believe she'd say yes?

He must have seen the hysteria likely etched across her face because he grabbed the box and recoiled. "Don't freak out. It's a small gift I've been meaning to give to you." He stood up, towering over Julie. "I know you've been working hard at the gym. This is just a little something I thought might keep you motivated."

Cautiously, Julie retrieved the box. She looked up at him and bit her bottom lip as she slid the top off. Inside, a small green teardrop-shaped electronic device sat in the foam impression.

"It's a Fitbit," he announced.

Julie's eyes lit up. "Oh my gosh. I freaking didn't know what to think," she sighed with relief. "Thank you."

"I figure with this, you can take baby steps before you run. You know, make yourself some step goals." Nico slipped his arms into the sleeves of his jacket and zipped it just above his collarbone. "Plus, I didn't think you could handle CrossFit just yet," he teased.

Julie rolled her eyes and reached out to playfully slap his arm, but Nico caught her hand and pulled her into him.

"Nico?" she breathed his name.

One more time, he kissed her lips softly and lingered for the faintest moment.

She inhaled his earthy scent and clung to his jacket. "I…"

"Goodnight, Julie." Nico turned back toward the door and took two steps at a time down the stairs to his truck.

THE NEXT DAY, a few scattered clouds still hung in the sky, but the air was warm with the thick tangy smell of barbecue smoke and the celebratory excitement of the Memorial Day holiday. By nine a.m., Julie had already gotten in six thousand steps at the gym, argued with her mother, and picked up the "couple of things" her mother asked her to get from the grocery store.

As it turned out her mother's "couple" was a little off. It equated to quite a few more than two items on her list. She ended up picking up the ingredients for the salad, a couple of fruit and vegetable trays, and enough meat for a party of twenty. Which was fine, except for the minor detail that it would only be few people coming to this "get-together."

"Mom, I'll be pulling up to the house in like two minutes, so get off the phone, open up the door and come help me," Julie said, accelerating at a green light.

As the bluetooth disconnected, the playlist Julie had been listening to before the call resumed. A mellow beachy song filled the car and she leaned back against the headrest, hoping to calm her nerves.

Apparently, Aunt Helen thought it would be in bad taste for her sister to invite anyone outside the family. Since Austin wouldn't be able to attend with Sophia, due to work-related travel. "It just didn't look right," her aunt had said. The debate whether it would be proper for even the Aunt Helen and Sophia to come was even a thing. Until she conceded based solely on her sister's ability to cue the waterworks and pour on the guilt trip.

"Good grief." Julie sighed as she brought the car to a stop. She popped the trunk and meticulously hoisted up the bags.

Now, Julie would be stuck spending the last day of her three-day weekend with her mother, Aunt Helen, and Sophia—about as cheery a bunch as a room full of depression patients.

This ought to be fun.

Still, she strung all ten or so plastic bags up her arms, used her head to nudge the trunk shut, and did a run-walk to make it to the front door in one trip before her arms could fall off.

With only her feet free, she kicked the bottom of the door a couple of times, in lieu of ringing the bell. "Mom!" she yelled. "Open the door. I'm here."

She waited a few more seconds before kicking again, finally deciding to use her elbow to poke the doorbell. By then, her wrists were beginning to burn and the crease of her elbow felt like it might snap.

"Mom!" she shouted, bordering on hysteria.

As footsteps neared, Julie clamped her hands together to hold the bags steady. Already some of the plastic bags looked like they might give way. It would really piss her off to have to sit all the bags down, dig in her purse for the key, and have to try again to get them all back up her arms without breaking or bursting anything.

Just as she stomped her foot and grunted, the door creaked open.

"What took you so long—"

"Don't you have a key?" Sophia materialized in the doorframe, big basketball belly in tow. As ever, her hair was perfectly coifed into a flawless flipped bob with a headband to match her pastel cruise wear, despite her being geographically out of reach of any real body of water.

"Honey, I would help you, but my doctor frowns upon me lifting just about anything these days." Her cousin laughed in a sneaky, impish sort of way and turned on her ballet flats. She kept moving toward the kitchen without offering to carry so much as the napkins or a platter, while Julie wedged herself through the door and kicked it closed.

When Julie made it into the kitchen, the women were all seated around the wooden dining room table with their eyes centrally focused on her.

"Wow. Don't hurt yourselves trying to help or anything. I've got this. No big deal," Julie said sarcastically. When she looked up, they hadn't moved an inch. "Everything...all right?" she asked, slow and cautious, but they remained quiet.

"Is the door closed?" her mother probed lightly as she stepped into the kitchen doorway and inspected the living room toward the foyer.

The lines of confusion strewn across Julie's face twisted into a big question mark. "Yes? Should I have left it open for someone?"

"Oh, it's just you?" Disappointment laced her mother's words at Julie's nod. "I thought you might invite your new fella," she said as she walked the few steps back to the table and plopped down. All traces of her best behavior were gone.

Instantly, the noise level in the room rose a few decibels. One or two of them was bad enough, but the three of them together was like siccing a rabid dog on an infant. By default, poor Nico had dodged the worst kind of bullet. Anyone would be hard-pressed to find a worse combination than the introduction of a handsome, virile man to a room full of hormonal and borderline-menopausal women, itching for attention.

Julie's failure to subject him to their claws was akin to dashing their hopes of having any fun at all. There would be no polite conversation or purposefully interjected tales of embarrassment from Julie's childhood. No inappropriate sexual innuendos.

And the biggest letdown of all—no reenactment of the Spanish Inquisition.

Heaven forbid they would have to wait to meet him until Julie decided what he meant to her.

"I'm going to try not to be offended by the fact that my own family is disappointed to see *just* me." An annoyed laugh slipped from her lips as she searched through the drawers for the lighter to get the grill started. "You know, Mom, after you told me it was going to be just us, I figured it might not be the best idea. After all, we wouldn't want Miss Sophia to be surrounded by anything other than polite company now, would we? I don't think it would be right to have another man around a married woman. Who knows what the people would say?" Julie mocked Sophia's badly imitated twang.

"Oh hush, now. For heaven's sake, Jules. You sound *silly*. We won't bite, now go on and invite your young man over. I'm dying to meet this new guy of yours," Aunt Helen said.

And though Julie had no doubts that she did want to meet Nico, she questioned her motives. Had it been anyone outside of the family, Aunt Helen would talk Julie up like a princess. Bottom line—it all stemmed back to Aunt Helen. She had a great niece, and the *best* daughter.

Behind closed doors—her sister's doors, in particular—Julie could be the princess, so long as Sophia got to be the queen. She did tit-for-tat better than anyone Julie had ever known.

Payback, Julie supposed. For her mother taking away Aunt Helen's spotlight a little over half a century ago.

The only child to a pair of adoring parents ready to spoil her on a whim, Helen reveled in her solo glory. Then, she had had a sister, Marian, a cheery cherub-cheeked cutie who came along and stole her spotlight. A younger, attention-grabbing, grubby-handed little sister who wrapped their parents around her bite-sized fingers.

The way her mother had told it, Aunt Helen had never lived it down. So, basically, having daughters close in age meant a long-awaited do-over.

On that note, Julie and Sophia slipped into the back yard, plopping down on a pair of poolside loungers.

"What do you think we have? Fifteen, twenty more minutes before they realize we're gone?" Julie asked her cousin.

Sophia laughed. "I'll be gone before they pick up on it."

Julie peeked over the side of the chair at the patio door where she could see their mothers going at it. Their sibling rivalry and now battle of the daughters was getting oddly specific and old.

By their standards, Aunt Helen was finally far out front. In the categories of relationship, work, wealth, and now the ability to provide grandchildren as fast as socially acceptable, Sophia was a head above Julie.

Julie pulled out her phone and began scrolling through her Instagram. "So what's on the to-do list today? A pressing fundraiser? A mandatory tea party?" Julie asked without looking at her cousin.

Julie could feel the steam coming off of her.

"Jealous much?"

They had been practically neck and neck in work, depending on which side of the debate you fell. If you considered self-employment versus gainfully employed, either one of them could take the category. Wealth was another one that came in with narrow margins. If only individual self-obtained streams of income were included, it could be too hard to call it.

"Of what? The piece of paper that says a man has to put up with you? No, that's not it. I must be envious of all the money and the baby. That's what you and Aunt Helen think, right?"

At the end of the day, the determining factors always came down to finding a man who could add value of some sort, and the ability to spawn golden children. In the past year, Sophia had secured her position as the leader in both, with a swanky Southern wedding and a questionably-timed pregnancy.

"It might do you some good to quit playing around with all these young boys and find someone who can afford to pay for his dinner and yours."

"Oh, okay, Soph because you know so much about the guy I'm seeing. Is that the conclusion Aunt Helen came to after talking to Mom for like five minutes. FYI she hasn't met him yet either." Julie rolled her eyes and peeked over at their mothers again.

To her cousin and her aunt, any hint that Julie might have found a man as good as or better than Austin sent the antennas up and the sirens wailing. They'd be happy if Julie settled for an unfortunate-looking, slightly overweight oaf with poor financial sense. If they caught wind that Nico had brains, brawn, and wit, they'd be forced to do something drastic to up the ante for fear of the scales tipping in Julie's favor. Given the propensity for Laurich women to birth nothing but girls, there could be a third generation of warrior women vying for an unworthy title.

Sophia, swung her legs over the edge of the lounger to face Julie. "Well, if he's so great. Why don't you bring him around? Like Mom said, we don't bite."

At one point, Julie had considered backing down and inviting Nico over to get the inevitable said and done. But she'd reconsidered just as quickly. "As awesome as that sounds, Soph—with the whole *not biting* bit and everything—I'm going to spare him the torture."

In a single fluid movement, she was up off her chair, headed back into the house. Dealing with the mothers was definitely the lesser evil.

A little over an hour later, Julie finally convinced her family that the world would not end as they knew it if Nico didn't join them. Still, they remained tried and true to their nosy ways, fishing for information on Patrick. That, and what the "new guy" thought about their broken engagement.

The older women, especially, harped on Julie's intentions for settling down sooner rather than later. Aunt Helen treaded lightly, asking what Julie thought her and the "new guy's" children might look like. Obviously, she was hoping to get an idea about Nico's looks from Julie's description of his physical features. *Nice try.*

As much as they seemed to be enjoyed the whole inquisition bit, Julie couldn't get passed the subject fast enough. There was only one topic more inviting to her nosy aunt and cousin. In fact, Sophia's favorite subject.

"So, how's everything going with the baby shower?"

Thankfully, Sophia bit the bait. "Oh. My. Gosh. You are not going to believe." She whipped out her tablet-sized phone. Swiping and tapping, the screen illuminated with multiple boards she'd created on Pinterest. At the top of the list, of course, shower games.

CHAPTER 28

"Just to give you an idea of what I'm looking for…" Sophia recapped her lofty expectations. She began swiping through endless images of overly-enthused women doing stupid things like wrapping the mommy-to-be in toilet paper and drinking alcohol from baby bottles.

"Uh huh." Julie wasn't exactly listening. Her eyes were on the screen and she gave a nod every once in a while, but her thoughts were on Nico.

Her mind reeled with images of their saucy kiss. Followed swiftly by the steamy, wet, hot memories of him in the shower. Then, him blazing a trail of kisses all over her body. Then, him…inside her.

"Earth to Jules?" Sophia snapped her fingers beside her ear.

"What?" Her heart was still racing. The sound pounding in her ears.

Sophia said nothing. She cocked her head to the mothers and Julie followed her line of vision. Her gaze swept around the table. By the looks of things, they had less than five minutes before round two began. Based on the number of empty wine bottles, maybe one minute.

"Goddamnit, Marian." Aunt Helen jumped up from her chair, leaving it wobbling in her wake. She double-fisted the bottles and tossed them in the trash. "This is exactly what I'm talking about.

Julie had no idea what she was talking about. She'd been too busy daydreaming about Nico's magic tongue to focus on what her mom and Aunt Helen were spatting about. Now, they were glaring at each other, sniveling like rabid dogs. Whatever it was, things were clearly about to get real.

She squinted her eyes at her cousin, furrowing her brow in question. Shoulders lifted into a shrug.

"Jules?" Sophia cocked her head toward the patio. Her voice was barely a whisper, but there was warning in her tone.

Reluctantly, and against her better judgment, Julie slowly stood up and slinked toward the backyard again. Man, she could think of so many better ways to use her time right now. Better positions.

When they were both outside, Julie rolled her eyes and plopped back down on the same chair she'd sat on earlier. "What are they arguing about *now?*"

"More of the same, but let's just say, for Aunt Marian, the chicken is coming home to roost," Sophia said, conspiratorially.

"It's 'hens.'"

Sophia face twisted at her.

"The saying. It's 'hens coming home to roost,' not chickens. Ugh, I can't wait until you get over this whole Southern phase you've got going."

Exhausted by this whole get-together, she released a loud sigh, bending her ear back toward the sound of the burning fuse being lit inside.

From what she could hear, this time, Mom had promised a member of their church congregation an "introduction" to her sister. Which, every Laurich woman knew was code for matchmaking. If history was any indicator, Marian had already given the man her sister's phone number, social media handles, and a list of places she frequented. It wouldn't be farfetched to assume she'd promised a date, either.

"I really want to get back home." Sophia checked her watch. "Austin should've landed hours ago and I want to check in on him."

Julie checked the time on her phone, too. "It's early. It's barely three. Give him another hour to get settled in, first," she said. "Your insecurities are showing.

It irritated her to no end that the strong, beautiful, confident cousin she'd grown up with, had somehow turned into this stage five clinger. Why did she need to have a play-by-play of her husband's schedule down to the minute? If she didn't trust him, then why was she with him?

Even as the thought crossed her mind, the irony buzzed over her skin. *Is this what I was like with Patrick?* She didn't to be like that with Nico. She just wanted to spend time with him. Be with him.

She unlocked her phone and tapped on the messages icon. Nico's name topped the recent list. He'd sent a message last night to just let her know he'd made it home safely. They'd exchanged a few emojis and proclamations of what a good time they had had, but it was the final message that she couldn't stop going back to. She'd read it a dozen times, each time with a new emotion.

Nico: I wish you were here

The way Julie and Sophia were wired said more about them and their self-worth than it did about the men who they chose. They both had daddy issues. One had left on his own accord, and the other without choice. But, Julie wasn't going to let her father's death dictate her relationships any longer. Not if she could help it.

She read the text again. Something about it warmed her insides. What they had was mutual.

She wished she was there, too. Even more so now. Despite a growing urge to protect Nico from the claws of the women in her family, she wished *he* was here. Julie wished that they could skip all of the pretenses and jump right into the comfortable stage of enjoying each other's company and the security of a *mutual* love. A lasting love.

By now, the mothers were going at each other with full-fledged rage and shrill venom on their tongues. On top of the name-calling, the personal jabs spat off like gunfire.

Julie and Sophia knew better than to insert themselves in the middle, so it seemed as good a time as any for Julie to make an exit. She swiped to Nico's message and began texting.

Julie: Are you busy?

The three little ellipses popped up, sending a flurry of anxiousness to Julie's stomach. Before he could finish typing. Julie replied again.

Julie: Can we meet?

Say yes. Say yes. Say yes. When Nico didn't respond fast enough for Julie's frantic nerves, doubt crept in. Maybe he was busy, or with someone else. She *hated* that was where her mind immediately went. They had gone over this just about every time they'd been together, but Julie still couldn't get Nico's words out of her mind.

Say anything.

Julie: It's okay. I know you're probably spending the holiday with your family. Call when you can.
Nico: Of course I want to see you. I've been thinking about you all day. I just have somewhere I need to go first.

Whether she wanted to admit it or not, a play-by-play was what she craved. She was being needy and she knew it, but she couldn't help it. As she typed her response, she peeked up at cousin sympathetically now.

Julie: I can go with you…

Desperate much? Loser. Why would you say that?

Julie: Sorry. Didn't mean to invite myself. Just…if you need some company, I'm game to come along.
Nico: Going to drop off some flowers for my dad. ???

This is what you get for being an addict. God, give the man some space.

Julie: I'm still in

These were the times that she was grateful for text messages. Words popped up on the screen, chipper and jubilant as rewards for instant gratification addicts—and Nico addicts— and it was up to the reader to determine how they should be heard. What kind of meaning hid between the spaces? Julie had said she was "in," when really, she was more "on the fence."

Am I jumping the gun?

"You leaving?" Sophia asked, jarring Julie from her thoughts. Her voice low and even as she nodded toward Julie's phone.

"Yeah."

Sophia looked at her sheepishly. "So, you really like this guy, huh? I mean, if you guys are spending so much time together. You were never like this with Patrick."

Julie's gaze met Sophia's. There was sadness in them. Hints of the cousin she loved. The cousin who'd grown up feeling more like a sister. She was intuitive and cared more about other people.

The way Sophia looked her, she wanted to share everything and tell her about Patrick and Nico, but so much had changed.

"It's new. We're just hanging out, but I like him." It was meant to be nonchalant, like she hadn't put much thought into it. The way it came out, even Julie heard the longing in her tone.

Less than a month had passed since Patrick, and she'd calculated timeframes down to the day that he must have gotten Celeste pregnant before their ties had been broken. And now, in the scheme of things, it hadn't taken her very long either to get over him and move on to the next. Which had an ironic side effect of making her question her own ability to choose the right person. While Nico had been great so far, Julie had learned to second-guess her radar.

When Nico had said he had somewhere to go, she assumed he meant an errand or two, or a favor for a friend. She hadn't expected a visit to his father's grave. Now it was too late. She would have looked like a wishy-washy flake to run the second things got serious.

"For the record, I never thought Patrick was good enough for you," Sophia said.

Julie eyed her now, reading her. It wasn't a lie or trick. She smiled back. She didn't have the heart to tell her she thought the same about Austin.

She wasn't sure what made her volunteer to ride along, but it just felt right. The thought of Nico visiting his beloved dad's grave alone left her empty.

This was the kind of thing people did in relationships that had been properly broken in, not on a whim with someone you just kissed a few times and shared a shower fantasy with once. But even if they ended up only being friends, a friend would be there for him in his time of need. One of the woes of having a conscience, Julie rationalized.

"Thanks."

Still, she had asked to see him. She would have to take it any way he'd allow, even if that meant spending time in a cemetery.

CHAPTER 29

He must've been nearby because it only took him fifteen minutes to get to her mother's house after she texted him the address. As instructed, he parked a few houses away and sent the thumbs-up emoji as the cue to come on out. By the time she dealt with a decent goodbye amidst her mother and aunt's fallout and managed to escape, another five or ten minutes had slipped away.

"Sorry I took so long. Mothers..." she scoffed with an exhausted laugh, climbing into the cab of the truck.

But, Nico didn't join in her playful criticism. Stone-faced, he flipped his wrist to check the time and put the truck in gear impatiently as Julie closed the door. Without waiting for her to buckle herself, he merged into traffic, cutting off an apple-red hatchback in the process.

Even at the honking horn, he flattened his foot on the accelerator. Julie clutched the oh-shit bar, instinctively pressing her own feet down hard against the floor mat. Her heart raced as she frantically scanned the lanes in front and on the sides of them.

Why was he driving so wild and reckless? Was he mad? At her?

It was a mistake to have come along, she told herself. But she was here now. He could've said no. He could've told her if he had changed his mind, but he didn't.

Whether it was the best time or not, she turned her body toward Nico and cut her eyes at him and said, "If you didn't want me to come, you should have just said so, instead of driving like a fucking psycho because you're pissed that I took too long to come out."

She took his silence as an admission of guilt. "Don't worry about me. Let me out at the next light and I'll get an Uber."

Her words were harsh, but Nico didn't flinch. He kept his eyes fixed on the road and swerved into a hard left. Down a block on the right side, the sign for the cemetery came into view. "Relax. It's not about you. I'm going to miss it."

For the life of her, Julie couldn't figure what he'd miss. Picking her battles, she resigned herself to let his attitude slide, given where they were headed. As he pulled into a space in front of an austere administration building in shades of cream and beige with sparse desert landscaping and sloped lawns surrounding it, she remained seated. She watched as he gathered a manila envelope with tattered edges and black writing on the front. He leaned over the armrest to grab a beautiful bouquet of yellow and white flowers.

She eyed him as he got out of the truck and patted his pockets meticulously like he was double-checking to make sure he hadn't forgotten anything.

He made it all the way to the curb before he realized that Julie hadn't followed him. When he looked back at her, in her usual head-strong way, Julie turned her attention toward the side window and didn't return it. Only when his face filled the glass before her did she meet his eyes.

"I'm sorry," he said through the tinted window. "Please come with me."

It could've been because she felt guilty for taking his time. Or it might have been the humble sweetness in his request, but she unlatched her seatbelt and unlocked the door. As he opened her door for her, he apologized a second time, traces of remorse evident as his voice trailed off.

In that moment, with her acceptance of his apology, their rough start to the day seemed to ebb away. Ever so gently, Nico locked the door behind Julie and settled his warm hand on the small of her back and guided her down the path.

Even as they had walked over to Nico's father's plot, Julie found herself playing a warped game of hopscotch, making a concerted effort not to step on anyone. Though she tried not to, she couldn't help figuring the ages at death. A couple of times she had to hang on to Nico to steady herself to keep moving in the right direction. There were people with full lives that she hoped were fruitful and others whose had been cut short way too soon. A current of emotions welled up inside her, overwhelming her in a way she wasn't quite ready for.

Julie stared at the headstone with a huge butterfly in the top right corner.

In Loving Memory of
Nicholas "Nico" Farfalla Sr.
Son. Husband. Father.
May 29, 1951 - September 26, 2012

It was his name. Well, his dad's name, but it was the same. His namesake. Nico was a junior, her butterfly.

Julie read further down and noticed the dates. *That's what Nico didn't want to miss—his birthday.*

"I'm so sorry, Nico." She clapped her hands over her mouth.

Suddenly, remorse settled in her chest. She had stalled and dilly-dallied with her mom and aunt over something so frivolous as a shared phone number, when Nico had the weight of his father's birthday on his mind. Julie mentally scoured herself for coming at all. She wished she wasn't here. She was no good at this kind of thing.

Not that cemeteries were really anyone's *thing*, but she hadn't had enough practice to know what to do with herself when it came to them. Aside from some fourth or fifth cousin who had died before she was born, there was only her father that she actually knew well enough to be sad about it, and her mother had kept her away from the burial. Her mom didn't want the scarring effects that funerals sometimes had on younger children for her daughter.

"It's okay. I'm okay here," he said.

Now, looking at Nico's name engraved in stone before her, it got to be too much. Her heart pounded hard against her chest as worry built up. They'd only recently acknowledged that there might be something beginning between them and now the very literal reminder stared her in the face—he could be gone at any time.

Julie backed away. Still in earshot of Nico with his father, she turned toward the main building. It would be devastating to have to hear *and* see him with such raw emotion. So, she listened.

Behind her, she heard the pendulum in Nico's voice swing from unfiltered agony at his father's absence, to pure elation as he recalled memories of times they shared. Mostly, it was the way the smallest things that he remembered—events which wouldn't even register with another person—that stuck with Julie. The words were so private and intimate, she almost felt like she was trespassing on their moment.

"Mom brought out the pictures from that Fourth of July at the lake," he began, releasing a robust laugh. He talked about the car he finally finished repairing that they started together. How he was taking care of his mother now and didn't want his dad to worry. His constant quest to make sure he was a person his dad would be proud to call a son. And when he trailed off, the confession to his father that he might have found someone important.

Over her shoulder she peeked at him now. His back was turned at an angle and she could see his profile. His voice was low and shaky. From where he rested on his knees, his watery eyes shimmered in the falling sun, a smile tugged at the corners of his mouth.

At first, it was hard for her to hear through the rustling of leaves in the light breeze, but as they settled, Nico's voice came in clearly.

"...Beautiful, and self-deprecating, and kind of a pain in the ass, but you would like her. She's clumsy and smart. She does this thing with her hair when she's nervous and it drives me wild." He laughed, totally comfortable like they had done this a zillion times. "And her eyes...they tell on her. Every little whim that crosses her mind flies through them and I can read all of them as clear as if they were my own thoughts."

Julie found herself squaring her body to him, her ears stretching further to reach as he continued.

"And she's perfect. She doesn't know it, but that's what makes her special. She's got this idea that she needs to change and reinvent herself, but for me, I'd take her just the way she is."

He paused for a beat and Julie whipped back around toward the building, careful not to tell on herself for eavesdropping. He must have known she was in earshot, but he either believed she had the decency not to listen, or he didn't care that she could hear.

Her heart pounded and every nerve-ending on her skin pulsed. Nico was...what? He liked her a lot? *Love?*

He began again.

"I guess my point in telling you all this, Dad, is...I need a sign or something. Is this how it was with you and Mom? How did you know?" he asked.

Julie turned on her heels at his silence. He must have been searching for the sign, stilling himself to hear a bird chirp or a whisper of the scattered trees in the wind.

She knew the quiet always seemed to hurt the most. When there was no reply, after you've emptied your heart and still you're alone. This outpouring of emotion was real for him, and Julie couldn't bear to see him crushed.

She ran to him, kneeled down in front of him and held him tight. "I'm so sorry, Nico." She trailed light kisses on his forehead and squeezed him, hoping to free some of his pain. And in her embrace, he cried freely, wrapping his arms around her waist as a white butterfly landed on her shoulder.

"I just miss him," he said, his voice strangled and hoarse. "He's supposed to be here, telling me what to do, telling me he's proud, that he loves me."

For the longest time, they kneeled there holding each other, blocking out the world around them. From the hard thud of their hearts beating, Julie could feel the weight of this moment, heavy on both of them.

"It's his birthday." Nico broke the silence. "We meet every year on his birthday at four. It was his favorite time of day. Once he told me it was when the colors of the sky were the prettiest."

Julie followed his eyes. Shades of pale pink and orange weaved through a somber cerulean blue, painting the sky a magnificent masterpiece. It left a melancholy stain on her, knowing it wouldn't last, as night had already begun to fall.

A little while later, Nico and Julie sat in his truck, still in the parking lot of the cemetery. Uncertainty and tension filled the cab. Something had changed between them today. Julie wasn't sure what, but she had a feeling that when he left her tonight, nothing would be the same again.

"Thanks for letting me come with you today," she said.

He turned toward her now. "I'm glad you came. It's never been easy coming here alone."

She nodded and shifted in her seat to face him. "I'm sure. I just... I don't know. It's really heavy, you know?"

Just as Nico opened his mouth to say something, the sky lit up. A vibrant, glittery display of fireworks filled the window before them. Julie let out a small gasp, in awe of the dazzling lights. "It's amazing!" she exclaimed.

Nico slouched lower in the seat to see the sky. "That's part of why I love coming out here each year. It just so happens that Dad's birthday fell on the holiday this year, so it's extra special. The fireworks are like the candles on his cake." He smiled.

"Yeah."

As they watched a rainbow of fire bursting into the air, Julie heard Nico expel a deep breath. "I think I'm falling for you, Julie," he muttered.

He didn't turn to her. There was no grand gesture or outburst of emotion, just a statement, a fact. A minor detail he conveniently forgot to mention. It was as if he had just said, "I'm going to pick up the dry cleaning tomorrow," or "grab me a case of beer while you're out at the store."

Oh, no big deal. No big deal at all.

CHAPTER 30

Later that evening, Nico and Julie had finished a quiet dinner in Downtown Summerlin. It was closer to home and they'd both agreed that the night was not one for the buzzing busyness of the strip after a day spent at the cemetery. The pace was slower and the night was light and romantic out in the open air.

They decided to take advantage of the warm breeze and the easygoing atmosphere. Plus, they weren't ready to head back home just yet.

Instead, they strolled hand in hand through the outdoor mall, window-shopping and talking as they passed by the upscale stores and small boutiques dispersed among a handful of restaurants.

Though Julie was enjoying the quiet time just being together, she kept going back to the fireworks and Nico's words in the truck. He had said he was falling for her. Whether she wanted to admit it or not, as scary as it was, she was about ninety-nine percent sure she was falling for him, too.

Ironically, allowing Nico into her heart wasn't the scariest part. It was the not knowing that left Julie feeling uneasy. Did she really know what it meant to feel something real? Could she let go? She thought she knew what it meant to be in love, but it turned out, she didn't know the first thing about it—not if she, at one point believed that's what she shared with Patrick.

This thing, whatever it was with Nico, was nothing like that. This quiet kind of ease and happiness with him? This was what she'd hoped for, wished for. Her hand at home in his was enough. The delicious weight of his eyes on hers filled her up and made her whole.

As they walked under a canopy of sprawling palms draped in twinkle lights, she turned her head toward a gorgeous red dress displayed in a window across the street. For a second it held her attention, but when Nico followed her gaze, it gave her a moment to really look at him without him knowing.

She didn't know exactly when it had happened, but he was becoming so important to her. This gorgeous man with the magical eyes and magnetic smile. He was sexy beyond any dream she had of the person she'd end up with, but he was more than that. Nico was a man who stayed.

Julie squeezed his hand and he looked down at her, a smile tugging at the corners of his mouth. "What's going on in that head of yours?" he asked.

"I was thinking about you?"

Nico narrowed his eyes. "Yeah? And what exactly were you thinking about me?"

"I was thinking about how much I like having you around," she said, biting her bottom lip. "And…"

"And?"

"And since it's Memorial day…maybe we can make some new memories."

Nico stopped in his tracks and pivoted toward Julie. He placed his hands on her shoulders and cocked his head, leaning in toward her. "Exactly what kind of memories are we talking about here? Like take a selfie by the fountain," he lowered his voice. "Or, like fantasies and dreams?"

Julie watched his tongue dart out of his mouth to lick his lips and felt a pull low in her belly. "Like, maybe you could tell me about your dream. Like exactly what I was doing in the tight black dress with my hair down and red lips, if I wasn't hugging you at the bar. And maybe, we could reenact your naughty little dream." Julie's insides flooded with warmth and her fingers tingled with the need to touch Nico all over.

A slow smile built on Nico's face as he swallowed, his Adam's apple rising to a bulge before dropping. He stroked his throat for a second, then he erased the distance between him and Julie. As he cradled the soft curves of her face in his hands, a jolt of electricity coursed through her at his touch. Every nerve ending on her body stirred and tingled with the craving to be touched by him.

Julie was practically floating on air as he took wide strides, dragging her toward the valet near the movie theater.

"Stay here." He gave her a wistful look before he covered her mouth with his, kissing her deep and hungry like he was starving and she was his to feast on. One of those, *I don't want to let you go* kind of kisses that left her breathless and a little wet. "The line is kind of long. I'm just going to turn the ticket in for the car and I'll be right back."

He disappeared into the curve of the queue and Julie was left standing there just outside the theater entrance. She took out her compact and applied a new coat of Ruby Woo lipstick. Already, she was feeling sexier as she took out her phone to check her Instagram when the one voice she didn't want to hear called to her.

"Hello Jules."

When Julie turned, there was Patrick with Celeste waddling behind him in a skintight mid-length dress despite her belly. This one was much the same as the white one she was wearing in Walmart, but in a coral pink that matched the lighter shades on her lips and cheeks.

She was stunning as ever, though her dark roots had grown out, color-blocking her platinum blonde hair in a way that only she could make look chic.

Suddenly, next to her, Julie felt frumpy in her shapeless brown sundress and simple sandals. "Hi," she muttered, looking back toward the valet line, then flitting between Patrick's fixed gaze and Celeste on his heels.

Damn, where is Nico when I need him?

Celeste landed on the curb beside Patrick and quickly wrapped her hand around his. "Honey, you know I can't move that fast with the baby." She dragged out the word *baby* like a trophy as her wicked dove-tailed eyes darted over Julie from head toe, before she forced a tight-lipped smile. "Hey, Julie."

"Hey," Julie said curtly, stifling the urge to roll her eyes. She wouldn't give these two the satisfaction of knowing how annoyed she was if she was offered a thousand dollars. She could be cordial, but they were *not* friends and she wasn't going to fake it either.

"So...uh, yes. How are you? Uh...how are you doing? You're looking well," Patrick said, wiggling free from the hand that Celeste held to push up his rolled sleeve. Which, as far as Julie could tell, was already up as far as it could go.

He squared his body to Julie, thrusting out his chest and exposing his scraggly-haired neck, and for once, she could see him. Really see him for what he was instead who she'd made him out to be in her mind.

Sure, he was good-looking enough, but there wasn't much else to him besides his height and decent bone structure. He looked dopey and ridiculous, like he was putting on airs. All that confidence she'd thought he had was just labels and height from the pedestal she'd put him on, but now she was seeing him down to earth.

Raising her brows, she said, "I'm fine, thanks," the annoyance clear in her sharp tone. She was so over him. What did he want her to say? It was just plain awkward.

Julie looked over her shoulder again. *Come on Nico.*

"We should probably get going, Hon. The movie starts in like ten minutes and I have a craving for popcorn and pickles." Celeste crossed her arms and released a heavy sigh. She was basically snarling and foaming at the mouth like a rabid nippy little Chihuahua.

She had a bone to pick and she was ready to bite the hand of anyone who got too close.

"Yeah..." Julie breathed the word, but she whole-heartedly agreed. Then, as she looked over her shoulder and saw Nico coming, her heartbeat sped up. She turned back to them, hoping they would say their awkward goodbyes and go fast.

Patrick's gaze flicked upward and Julie could see the visible tension in his neck and shoulders. He opened his mouth likely about to criticize Celeste, but stopped short. "Well, I guess we better be going then," he said, sarcasm dripping from his lips. "Wouldn't want to miss the *previews*." He rubbed his brow as if to ward off a headache and turned away just as Nico arrived.

"Should be about ten minutes, the guy said." Nico slipped his arm around Julie's waist and kissed her on the cheek. "Hello, I'm Nico, and you are?"

Before things could really get awkward, Julie chimed in to introduce them. "Nico this Patrick and his wife, Celeste—"

"Girlfriend—" Patrick corrected her just as Celeste corrected him.

"Fiancé." Her lips pressed into a white slash. "Lovely to meet you, Nico. And you are?"

Nico and Julie both stared at each other. They hadn't exactly decided what they were. What were they? Friends? Falling for each other? Lovers? Were they even in love?

"Julie is my girlfriend."

Bam.

He'd said it without doubt or question, and almost immediately Julie's insides flooded with a fluttery kind of excitement and joy. Just like that, she'd become his. He'd claimed her to the one person, who deep down, Julie knew believed he still owned her—believed he could have her back anytime he wanted her.

Softly, Nico brushed his lips over Julie's. When he returned his glassy gaze to Patrick, who was now glaring at him, Nico jutted his chin out and stood taller.

Patrick was scowling at him, and Julie. He cracked his neck and inhaled a slow, measured breath. His nostrils flared and his murky brown eyes were cold, hard, and flinty. "Ah. Julie hadn't mentioned that she was seeing anyone." He folded his arms over his chest and cocked his head, now extremely interested and apparently going nowhere anytime soon. At least, not to the movies.

"That's because we don't talk, Patrick," Julie said plainly and more than a little irritated. She swallowed hard and prayed for them to leave. "Anyway, look at the time." She didn't even glance at her watch. "Celeste, weren't you just saying you wanted popcorn?"

Before Celeste could get a word in edgewise, Patrick continued on his weirdly jealous probe. "I was just telling her the other day at the bank that we should get together soon. I didn't know you existed, but now maybe we'll have to make it a double date." *Says the guy with the pregnant, sniveling fiancé beside him.*

Patrick made a point to flicker his gaze to Julie's bare ring finger, which along with her other fingers she was using to draw blood from the skin of her other hand. But, this was the precise reason he annoyed the shit out of her. He'd said it as if she needed pictures of Nico plastered across her desk and a sign on her fucking head to let people know she was taken. She didn't need a ring or pictures or any other advertisement, plus what concern was it of Patrick's?

Ugh, Patrick. Seriously, now you want to be jealous?

"When were you at the bank?" Celeste badgered. She was whining with her bottom lip trembling as her eyed bugged out of their sockets. "You didn't tell me you saw Julie at the bank?"

And just when Julie thought things couldn't get worse than her jealous ex and her whimpering ex friend about to claw at each other, Nico added another log onto the fire. "No. She didn't tell me she saw her *ex* either," he said calmly, his gaze narrowed on her. This was going to be a thing. God, why did it have to be a thing?

"It wasn't a big deal. He showed up out of nowhere saying he missed me and I asked him to leave. That's it. Nothing else happened, so why would we need to talk about it?"

"You *miss* her?" Celeste asked Patrick. To look at her, she had to be seeing red the way her fists clenched. She was either going to go into labor right there on the sidewalk, or beat the shit out of him.

He clamored backward and raised his hands, palms up, in defense. "We need to get going. I thought you said you wanted popcorn and pickles before the movie starts," he said deflecting like the coward that he was.

For a split second, Julie actually felt sorry for him. Until, she met Nico's gaze which was trained on her.

"I think you *should* get going," he said to Patrick and Celeste, but his tone was unmistakably directed toward Julie.

CHAPTER 31

J ulie looked at herself in the reflection of her car and tugged at the bottom of her blazer. Despite the distorted image, she looked professional and well put together. She'd chucked her gum already *and* managed to remember to bring two extra copies of her resume. What's more, she was early. And thanks to a second cup of coffee, she was extra alert.

As she waited for the bank to open, she inspected the glass building and the cars parked out front. In all of its newness, it was a neighborhood designed for and inhabited by the affluent. Doctors and lawyers and accountants. Maybe a small business owner or a teacher among them. All driving their luxury class sedans and souped-up soccer mom-mobiles.

The bank itself, though, was similar to Regions with its linear minimalist design and brightly colored marketing panels glazed over the windows, each with cliched images of nuclear families cooking and traveling together. A small shaggy dog propped up on a pristine living room sofa, or a set of hardworking newlyweds painting a room in their newly mortgaged home with half-opened boxes strewn about. All banks had them in varying versions, complete with slogans and phrases dabbled over them going on about accruing wealth and family riches. Along with bank accounts, they sold the dreams.

Certainly, Julie counted herself among those who had bought them. It was the reason she was here. She had a detailed vision of the life she wanted to live and being a bank manager was an integral part.

A young guy in a plaid button-down and slacks with a coordinated polka-dot bow tie opened the front door and the first crowd of people rushed to the teller stations. Julie fell in line and veered off to the left toward the lobby waiting area where she sat patiently with her legs crossed at the ankles and her hands folded.

Within a few minutes, a tall slender black man with a nicely tailored suit and freshly polished shoes came out of the office at the far end of the building. He stood directly in front of her with a blank expression and stretched his hand toward her.

"Avery Beckstand," he announced in a deep echoing bass. "And you must be Julie Laurich. Pleased to meet you."

That name. Why do I know that name?

Julie rose to her feet and extended her hand. "Yes. Thank you for seeing me today, sir," she said aloud as her thoughts froze. Her mind raced to place the name.

His lips moved again, but she couldn't hear what he was saying.

"I'm sorry…what did, what did you say?"

Mr. Beckstand cleared his throat. "I asked if you were ready?" he repeated.

"Am I ready?" Sweat beaded at Julie's brows. "Oh. Yes. Sorry. I thought you said something else. Yes, I'm ready," she answered quickly, blinking rapidly.

He turned toward his office and gestured for Julie to follow him. On his heels, she took staggered steps, still trying to place him. She was certain that they'd never met. She would have remembered his face. But his voice? His voice was oddly familiar. That name, she knew it, *well*.

Is he a customer?

His body was slender, but he didn't look like a gym rat. Definitely not from school, he looked older than her by at least five or so years.

Maybe the grocery store?

As she took her place in the sleek wood-grained chair facing him, she plastered on a tight smile and nodded. First things first. The job was why she was here. It came second to nothing, especially not placing a face that might not have been meaningful anyway. She'd have to figure out how she knew him later.

"So, Miss Laurich, I've had a chance to look over your resume. Tell me why you're considering leaving Regions?"

Julie cleared her throat. *Time to get serious.* "Well, Mr. Beckstand, I'd prefer not to leave Regions. However, there isn't much room for upward mobility that I've experienced. I'm looking for career growth and I believe that American Bank could be the place for me to recognize my potential."

He tilted his head to the side and pursed his lips together. "I see. And what makes you think you'll be a good fit for American Bank?" he said, as if he had literally thrown the ball back in her court.

Julie knew all about this tactic, though. Elise had let her sit in on a few interviews over the years. She'd said that it was always best to keep the candidate talking. Her 80/20 rule. The interviewee should be talking eighty percent of the time and the interviewer only twenty.

Elise would focus on open-ended questions and listen for what she called "fluff"—any answer that included non-experiential prefixes such as "I would," "I might," "I usually." These answers were a dead giveaway. The people who used them had no experience and they were only saying what they thought the interviewer wanted to hear, Elise explained.

Half of the time, Elise had counted people in or out from the second they walked in the building. At the top of her list were time of arrival, level of appropriateness for professional attire, gum-chewing, and whether they had a copy of their—hopefully one page

—resume with a relevant objective and up-to-date contact information.

Believe it or not, most candidates failed upon entry in her book. The biggest mistake, she mentioned, was when the candidate hadn't read the job description for which they were applying.

Whether or not Elise wanted to help Julie succeed, she already had.

Both for the sake of time and to increase her chances, she cut straight to the chase and laundry-listed her qualifications.

"Mr. Beckstand, over my combined seven years of banking and sales experience, I've had an opportunity to partake and assist in overseeing the running of a branch from all perspectives, including, but not limited to meeting tough sales targets, ensuring that the branch is operationally sound, and developing business. I'm versed and trained in consumer and business account opening and lending. I have a NMLS number for property-secured lending. I'm a notary. I'm not licensed for investments, but I'm a top referrer and efficient at recognizing when our high-value affluent clients might benefit from having an advisor. If you require them, I have multiple references and I have these." She pulled out a file, bulging at the spine and slid it over the desk to him.

"And what are these?" he asked with raised brow seriousness.

"Please open it. I've taken the liberty to provide you with a copy of my ranking over the past two years at Regions, my annual reviews, certificates of achievement, service letters from clients, and regional recognition from two district managers."

His lips parted, and seconds later, his expression softened. With his focus on Julie, he leaned back in his chair and let his posture open up. Still, he said nothing; but as he released a sigh and drummed his fingers on the top of the desk, his eyes brightened.

For the next twenty minutes, he seemed to be going through the motions for the sake of going through the motions. His mood lifted considerably, as if he'd taken off his interviewer hat and put on his colleague hat. Almost to the minute after Julie stepped down from her soapbox, he became a regular motormouth, talking about the fickle weather and the chances of his Astros making it to the World Series, despite Julie's being a Cubs fan.

He'd already discussed benefits and how the variable compensation worked, when he started winding the conversation down. "Which branch are you at? Is it the one over on North Decatur?" he asked.

"Yeah. Not too far from here," Julie added.

"Oh, so you're with Elise Tisdale," he said. But it wasn't what he said, it was how he said it, the way his chin suddenly jutted out. He squinted with a hard smile—a look that radiated superiority. Beckstand let out an arrogant laugh and clasped his chin as if he was struck by deep thoughts.

Up until that point, he seemed like a good guy. She'd written him off as a little dramatic and overly-confident, but it wasn't enough to crucify him. Now she remembered why she knew that name. He was the eggplant. The other half of Elise's phone sex conference calls. The frequent-caller with the deep bass voice.

Suddenly the fog cleared. The secure feeling that Julie had, telling herself she was a shoo-in a few minutes earlier, was gone. Either this guy was as big a tool as her gut told her he was, or he and Elise were playing her.

Julie sat up straighter now. "Yes. She's my manager." Her mouth pinched with the tension in her jaw.

Beckstand fussed with a piece of lint on the lapel of his blazer. "And does she know you're here?" He projected his voice now, as if to reinforce his upper hand.

She clasped her hands on the desk, betting on the former of her suspicions. "No," she stated firmly.

Time stood still in that moment as they stared each other down, waiting for the other to call their bluff. Beckstand blinked first.

"Miss Laurich, I can't make any promises right now, as protocol requires that I consider all eligible candidates who have submitted resumes by this coming Friday..." He lifted his chin. "However, I'd like to unofficially offer you one of the positions for bank manager at American Bank."

He rose to his feet with perfect posture, shoulders back, and exposed neck. Once again, he extended his hand toward Julie.

One of the positions?

Julie let his hand hang in the air. "I'm sorry, how many positions do you have open in the northwest?" she clarified. "I thought you only had one branch in the northwest part of town." Her eyes narrowed.

In the back of her mind, she scrolled through the job posting. It had said Northwest, she was sure. Her chest tightened now. Had she read it wrong?

Lowering his hand, Beckstand took his seat again. "I apologize for any confusion, but I was certain you read the location details. We have two branch manager positions available currently, both in the Northwest *Region*," he dragged out the word. "One here in Centennial Hills in northwest Las Vegas, Nevada, and one in Portland, Oregon. We're expanding our footprint as a bank," he explained.

Julie plopped down on the seat and let her purse fall beside her.

"Miss Laurich? The recruiter should have mentioned that we've already made an offer for the Las Vegas branch. I'm sorry. Would you still like to be considered for the position in Portland? I know that's a big change of scenery, but we do cover relocation expenses."

The right words didn't quite come to her. "Hmmm." She opened and closed her mouth, pulling in a deep breath and releasing it. "This is a tough decision."

Damn it.

The pros and cons flashed by in rapid succession as she weighed all the things that mattered to her. Besides the obvious, her mom and Liz, now there was Nico. But, if there was a time to end it, it was now, before things got any more serious. Especially, after last night, she didn't want argue any more than she wanted to depend on someone new.

On the flip side, Patrick and Celeste would always be there flaunting their new baby in front of her. She'd keep running into them.

Plus, Portland was self-proclaimed weird. Ugh.

A frog-like croaking sound echoed from her stomach and she squeezed her arms around her waist. She needed time to think. Then Liz's voice replayed in her ear. "Study long, study wrong," she often warned.

And just like that, Julie grimaced, and nodded.

What the fuck did I just do?

Julie raced through traffic. Day one and she was already going to be late to Kid Savers. How in the hell was she supposed to teach children about responsible finance and saving when her mind was a mess? She'd just committed, not only to a new job, but to an entirely new state. A state she'd never even been to before. This was crazy. She simply wasn't in her right mind.

It occurred to her to call Elise and cancel, but what was she going to say? "Sorry, I can't do your Kid Savers stuff because I'm mind-blown that I just accepted a new job? Oh, and by the way, it was your phone sex buddy who hired me?" Great. Just great.

Sweat greased her palms on the steering wheel and she wiped them on the seat. She checked the clock on the dash again. Nine forty-five. Fifteen minutes to get to Evans Elementary safely, find parking, check in, and find the damn classroom. *Awesome. Fuck.*

"Great, Julie. Why not just crush everyone you know and love under your ugly heel," she scorned herself. "Damn it, damn it, damn it," she screamed in the car.

On her left, in the car beside her, a perky pony-tailed mother with her matching cardigan set stared at Julie, who frankly couldn't care less at the moment. There were more important things to worry about now. Like how she was going to break the news to Nico. Gorgeous, sweet Nico, who had poured his freaking heart out to her. Nico, who had said he was falling for her. *Ugh.*

Totally out of line with her luck, Julie made it. In fact, in record time she'd passed through three green lights. And not just that, she happened to pull into the parking lot just as someone was backing out of a space directly in front of the main office. To top it all off, a pint-sized classroom representative with a backpack bigger than she was awaited her with a name badge to escort her to her assigned classroom.

It was like the stars had aligned to ensure she kept her promise. If you're going to jump at a new opportunity without regard for anyone else's feelings, get to the heartbreak stat. In Julie's case, she'd opted for Portland, so there was no sense in the universe delaying the inevitable. She'd have to tell Nico, sooner rather than later.

Only, she was sort of hoping to tell him much, much later. Like, ignore him until it was time for her to leave and then maybe place a note on the windshield of his truck. She was hoping for the kind of letdown that avoided face-to-face contact. That was going to be damn near impossible.

If she hadn't been sure before, she was one hundred percent certain now that the universe was working against her. As soon as she opened the door to the classroom, there was Nico. Mr. Farfalla. The teacher she'd be assigned to for the next week. Nope, the universe was not on her side at all.

Gorgeous as ever in khakis with a baby blue gingham button-down and a panoramic view of his dimples. How was she going to tell him about the job offer now? *Oh by the way, I'm taking a job offer that's going to move me out of state, which means you and I are over, pal.*

The second he turned his attention to Julie, his lashes did a fluttery, wispy fanning motion, pulling a smile from the corners of his liquid brown eyes.

Why does he have to be so damned hot? If he were uglier, this would be easier.

For the next half hour, Julie muddled through her regimented lesson plan provided by the bank. She hemmed and hawed about the importance of saving. They went over a glossary of definitions that included words like money, currency, interest, and banks. The material wasn't a Pulitzer Prize-winning grade, but the kids seemed to enjoy it and it gave her something to do to avoid eye contact with Nico.

Elise didn't need know, but Julie actually enjoyed herself, playing games and giving the kids treats and prizes for their participation.

When the day wound down, she found herself wishing it wasn't over—that she had more time with the kids. Seeing them absorb the information—learning—she wanted more of that. More purpose to her work. It was validation that she should be a manager. She should be giving back to the community, and helping people understand and excel in finance.

Elise may not have seen it that way, but Julie did. Which only further validated her choice to move on from Regions. Even *if* that meant relocating to Portland.

With a renewed sense of determination, Julie closed the door after the last kid left, and turned to Nico.

"What are you up to after this?" she asked, hoping to break the ice. They'd been in professional mode all day.

He locked his desk drawer and slid a stack of papers into a folder. "I, um…" he started, still focused on the task at hand. "I'm just, uh, going to throw this stuff in my bag here and then I'm going to take you somewhere and feed you a good meal, if you'll allow me to," he said in his trademark nonchalant way. It was as if he was talking about mundane housework and errands, not a meal or quality time.

Julie's heart beat heavy and hard. She could almost feel her blood moving through her chest, slow like sludge. This was just what she needed—a heart attack. She held her chest and prayed for the best, even though she expected the worst.

"Actually, I was hoping we could talk," she said quietly. Her shoulders curled forward, caving her chest inward. She hadn't noticed it before, but her hands were trembling now. As much as she wanted to run, she couldn't. She had to do this. It would only be worse, the longer she waited. When it came down to it, hurting him was the last thing Julie wanted to do.

Nico seemed none the wiser to Julie's impending heart failure. His bag was zipped and ready to go. In the amount of time she'd spent hyping herself up to break the bad news, he'd nearly cleaned the whole classroom.

"What's on your mind? Thinking about your boss, or the pregnant cousin, or the ex?" His ears perked and brows raised, awaiting her usual playful response. "Oh, or is it the pregnant ex-friend?"

Dizzy and a little shaky on her feet, Julie grabbed hold to one of the small chairs and used it for balance.

"Is it that bad?" Nico glanced up at Julie, but when he got a good look at her, the laughter in his eyes faded quickly only to be replaced by worry. He rushed over to her, just as she drained into the chair. "Have you eaten anything today? Look at me. When was the last time you ate, Jules?"

"No."

In seconds, Nico pulled a water bottle from the side pocket of his bag and twisted the top off. "Here. Drink this. You don't look so good." He rubbed her forehead and pushed her hair back. "We've got to start taking better care you."

At the word "we," Julie began to hyperventilate. Where before her heartbeat had been sluggish and heavy, it now raced. Her skin tingled and her vision blurred. It seemed the closer she got to saying the words, the harder he made it for her to let the words graze her tongue.

"I'm going to be fine—"

The words slurred, and suddenly everything went black.

Images flashed before her, mostly Nico in different settings. In the classroom. In the car. Before long, in her condo, up close as he sat on the edge of her bed.

Then, nothing.

CHAPTER 32

The refrigerator was empty. Clad in an oversized t-shirt, the fluorescent white light of the refrigerator painted Julie in a relatively ethereal glow. The bottom half of her body hung outside the door as she leaned further inside. She searched behind plastic containers full of leftovers for something, anything edible. She had been meaning to go grocery shopping, but between the gym, the holiday, her family, and Nico, there was no need or time. There had been plenty of food to go around all week, which seemed to conspire to reshape her curves. Still, she had nothing left in her fridge.

Behind the jar with two rubbery pickles floating in seedy juice, a low-fat organic blueberry yogurt peeked through. She pulled it out and twisted it until the faded blue ink faced the front.

"Damn. Expired," she muttered to herself.

Given her limited options and the two-week old expiration date, Julie lifted the aluminum top and sniffed. It didn't smell too bad and she was starving, so she dipped the tip of her tongue inside the plastic cup and tasted it.

Almost instantly, she regretted her ill-advised decision. Rancid wasn't even the word. Grossed out, she tossed the cup in the trash and ran to the sink where she began spitting.

"You going to be all right in there?" a groggy male voice asked, startling Julie.

She let out a scream worthy of a good horror movie and clapped her hand over her mouth when she saw Nico sitting up on the couch.

"Nico?"

"Yes?" he mocked her disembodied voice. "Who did you think it was?"

His normally sleek tamed curls, were all over the place and he was still wearing the khakis with the blue gingham button-down, although his sleeves were rolled midway up his arms and he'd taken off his shoes. And now, his upturned brows pointed at Julie with sincere disbelief.

Whether she meant to infuse so much shock in her words, or not, they came out that way. "You stayed?" she said, as if she couldn't fathom the possibility.

The fact she couldn't wrap her mind around the notion that a man had hung around to check on her wellbeing was telling in two major ways. For one, it said a lot about the guys she had dated before Nico, dressing them in a less-than-favorable light. And two, it highlighted a distinction between Julie and Nico in a bold way. Where he went through life mostly unfazed by the curveballs life threw at him, just about everything shocked the hell out of her.

True to form, he had shaken up her life and seemed content to let things fall where they may.

He stared blankly. "Where else would I go? You needed me," he stated matter-of-factly, as if it were the only probable answer. Leaning back on a stack of throw pillows on the couch, he stifled a yawn and let his sleepy eyes glaze over.

Dumbfounded and slack-mouthed, a sputtering laugh escaped her lips. There were no words for the audacity of this man. It unnerved her that he could take anything that she freaked out about and belittle it—dumb it down to a grain of sand. Even more, she hated that she kind of loved that about him, his calming effect on her.

"By the way, Miss Year-Old Yogurt, there's food for you in the microwave." Nico turned on his side and pulled the sky blue chenille blanket that hung on the back of the sofa over his shoulders. And just to rub it in that he had rescued her once more and she'd shown her gratitude by banishing him to the couch, he shivered aloud and let his teeth chatter as he let out an exaggerated, "Brrrrrr."

Julie gagged aloud. "I hope you know I had furry mold on my tongue," she laughed. "And it wasn't a year. It said May fifteenth. That's two weeks."

"May fifteenth two thousand seventeen."

Again, she shuddered, thinking year-old yogurt had been in her mouth. "Ew. That's so disgusting," she reiterated as his whole body rumbled with laughter beneath the blanket. "Okay, it's all funny now, but don't be mad if I throw up all over you."

"Been there, done that," he retorted.

Touché.

"And keep it down, will you? I'm trying to catch a few winks over here," he said.

In the microwave, she found a full plate with rice and green beans and a grilled chicken breast. As she held the plate in her hand and let the door close, she checked the time on the panel. Ten twenty-three p.m. She'd been out for hours and in that time, he had cooked for her. And not some heat-it-up-in-the-microwave-for-three-and-a-half-minutes dish, either. Nico had boiled water and marinated and sautéed for her. What was he doing, going for best boyfriend of the year? Was he even really her boyfriend, or had he just said that to mark his territory in front of her ex?

While she contemplated the answers to her questions, she ate in silence, watching him as he feigned sleep. With each bite, she thought about balking at the carbs and salt, but the flavor had silenced her. And in between bites and audible moans of hunger satiation, her mind drifted back to the inevitable and unanswered prayers.

On her knees, she had begged for Patrick to come to some grand epiphany and realize the error of his decision. But it made sense now. There was a reason her prayers had remained unanswered. There was someone else out there who cooked and cared and saw all of Julie's flaws and still seemed grateful to have met her. His world was better with her in it.

Julie had depended on her dad and felt lost when he died. She'd tried to depend on her mother, but she wasn't exactly a role model for standing on your own two feet. She'd even depended on Patrick, and he was sick and tired of her. All this time, she'd been doing her damnedest not to have to depend on anyone else, but it wasn't forced with Nico. It felt nice and natural to be there for him and let him be there for her in return.

A little while later, Julie hung onto that realization as she cleaned her plate over the trashcan, foregoing the garbage disposal for fear of waking Nico, who now seemed genuinely asleep. As she rinsed the plate and placed it in the left sink basin, she kept a watchful eye on him. Did she have to hurt him just because *she'd* made a rash decision? Long-distance relationships had worked for some people. She didn't know any of them, but they could be the first. They'd already been through worse things than most new relationships. Hell, when a man tells you that he's falling for you, you don't take that so lightly, as if it meant nothing.

He'd come to mean more to her than any of the men she'd known before him.

Slowly, she made her way over to the couch, grabbed the remote off of the table, and sat near his feet. "Are you awake?" she said quietly.

"Hmmm huh," he mumbled with his eyes still closed. "How're you feeling?"

By his question, she knew that he meant her hunger, but all she could think about was her heart. "I really need to talk to you." Her voice was low and strangled.

Nico shifted onto to his back and cracked his eyes toward her. The room was dark except for the strains of light through the sheer curtains and the glare of the muted television. "I'm listening," he said, clearer, expectant.

"I don't really know how to say this." Julie pulled a pillow to her chest and wrapped her arms around it to occupy her hands. "I don't know what to do about you? I heard what you said in the car the other night, and to be honest, it kind of scared me."

As if figuring where the conversation was headed, based on her grave tone, Nico sat up and scooted next to her, so that their shoulders were touching. He could've opted out or asked questions, but he remained silent, giving her the floor.

"One second, I want to yell at you and give you a piece of my mind. And the next, I can't imagine...what I would do without you." Surprise laced her tone now and she turned to him. She'd planned to be honest and upfront with Nico, but evenly, carefully, a little at a time.

At the blank expression on his face, dread crawled up her throat and lingered there. She'd said too much; the words, now that they were out, seemed irrevocable.

Abruptly, she closed her mouth and inhaled. As she lifted her chin to him with feigned confidence in her decision, he met her eyes in the dark. His were pitch black and liquid, but in them she saw something she couldn't quite name. She wasn't sure whether it was hope and reassurance, or the kind of fear that gave most men pause as they figured the fastest way out with the least collateral damage.

Calm and cool as ever, Nico blinked a few times.

She wished he would just blurt it out, whatever he was thinking —instead of sitting there while he watched her internal tantrum unfold. She'd kick and scream, if that would get a real reaction out of him, but he had mastered the art of torture by silent treatment.

"You said, you don't know what to do about me?" he asked finally, looking down at his hands. "Well, what are your options?"

Even without light, Julie heard the questions in his voice. Something about his collected response set the rage in Julie's blood ablaze. "That's all you have to say? You and your cryptic responses. I'm pouring my fucking heart out to you, and you're talking about options. What the heck are you even talking about?"

Her voice shook as annoyance lifted her volume to near-yelling. "This. This is why I know it's not going to work between us." Julie lashed out at him and slipped her feet beneath her, sitting up on her haunches in the corner of the couch. She faced Nico, tight-eyed, bubbling with irritation.

Even more infuriating than yelling back at her, he tilted his head up with a smug grin stretched across his reddened face. "You about done?" he asked, minutely shaking his head.

Something in his question gave her pause. Julie caught herself, vaguely reminded of the day that she had ignored and dismissed Patrick at the bank. His lost look of disbelief and shock that she hadn't been the hysterical mess with him the way she used to. She hadn't reacted. Out of character, really. The way his eyes bulged out, she knew no one had ever not talked to Patrick that way. That, coupled with her request to never see him again? It was a breakthrough. By saying very little, she'd spoken her mind and stood her ground. Everything about that quiet protest was right, felt right, which was why she knew it was warranted.

But this? Nico hadn't done anything that warranted her shameless attempt to find something to balance out the scales. She'd stooped low, all so she'd feel better at ending things between them. Nothing about it felt right.

Julie's cheeks burned as she fell back on the arm of the couch and pulled her arms and legs toward her core. She let her head fall on her knees and let the brimming tears trail down toward her nose.

"Jules?" Nico whispered and laid his head on her shoulder,

nudging her to come out. He stretched his legs the length of the couch. "What's going on?"

When she lifted her head slightly, their eyes met.

Nico searched her eyes, likely finding the endless pools of wariness she could feel draining from her. "What are you trying to tell me?" he asked, his words hurried and drenched in urgency. "Why are you torturing yourself like this? Please stop fighting it."

Before she could let her mind take hold, she took a deep cleansing breath, leaned in, and caught his lips with hers. She brushed them softly together, tasting him, memorizing the lingering taste of sweetness and the faint scent of soap and minty aftershave on his cheek. Light moans seeped from her mouth as the need to be with him clawed at her. She squeezed her eyes tight.

Why was she punishing herself like this?

Julie drew in closer to Nico and rubbed her hands over the stubbly squared edges of his jaw. She needed to feel that this was happening, simultaneously pulling him toward her as she resisted the urge to push him away. She peppered his lips with soft, tentative kisses, then urgent, hungry ones.

Her mind raced with imaginings of what was happening. How he would make love to her. Whether he would be gentle or hurried with anticipation. If they would both enjoy it, or it would be one-sided pleasure. She prayed she wouldn't have to fake it for his ego's sake, and by some strange bout of grace and mercy, she might feel something. Something real. Real experience-shared pleasure.

What happened next she knew would be a line in the sand—a point of no return. A fork in the road with two very distinct paths that they would never cross again. A choice.

And though it may or may not have been that simple, in her mind's eye, she had to choose: career or love.

Somehow other people made it appear to be so easy to have everything. The man, the career, the family and the house. And while she knew love and a livelihood weren't mutually exclusive, the fog was too thick to see how they might intertwine. She'd have to figure it all out once she could think clearly. But for now, she leaned into the kiss. The kind of kiss that lasts for hours.

Julie nodded as if giving herself permission to relish in the moment. Her heart pounded and ached at once.

Gently, Nico circled his arm over her legs and pulled her body flat beneath him. As he centered himself on top of her, he kissed her deeper still—the slightest tremble pulsing over his skin. When he seemed sure that her lips had received enough attention, he trailed his magic tongue down the curve of her neck, while he worked her T-shirt up. As he slipped it over her head, he let it drop to the floor.

At the sight of her bare breast and soft curves in only her panties, Nico exhaled and bit his bottom lip. "What do you want to do?" he asked.

On limited air supply and with hazy brain function, Julie writhed beneath him. "I just want to keep on torturing myself."

Without argument, Nico scooted down her body and took her nipple whole in his mouth. He suckled gently, circling the tip with his tongue before teasing it with his teeth.

She parted her legs and squeezed his waist between her thighs. "Please," she moaned. She was begging him to take all of her pain away.

As Julie clung to Nico, her fingernails digging into his back, she couldn't bring herself to let him go. It was the kind of attachment that held steadfast as the fear of losing him coursed through her, masking wariness with heated passion. The kind that if she let him go, she might never heal. She was about to let go of a part of herself, her soul.

This dread filled her while they searched each other's bodies on the couch and rolled to the floor before she finally led him to her bed. It didn't end as she pushed and pulled him, wrestling with the underlying meaning of what tonight meant. It didn't end as they reached their peaks together, worn and breathless. It didn't even end when he lingered inside of her, showing her exactly how real this thing was between them.

Julie awakened the next morning to the sound of her cell phone vibrating on the nightstand. Still tangled in Nico's embrace, she stretched her arm over the side of the bed until the tips of her fingers were in reach. Slowly she dragged it closer, careful not to rouse him in doing so.

Before she unlocked the screen, she dimmed the brightness and swiped to open up a message from Liz.

Liz: Earth to Jules?

It had been something close to a week since she'd checked in with Liz, which was basically unheard of for them. They never went a day, let alone *days* plural, without speaking, which was a dead indicator that something drastic had happened.

Aside from her own shenanigans with Nico, she had suspected Liz needed some time to wade through the muddied relationship waters with Derrick. And as much as she really wanted to talk to her and advise her, Liz and Derrick had to work things out for themselves. So, she'd given them the obligatory amount of time that friends should give, and now, she was thankful to hear from her.

Julie: Hey
Liz: Um, so you're alive, then?
Julie: Don't even try it. Been waiting on you and your drama all this time. Sounds like someone got some the eggplant. Glad you and Derrick are back together. So…do I need to pick out a bridesmaid gown?
Liz: Girl?!?!?! We have basically been locked up in the room for like a week. No time soon on the nups, I finally got it through his thick skull that I need some time. Plus, you're going to be the maid of honor, obvi! Or, should I say, maiden of honor?!?! You still in drought, or did you finally go ahead and get busy with Nico and now I need to pick out some hideous taffeta eyesore for a winter wonderland wedding?

Julie: Uh, no. As far as smashing, I wouldn't exactly say dash, but…
something did happen…
Liz: Yaaassssss! Finally. It's about time. If you're not going to marry
him, then he's a rebound and now that you've gotten it in with a
good rebound, you can get out of the funk you've been in. Maybe I'll
get my friend back.

A text with clapping hands and halos came through on Julie's
phone. Liz was celebrating. Meanwhile, Julie still hadn't conjured
up the nerve to tell Nico about the job offer. Maybe Liz would
know what to do.

Julie peeked over her shoulder at an adorable sleeping Nico and
replied to Liz.

Julie: I'm ignoring you. BTW I'm not going to make it to the gym,
but can you meet me around 5:30? I'm going to need a shoulder.
And a glass of something. Just sayin'
Liz: You good, Jules?
Julie: I am for now…
Liz: ???

Julie stole a glance at Liz's text and stuffed the phone under the
pillow as Nico shifted and tightened his arm around her waist.

"Mmmm. Good morning," he mumbled against her hair,
pressing his morning wood hard into her backside. His husky
hoarse voice stirred her insides with memories of the previous
night.

"Morning," she said. Fresh worry and yearning careened through
her. Just hours ago, the two of them had been wrapped in a mess of
roaming limbs, shallow breaths, and insatiable hunger for one
another. And now Julie's chest tightened for a different reason, the
same reason that had given her pause since their night of fireworks
beneath the stars at the cemetery.

They'd been moving too quickly for any of it to seem real or right. And as if affirming that belief and etching it in stone, Julie had told Beckstand that she wanted the job in Portland, only making things harder still.

Now, she'd taken difficult and made it impossible.

She had to do it before she could talk herself down or tell herself that he probably wasn't worth her worries. She could tell herself that Nico Farfalla was nice enough, but not for her. Before she'd spent the night making love in his able arms with those warm brown eyes pouring into her, she could lie to herself. But now, the lies would never outweigh the truth—she was falling hard and fast for him.

In her heart, she wanted to depend on him.

She played worse-case scenarios in her mind, rightfully blaming herself for the position in which she now stood knee-deep. Time seemed to slow down as she replayed the events that had put her there, and scrounged through quick fixes to avoid hurting either of them.

Nico raised himself up onto his elbow and pulled Julie's shoulder, so that she laid flat on her back.

Under the weight of his stare, she squeezed her eyes shut, praying that if she closed them tight enough, maybe she could remain calm for as long as it would take to face her own demons.

"Uh, you going to open your eyes, or do I have to use some of my methods from last night to get you to open up?" Nico teased, leaning down to kiss the curves of her neck.

Her heart beat erratically as she stilled her body against his wet hot lips. "Nico?" she breathed his name.

"Yeah?"

"I—"

Before she could unburden herself, he interrupted her and spoke the words she couldn't unhear. "I love you."

Julie sucked in a chest full of air as her heart stalled. Words clogged in her throat. She gave him an unblinking, weighted stare. "Don't," she pleaded. "Don't."

Every line in his face hardened. "Don't what? Don't tell you that I love you? It's too late," Nico snapped. He sat up, all traces of his gentle, loving demeanor gone now. "I know you like to try to control everything and everyone. You want to be everything everyone else wants you to be. Well, this isn't yours to control, Jules. You can't control *my* feelings."

At the change in Nico's tone, Julie immediately regretted her words. She wished she could take them back, stop them from piercing his heart and spreading small fissures. Underneath his rough, gravelly voice, his words were wobbly and brittle, as if they were a dam holding back the tears on the edge.

"I'm sorry," she muttered shamefully.

He stiffened at the remorse in her tone and cleared his throat to begin again. "I know how hard-headed you are, so I should've guessed that you'd make me spell it out for you." A playful smile crossed his face. Squaring his body to Julie, he said, "I love you, Julie. I want to be with you. Just you. Just the way you are. And I don't need you to change for me. If you want do some crazy new hairstyle or hire a trainer to get healthier, fine. But, it will be because that's what you want. I'm happy just being with you."

The way he looked at her, she couldn't tell what he was thinking, only that his message was instructional and urgent. He searched her eyes for understanding, waiting for a response from her. Some sign of comprehension.

When she said nothing, he asked a simple question. "All I need to know is do you love me too?" He paused. "Or, do you think you could grow to love me too?"

This was what she didn't want—the sad eyes lined with the questions she wasn't prepared to answer. He wanted something from her she didn't trust herself to give. Somewhere in her tight stomach and her aching heart, she knew the answer. It had been growing stronger every day, every minute she'd spent with Nico. But what good would it do now to acknowledge it?

"I'm leaving," she said.

Vacant eyes met hers for a heartbeat before he lowered his chin to his chest.

"That's what I've been trying to tell you, Nico. I'm leaving. I had an interview yesterday and there's a bank manager position in Portland and I'm going to take it. So, you see? You can't love me...and I can't love you back."

CHAPTER 33

"**E**veryone think about a time when you wanted to buy something, but didn't have enough money to pay for it." Julie stood at the dry-erase board with red and green markers in her right hand and her lesson plan in the other.

All twenty-six children's hands flew into the air, eager and restless. Squeals flipped between pint-sized "ooh oohs" and "pick me." Usually, Julie was inclined to choose a kid who was quiet with averted eyes, but today, she thought, why not? Why not choose the little brown-skinned girl with the curly pigtails, who likely studied until she knew things backward and forward? The kid who was often passed over as a know-it-all?

She eyed the three-fold poster card in front of the girl that read Jasmine, and pointed her markers toward her. As the overzealous Jasmine squirmed on the edge of her chair, flailing spirit fingers over her head, Julie nodded. "Okay, Jasmine. Can you tell us about a time when you wanted something, but didn't have enough money?"

Almost instantly, the fire that was bursting from Jasmine fizzled as she began to share her story. With downcast eyes and antsy feet, she began speaking. "When I was a little girl," she explained, as if the time had been so long ago. "I asked my mom for a bed of my own, but she said we didn't have enough money and I had to wait until I was older. So, I have to share a bed with my sisters."

Julie's words caught in her throat as her eyes darted around the room. She had expected a rumble of laughter from the other kids, but as she took in their small innocent faces, there was nothing but understanding in their eyes.

She'd expected video games and electronics, or dolls, or the latest shoes, but a bed to call her own? Suddenly, Julie felt embarrassed by her shock. This was normal for these sweet children. It was the hand they'd been dealt, still they smiled and laughed freely, offering their good nature as their only means of bartering.

In the corner, her eyes found Nico's whose were serious, and—if she wasn't mistaken—empathetic. He gave her a light-hearted smile and returned to his paperwork on the desk.

"Good, good job." She cleared her throat, searching for her place in her lesson plan. "That's an excellent example," she said.

For the remainder of the class, she couldn't help wanting to be close to the kids. She wanted to build up their self-esteem and encourage them. She listened with a discerning ear and observed them, wishing she could do much more for them than teach them about the difference between wants and needs.

All of their lives, she was sure it had been instilled in them through hand-me-downs and shared everything, wishing for just one thing to call theirs and only theirs. Though she knew it was an important lesson for them to learn, half of her wished they didn't need to know how to scrimp and scrounge, saving their pennies. That they had the luxury of wanting the latest Black Friday toy, and not food, new clothes, and a bed they didn't have to share.

When the bell rang, Julie exhaled a sigh of exhaustion. She had come into the class today, dreading the sight of Nico and their awkward exchanges. It hadn't occurred to her that she might be so involved in the kids and the lesson that she would think of him only in passing glances.

Though it was strained between them, he had remained professional and kept their personal issues out of the classroom. But now, as she hugged the kids and told them how much she was looking forward to seeing them tomorrow as they filed out of the room, the tension in the air thickened.

She glanced over at Nico, gathering her purse. "Thanks for today. I really enjoyed the time with the kids. They're so smart and sweet." She bit her lip, her mouth growing dry.

"You did a really great job with the kids. I think they enjoyed it, too," he said.

"Think so?"

His face reddened and his jaw clenched as he sighed.

"I'm sorry," Julie said.

"Don't. Don't apologize. Just..." His voice was curt and controlled at first, then it trailed off and he darted his eyes toward the door.

Julie followed his line of vision and turned, thankful for the interruption. Jasmine, the eager little girl who reminded Julie of her younger self, stood at the door with a backpack twice her size hung over her shoulders.

"Hi Jasmine. Did you forget something, honey?" Julie asked, searching the desk tops and chairs for a jacket or pencil box left behind.

"Um...I wanted to ask you a question, Ms. Laurich?"

Surprise washed over Julie. She blinked hard and clapped her hands together, unsure what else to do with them, then she bent down to the girl's height. "Oh, okay. Sure." She flashed a nervous look over her shoulder at Nico before returning with a wide grin. "What kind of question do you have for me, sweetheart?"

"You work for a bank, right?" she said.

"Yes, Jasmine, that's right." Julie agreed hesitantly, unsure where the girl's questioning was going. "That's how I earn money. Remember we talked about how adults have things they have to pay for with the money they earn?" As the girl nodded, Julie asked her to recall the term they had learned.

She lit up with the glow of a person who knows the right answer. "Monthly expenses," she said, seeming pleased with herself for remembering.

"Good job." Julie continued. "Now what did you want to know about banks?"

She shifted on her feet. "Are you the bank manager?" Something resembling hope twinkled in her eyes.

"No, Jasmine, I'm not a bank manager yet, but I hope to be one sometime soon." Julie lifted her shoulders to appear as cheerful as possible for the girl's sake. In the back of her mind, she hoped Nico was listening. Maybe he would understand that she needed to pursue her dream as much as he needed to be here for his kids.

"I'm a personal banker. Personal Bankers help the customers and open checking and savings accounts," she explained.

"Can you help me learn how to become a bank manager?" Her eyes cut to the door where another little girl who looked like a slightly taller version of her with a single side braid waited in the frame.

With renewed resolve and the faintest hint of flattery, Julie told the girl that nothing would make her more proud than to be her mentor. In fact, tomorrow, she would bring her a junior bank badge and they would begin their training. As she left with a noticeably bouncier pep in her step, Julie couldn't help brightening, too.

Except, when she turned around, Nico stood directly behind her.

"That was nice what you did for her, but please don't make promises you can't possibly keep," he warned. Though she understood the downfalls of giving kids false hope, she had a niggling feeling that they weren't talking about kids any longer.

"I just wanted to help," she muttered.

His eyes were cold and his skin flushed. "False promises only end up hurting," he continued to berate her. He crossed his arms. "For the remainder of the time that you're here, I'm asking you, please just do the job you're here to do. Teach them about saving. Engage them. Let them participate. But, don't go answering any questions that are not directly related to the lesson plan. Do you understand?" he instructed.

Everything about his words and his tone was condescending and full of contempt. He was reprimanding her like one of his children and she felt as small as a grain of sand. All she wanted to do was run away.

This can't be happening.

A small laugh escaped her as her eyes welled. She pressed her lips tight and gritted her teeth. "Look Nico. We both know this isn't about what I said to Jasmine. If you want to take it out on me, fine, but don't shoot me down for trying to help out a kid. I know that what I did to you wasn't right. I should have told you how I was feeling, but *I* didn't even know what I was feeling," she cried.

Nico stalked off to his desk. He propped his hands on the edges and let his head hang between his shoulders. "I don't want to hear this," he muttered.

"What don't you want to hear? That I love you, too? Is that what you don't want to hear? Huh?" she yelled as tears trailed down her cheeks. She closed the distance between them with slow measured steps, weaving through tiny desks and chairs, and stood behind him.

With softened words, she began again. "I didn't know this was going to happen. I didn't plan on you. How was I supposed to know? I've been working toward this career goal, meeting road-block after roadblock and finally a door opens, and now I have to choose between the only two things I've ever really wanted? It isn't fair."

Julie plopped down on a desk at her right side, feeling drained and exhausted. All of her cards were on the table now. It was up to Nico to decide what hand they would make with them.

After a few minutes, he stood upright and turned to Julie.

A tight smile crossed his face as he drew in a slow, steady breath. "So, then I'm glad you understand. Sounds like we both know just how much false promises hurt."

~

THREE CALLS SENT TO VOICEMAIL, two letter-length text messages, and one hour later, Liz showed up at Julie's front door, armed to the hilt with what she considered post-breakup must-haves. She had a year-old bottle of cheap wine, a pint of pralines and cream, and her Netflix password.

Barely a foot in the door and she smothered her best friend in a stifling bear hug, running off at the mouth about "no-good assholes" and "smug bastards."

With her and Derrick doing so well as of late, Julie felt bad dragging Liz into her mope. In some form or another, he'd be the one who suffered from their man-bashing session. Besides, Julie really couldn't be mad at Nico. He wasn't the one who had decided to pick up and move when things were just getting good.

Julie had hoped to be alone to wallow in her own self-inflicted torture, but hearing her friend ante up for battle on her behalf filled her empty insides. Liz had a fierce loyalty that gave Julie life at that moment.

"Liz, you know I love you, right? But, I just want to crash tonight and not think about it." She scrunched her nose and looked up at Liz with a sheepish grin. The last thing she wanted to do was hurt her best friend's feelings, but Julie prayed that Liz would understand what she was going through.

"Um, no. That's not going to work for me," Liz stated. "Fine. If you don't want to try my sure-fire cure to the break-up blues, fine." She padded over to the refrigerator and stuffed the ice cream in the freezer. "But you need wine," she said definitively, as if she were talking about something as dire as medicine.

Julie pursed her lips and tilted her head to the side, too exhausted to debate effective vices for speedy healing of relationship rifts. "Okay, but let's at least take the wine out on the balcony. It's nice out."

"That works. You know you need to take advantage before we get up to the triple digits."

From the top shelf in the cupboard, Liz pulled out two stemless wine glasses and a bowl. "Grab those pistachios, too. I need something to snack on while we get to the good stuff because I'm giving you exactly twenty minutes to get all that Nico shit off your chest and then I'm going to unload on you."

"About what?" Julie asked.

"That's for me to know and you to find out. So, start thinking about what you have to tell me, including why you decided to up and skip town without consulting me." She rolled her eyes and smacked her lips loudly. "I'm expecting some legit answers, too. Better not have anything to do with some asshole, either."

Julie shook her head, unwilling and unable to come up with a response for Liz's bossy comments.

In the small junk drawer at the end of the island, she pulled out a citronella candle and a matchbook. Along with the pistachios and her Bluetooth speaker, she took them out onto the balcony and proceeded to set up their makeshift gossip lounge.

By the time she took her place, Liz was already seated facing her with feet curled up into the chair, ready. Liz glanced down at her watch and flashed her attention back to Julie. The clock had started ticking.

At first, Julie thought she might be joking, but the blank stare was all business. The unloading was yet another one of Liz's breakup-cure must-haves. Once, after Liz and Derrick had split earlier in their relationship, Liz had called an emergency meeting with Julie just to vent. It was structured, timed, and cathartic, by design, meant to unburden her of the negativity and figuratively unclog her heart and mind. She had book references earmarked to the sections on the psychosomatic effects of stress and anguish. According to her paraphrased findings, if she didn't spill the beans, she could die of a broken heart.

Now, Julie found herself taking note of her lost appetite and the heavy tightness in her aching chest. The sense of hopelessness she couldn't seem to escape. She took a long swig of her wine and let the air in her chest funnel out in plumes.

Staring at nothing in particular, Julie said, "I think I might have fucked up."

CHAPTER 34

By the final day of Savers Week, the kids had each earned a paycheck for one hundred Kid Saver dollars from their assigned jobs. Some were doctors and postal employees, others worked at restaurants and law offices. There was even one teensy rambunctious bank manager with pigtails and a junior bank badge.

From Mr. Farfalla, as the kids called Nico, the class had been given an account register book, four utility bills, one parking ticket, a choice of bus fare or gasoline cost, and a list of groceries the previous day, with the assignment of balancing their checking accounts. Today they were going to be adults, budgeting and determining the difference between needs and wants.

It really was kind of a big deal. Over the full school year, art classes had worked on painting and constructing miniature city sets, complete with cardboard buildings and cars. The whole school got involved. Everyone wore costumes or uniforms suited to their careers, including the principals and teachers, who really got into their roles as "the law." The whole class had been transformed into a new world to allow the kids to manage their expenses and decide whether to save or buy themselves treats at any of the tiny stores.

Julie got in on the fun as well. She put on her best navy blue suit and heels, and proudly clamped her badge over her breast pocket. Armed with business cards and a box full of piggybanks, books, and candy, she greeted the children by Mr. and Ms.

In her most professional voice, she assisted her mini-manager Jasmine as they opened checking and savings accounts and offered twenty-dollar loans. Her heart filled with joy as she laughed with the kids and mingled with the staff and faculty.

She was armed with a basket full of plastic groceries at the checkout, when she looked over at the post office, formerly known as Mr. Farfalla's desk. He stood there with a sack full of envelopes addressed in large wobbly print. Seemingly lost in conversation, his lips continued to move as he spoke with the principal, but his mind appeared to be somewhere else. Over the principal's shoulder, he wore a slack expression on his face and his attention was focused on Julie.

In the crowded room, over the din of joyously shrieking children, their eyes met.

Suddenly, Julie's skin pulsed with the memory of his gentle touch. She could feel the blood in her veins racing. That's when it all came into sharp focus. She knew the difference between a need and a want. In her mind, she wanted him. In her heart and in her bones, she needed him.

Love wasn't a want. It was an urgent, life-threatening melding of the mind and body, psychosomatic need.

The realization slapped her in the face. She had to tell him, now.

In the middle of the line, she sat her groceries on the makeshift conveyor belt and walked away. The cashier made a point of yelling, "you haven't paid for this," loud enough for the other store patrons and city workers to hear.

It even got the attention of Mr. Farfalla, who excused himself from the principal and closed the distance between himself and Julie.

"Everything okay?" he asked with genuine concern.

"Uh...yeah." She twisted her watch on her wrist, then clutched her fidgety hands together to keep them from driving her crazy. She took a deep breath. "I just, I need to talk to you for a second. Do you think they'll notice if we step outside for a few minutes?" she said, her eyes pleading with him.

A flash of worry crossed his face and he nodded emphatically. Over his shoulder, he notified another teacher that he'd be right back and excused them as he guided her from the room with his hand on the small of her back.

When they reached the side of the building, he exhaled and seemed to brace himself for whatever it was she was going to say.

She didn't want to alarm him or make him think anything was wrong with any of the kids. "This has nothing to do with the class," she explained.

Almost instantly, he deflated and puffed up again with fresh annoyance. "Don't do this. We've already run this thing into the ground. Let's just leave it at that." His gaze flicked upward as he shook his head.

"Please."

"I'm not doing this here. This is where I work," he scoffed.

All she heard was "here." Maybe this wasn't the appropriate place or the time, but this was where it all made sense. Seeing him with the kids and being around him only made her so much more aware of his absence—how he'd filled a void in her life that she hadn't known was there.

As he walked away, desperation pumped through her.

"I'll stay," she said. She hadn't had much time to think anything through, but it seemed the only option that fit.

He stopped, but he didn't turn to her. His body appeared weighed down, despondency an incomprehensible burden.

"I love you, Nico. Please talk to me, butterfly..." Her voice cracked. In that moment, her body felt boneless as her shoulders curled over and her spine bent. She was breathless, waiting for him to say something, anything.

And when he did turn to her, she knew she was willing to do anything.

Slowly, he walked to her and stared down into her forlorn eyes. "Is this a game to you?" he asked, his words laced with two parts disdain and one part agony. Between each word he paused, as if tasting them on his tongue. "Because it's not for me. I imagined the kind of lifetime love my parents had, but for you, that means nothing. It's all a game, isn't it?"

She shook her head. "No."

At her answer, he ran his hands through his hair and dropped his face into his hands. "What are you doing, Jules?" he questioned, low and exhausted. "Do you even know what you want?" Now he sounded desperate and anguished.

Her chest rose and fell to a hurried staccato beat. "You. That's all I want is you." Tears streamed freely over her cheeks.

A light breeze rustled the swings across the playground, setting off a squeaky tick of the clock. This strategic chess game measured in moves. Every choice would have a consequence, and they each hesitated in anticipation of the other's move. She had made hers. Now, it was his turn.

"Do you know what bothers me the most?" Nico asked. His chin lifted now as he trained his eyes on Julie. "That you were willing to give up so fast. And I know that most long-distance relationships don't work, but you didn't even consider it. You threw every option out the window before you even talked to me. How do you think that made me feel?"

"I know and I'm sorry." Julie reached for Nico's arm and he moved away.

As if he had been compiling a list, he began shooting off his questions. "Have you ever been to Portland? Do you know anyone there? Most people don't just decide to up and leave everyone and everything they know. Was it for the experience, or was this some kind of test that I didn't pass? Huh?"

As much as she did, it seemed he needed to make sense of things, too. She had to make him understand where she was coming from.

"Nico, it wasn't *about* Portland. I've been wanting this for so long and finally someone said yes. 'We believe in you. You're good enough.' And it felt so good to have my hard work and dreams validated, if you can understand that." She turned on her heels and paced a few steps. Then, her tone low and careful, she treaded lightly. "I've had promises of love before and I've had my heart crushed. I didn't know where this thing with us was going. I was scared. I'm scared," she admitted, biting back tears.

Behind her, Julie felt the warmth of Nico's chest hard against her back. As his arms curved around her waist, he leaned his head down in the small of her neck.

"I'm scared, too," he whispered, squeezing her tight.

He trailed soft kisses behind her ear along her hairline and turned her in his arms until they were face to face.

Julie's lips parted and she inhaled deeply before she began again. "This is scary and I *have* been hurt, but no one has ever made me feel like I feel when I'm with you." She held onto his arms and lifted herself up onto her toes.

With every touch of his lips on hers, her skin tingled. She'd been gone. The wind knocked from her. Pieces of her had died, but with one kiss, he was giving her life again.

Air flowed through her lungs. She could breathe again. Her heart beat buoyantly, for once not at war with her mind. And though there was still the matter of trust, the gumption to try for him was abundantly present.

"I'm willing to take a chance, if this is real," Julie said. "If they're not just words. I need you to tell me that if I stay, that we've got a real chance. That I'm not just giving up on my dream for something you've only got a halfway feeling about." She looked at him expectantly, awaiting the answer she needed to soothe her angst.

In her mind's eye, she imagined a dramatic profession of his unfiltered, undying love. Maybe a lone glistening tear as he confessed that he'd waited his whole life to meet her. And somewhere in the wildest of her dreams, he'd kneel and another small box—possibly in a pastel shade of teal blue—would materialize in his hands as he suggested they stick together. Oh maybe until they sprouted silvery hair and their skin lost elasticity. Nothing too formal, just forever.

But Nico didn't tap into any of those fantasies. True to form, he put his own twisted spin on it.

As cute as he was in his blue and gray postal uniform with the mail sack, Julie had figured it was all in good fun for the sake of the kids. She had no clue that it was all part of his finely detailed plan.

From his sack, he pulled out a stack of packages and envelopes, all in that same adolescent script. He rifled through them until he found one written in red crayon addressed to Ms. Laurich with a yellow butterfly drawn in the top right corner. He handed it to her and folded his arms over his chest.

The expression on his face wasn't exactly smug, but it definitely had the telltale signs of confidence and a challenge met. She imagined him accepting her wager and raising her one Kid Saver postal envelope for the win. He was all in.

Julie tucked her right index finger under the corner of the envelope flap and slid it the full length until there was a slit wide enough to retrieve the letter inside. It had to be about five or six white pages thick, folded in half. She pulled the stack free and flattened the pages as she scanned the text.

At first, it looked like some kind of Google search or a bibliography, the way the results were spaced on the page. But, as she looked closer and read the search criteria, her eyes watered.

"I didn't know if you would, but I hoped you'd stay," Nico said.

Julie flipped through the pages, eager to see all the work he had put into it. "You did this for me?" she asked. A mix of laughter and amazement bubbled up inside of her. "I can't believe you literally found *every* branch manager opening within a fifty-mile radius. You're crazy, you know that? And amazing."

She threw her arms around his neck and pulled herself up high enough to wrap her legs around his waist.

This was what real felt like.

It wasn't rainbows and fireworks by any stretch. She recalled the instaspark she felt just looking at Nico in traffic. The image and the man she'd built up in her mind. Her first impression of him at the gym. How she'd misjudged him based on her own blindness. How no matter how much he'd proven himself otherwise, she'd kept finding her way back to her perception of him as a player. From their night at Nora's Italian and their chaotic exchanges at the gym, she'd held on to the words between Nico and Dane over everything else.

Now when she thought about it in such an epiphanic moment, it never was about the words.

For too long, she'd relied on the words instead of finding her way back to the actions. Patrick's words, for one, never held their weight. His forever was something akin to two and half years of infidelity and constantly stripping her of her value and worth. His words were loud, but his actions should have been her focus.

Her heart beat now with urgency, with hope. Like a magnet, she was drawn to Nico. Like she hadn't fully understood her purpose until she felt the undeniable force of his pull.

Nico lowered Julie down onto her feet without letting her go. "So, you're staying?" he asked, averting his gaze. A mischievous grin tugged at his eyes and mouth.

A silent pause buzzed in the air.

"Wait a minute." Julie muttered, her mouth agape. She could feel her eyes widen and her pupils dilating. "Wait, just a minute." She emphasized each word and pulled his chin down so that he had to face her. "You are *so* guilty."

Playfully slapping him on the chest, she could barely contain her shock. But, even as she touched him, a bout of giggles bubbled up inside her.

He burst out laughing.

"I cannot believe you. This was all a big game to you. You had this printed out and sealed in this envelope." Ear to ear grin, Julie shook her head in disbelief at how slick he was. How he had played her.

"You even involved the kids, you dirty sneak." She narrowed her gaze. "You knew you were going to get me to stay, didn't you? And you still put me through all of this, let me keep going on and on and on?"

Nico clutched her upper arms and drew her into a hungry kiss as he chuckled guiltily.

Her skin pulsed beneath his strong hands leaving her dazed and short of breath as his deep bass rumbled into her mouth. She trembled, her heart fluttering like a hundred butterflies were caged in her chest.

A surge of fire ignited in her feet and coursed upward, electrifying every nerve ending in her body as she kissed him deeper still.

"I love you," he said between kisses. "But, I had to know your reasons, your why—see if you meant it and what changed your mind. I was never going to let you go."

EPILOGUE

Julie and Nico took in the floor to ceiling brick walls sandwiched between panoramic windows. Curtains in silky luxurious fabrics were draped from the chandelier to every corner of the room. Between them, gigantic paper pom-poms hung in varying lengths. Julie's nose warred between the sweet lemony scent of cupcakes and Harman lemonade, and the potted Jane magnolia trees lining the edges of the room. It was an explosion of pinks and yellows, from the linens to the food.

Perfectly aligned in a half circle centered around a singular chair were at least ten large round tables skirted in matching pink tulle with elegant pink-padded gold Chiavari chairs. Floral arrangements included vases filled to the top with pearls, pink hydrangeas and magnolias towering in the center of the fully dressed tabletops.

Apparently, as dumbstruck as she was, Nico let out a small whistle. He squeezed her hand and kissed Julie on the head.

"Your cousin really knows how to bring a baby into this world with a bang, doesn't she?"

"You should have seen the wedding."

He scanned the room again. "And you're sure this is a baby shower and not a wedding reception because this place is right out of some warped princess royal ball fantasy. Should I bow when I meet her?"

Julie elbowed him in the ribs and slipped her hand back into his as she spotted her mother. Despite her strange bout of nervousness, Nico's presence calmed her. In the month or so since Kid Savers ended, their relationship had grown stronger, happier. Just about every waking minute they spent together at her apartment or his home visiting with his mother and brothers and sister. Somehow out of this she'd gained another family who loved her, mishaps and all.

Since his mother's health had improved, and Julie's lease would be up at the end of August, they'd been looking at condos and apartments with enough space for her shoes and a quiet nook for him to grade homework.

They still went to the gym regularly, but with Nico's cooking, she'd come to embrace food *and* her curves. He made her feel beautiful inside and out. Ironically, the more she fell in love with Nico, the less she cared about labels, pant sizes, and how fast she made it down the aisle.

They broached the subject in passing conversation a few times, but they agreed there was no rush. And that was fine by Julie. She was happy just being with him.

"Oh honey. You look…you're gorgeous," her mother said, when they reached the dessert table. "And isn't this just breathtaking? Did you see the paper flower backdrop? And the *A* monograms? They're everywhere."

Her mother gestured around the room, pointing at the smallest details, seemingly with a glint of whimsy in her eyes. Who knew, since her mom had been on a couple of promising dates recently, maybe in a few months she'd have a celebratory occasion on the calendar.

Julie's mother took a bite of a pretzel stick dipped in pink chocolate with gold flakes. "Look at this," she said, examining the pretzel. "Your cousin thinks of everything."

Julie shrugged, unsure what else to add. If anyone were to ask what was Sophia's sense of style, there would only be one way to categorize it: over the top.

"I'm so sorry. How are you, Nico? You're looking handsome as ever, sweetheart."

Nico untangled his hand from Julie's and hugged her mother. "I'm doing fine, Mrs. Laurich. Nice to see you again," he said as he kissed her cheek.

Right on cue, someone slid the glass doors to the patio open and in came Sophia in a downright stunning white chiffon maternity dress—more like a ball gown.

As for the rest of her? She looked as if the third trimester had gotten the best of her. Every inch of her body was bloated. Her face was oil-slicked with the early July Vegas heat, and her expression was tired and uncomfortable. Other than her greasy cheeks, nothing about her glowed with the ethereal glimmer of motherhood that so many women boasted about.

In the middle of her grand entrance, Aunt Helen materialized behind her sister and her niece, and whispered, "Isn't that dress glorious on her? And we got it for a steal. I've known the designer for years. He wanted Sophia to model his latest line for him, but we simply didn't have the time and now she's a puddle-jump away from giving me the granddaughter I deserve," she said, simultaneously bragging on Sophia and name-dropping subtle as a brick through a windshield.

"It's lovely, Helen," Julie's mom muttered to her sister, her voice flat.

Nico gave Julie a knowing look as he rolled his eyes. He'd heard the stories of the terribly fabulous Aunt Helen who bragged on her daughter relentlessly, and for whom no opportunity would be missed to rub anything in her sister's face.

Julie stifled a laugh at the funny face he made over Aunt Helen's shoulder and tilted her head toward the food table, indicating that they needed to get out while the getting was good. But it was too late.

"Now, Julie, I heard that you didn't get the branch manager position in Portland," Aunt Helen said, with squinted eyes and puckered lips, as if it pained her to know that Julie hadn't advanced at the bank.

The satisfaction was too great to miss the opportunity, so Julie went for it, further drawing her aunt in. "No...I turned it down, but American Bank had a position re-open in northwest Las Vegas. The candidate that they offered the position to didn't pass the background check, so they gave it to me. I started a couple of weeks ago." Julie's insides filled up with pure elation at the tight grin on Aunt Helen's face.

On that note, Julie moved over to another table where she grabbed one of about fifty monogrammed "A" mason jars. She inspected the pink lemonade garnished with a lemon slice and a pink and white-striped straw. After a long swig, she filled a small plate with cucumber tea sandwiches and two raspberry macaroons before turning to Nico who had trailed behind her.

"I think we need a code word," she said.

Nico's brows raised as he nodded emphatically. "Definitely. The minute you give me the go-ahead..." he snapped his fingers, "... we're out of here."

"Red bluejay, too much? Or, should we go with something more apt for the situation, like rubber ducky or binky? But, you've got to act quickly. No hesitation."

He seemed to consider the options with serious concern. "We better stick with the red bluejay. With the stuff they've got set up for the games over there, you might end up saying some of the other ones by accident and get me excited about an early exit."

"You're right. Okay, so we've got that taken care of. Now I just have to wait until Sophia grants us permission to start the games and we can sneak out during the gifts."

Nico nodded without looking at her and bent his ear to her. "Who is that?

Julie followed his line of vision. Her heart came to a screeching halt. "Uh...that's Austin, Sophia's husband. But, I don't know who the tall redhead is on his arm," she said, barely able to catch her breath.

"We better grab a good seat, then. Things look like they're about to get interesting." Nico guided her to the closest round table to Sophia and pulled out a chair for Julie before scooting in close.

From where Nico and Julie sat, it was difficult to hear as Sophia, in hushed tones, accused Austin of being unfaithful. Even more, she did it in front of the woman who had bounced in holding his hand. All of her minimal radiant mother-to-be extra glow was replaced by blotchy redness creeping from her neck to the irises of her eyes.

Julie was practically seeing red for her. She strained to make out Sophia's words.

"We need to talk, now. Alone," her cousin barked.

The woman obliged, finding her way over to the dessert table, wearing a downtrodden expression. When she was gone, Sophia stabbed her finger into Austin's chest and whisper-yelled inches from his cheek.

Anyone else might have seen a playful spat or a tug-of-war for names. Sophia's insistence on Raleigh or Emma Grace, and Austin's request to name their first-born girl after his mother Loretta. Or, maybe a second guess on the name Ainsley, on which they'd settled.

What Nico and Julie got to see were the tiny tears in a distressed relationship. Suspicions confirmed. A blip of waning trust in the perfect life they had built together, as it took a final dip before flatlining.

Sophia could be a pain, but she didn't deserve this.

"I should go check on her," Julie whispered to Nico, getting to her feet, but he gently pulled her arm down. "I need to be there for her. No matter what, she's family."

"You don't want to get involved in that," he warned her.

"But she's pregnant." Her mind immediately went to an image of Sophia going into early term labor and she panicked. She squeezed Nico's hand and met his imploring gaze.

He simply shook his head. "She has to figure it out on her own," he said.

In that moment, as she watched Sophia's choices coming to a head, Julie thought about her mother and how her words always seemed to come to mind at crossroads. A few months ago, her mom had hinted about regret being a funny thing and Julie had read it wrong. She'd meant that Julie would regret staying with Patrick and she had been right in every way. Julie had reluctantly started over again and the stars aligned when Nico came into her life. He fit. He was the missing puzzle piece that helped all the other pieces fall into place, and the big picture had never been clearer.

"I need to do something."

"All you can do is be there for her when it's over," Nico said. Julie knew he was right, but it sucked to have to sit back and wait for the other foot to drop.

Now again, it was her mother's words that came to her as she looked on at Sophia sympathetically knowing the rocky road ahead, no matter what path she chose. Julie had heard the quote before, but it was something about the way her mother had said it that made it stick with her. The way she'd said it was so wise and definitive, it seemed she'd been speaking from experience. What she'd been talking about was karma and letting go of the things we're so hell-bent on holding onto.

"No need for revenge," she'd said softly. "Just sit back and wait. Those who hurt you will eventually screw up themselves, and if you're lucky, God will let you watch." But, there were always two sides to a coin.

On one side, this, the crossroad her cousin faced was that of a wife, already feeling her frumpiest and least sexy, made to feel worse by a beautiful replacement. Julie knew it was karma in its ugliest, purest form, at the worst possible time.

But, on the other side of the coin, karma could be whimsically beautiful as it unfolded. Around the point when Sophia slapped on her Facebook happy face and neatly unwrapped her gifts, karma flared up in the best of ways and it had nothing to do with Julie's cousin.

"Look what the wind blew in," Nico said under his breath.

Sophia had just taken the lid off a blush-pink box with a silk ribbon and pulled out a onesie that read "I'm fix in' to cry, y'all" in pink glitter, when Celeste stumbled into the hall, perfectly round belly and raggedy asshole Patrick in tow.

It wasn't that long ago that Julie had obsessed and cried and prayed over Patrick. She tried to understand what happened. She questioned everything about herself from her worth to her looks to the value of her life. Hell, she had gained weight over this man.

Julie scrunched her nose. "Is it too early for a red bluejay?"

Nico flashed her a disarmingly sexy full teeth grin and her insides got all gooey.

Thankfully, Patrick hadn't taken the last of her luck.

The eyes she thought were only meant for him had changed focus. People had said one day she'd get over him, but at that moment—that very glorious instant—with Nico by her side, Julie wondered what she ever saw in Patrick.

Sure, he was tall and had symmetrical features, but so did skyscrapers. The way his low-hung brows seemed to overpower his deep-set eyes and the way his posture sort of hunched in that creepy way, like the alien's did in Predator, grossed her out. He didn't even have the benefit of a sexy walk to boost him up a bit.

As he stumbled into a table causing a loud clatter, Julie tossed a glance over her should once more. "What a hot mess. I'm pretty sure he's drunk."

All the things she thought made him so suave and unique were now the same things she hated, couldn't bear to look at. In fact, she was *sick* and *tired* of seeing him. *He* was boring.

Julie's eyes darted straight across the room to her mother's, which were glazed over with worry and shock that he'd dared to show his face. By now, the man formerly known as Mrs. Laurich's Perfect Patrick had dropped in the ranks to a no-good dirty loser who didn't deserve her daughter. She adored Nico now, who wasn't perfect, but he was perfect for Julie.

She turned in her chair and prayed Celeste and Patrick didn't see her.

For the most part, it seemed Julie had managed to stay under their radar. Or, at least they had the decency not to talk to her. The games went off swimmingly, which a few of Sophia's friends made it a point to come tell Julie, raving on about how hilarious it was drinking alcohol out of baby bottles and scavenging for junk in their purses.

I might just make a clean getaway.

Celeste and another pregnant woman with blonde hair and cankles were poolside on the patio. Meanwhile, Nico chatted up Liz and Derrick near the bar as they downed another round of Sophia's pink cocktails made special for the shower. It was the first time of the day that Julie had been left alone.

She took the time to visit the dessert bar and actually eat one of the cupcakes that everyone had raved about.

Admiringly, she observed the table filled with cake stands in varying heights and apothecary jars as she peeled back the cupcake wrapper and took a bite. Not only was the cake moist and filled with lemon creme, but the frosting was light and fluffy and buttery with a hint of strawberry. In pure bliss, Julie let her head hang back with her eyes closed, and moaned with the satisfaction that usually comes with sex or chocolate.

Warm breath blew over her bare shoulder. "That good? I wish I was that cupcake," a familiar bass-filled voice said.

Julie opened her eyes to Patrick, standing so close to her that she felt cornered. No one else was at the dessert bar and the way he'd wedged himself next to her, anyone looking who didn't know them would just think they were two old friends catching up over baked goods.

"Hello, Patrick." Julie inched backward against the table.

"You weren't going to speak?" he asked. "I've been watching you ever since I got here, but this is the first time you've been alone. Are you serious about this guy? I mean really, who is he?"

She smiled a calm, easy smile. "You already know he's my boyfriend, so why do you care? Not that it's any of your business. I don't owe you any explanations."

Patrick wore a tight expression and drew in a slow, steady breath. He looked around the room before gazing back at her, his eyes shooting daggers. In the past, this had worked. Almost immediately, she'd cower and try on different responses to calm him. Most times they'd end up tangled in sweaty sheets with sore muscles the next day and the problem swept neatly under the rug. But today, Julie lifted her chin to him.

On some level, Julie had been waiting for this moment. The chance to get her questions answers. Some warped form of closure that she needed. She loved Nico with everything in her, but it couldn't hurt to know the truth.

"Look, Jules," Patrick began again. "I still love you," he said, swallowing hard. He pressed a fist to his lips and exhaled through his nose.

"I don't—" Julie started.

"Let me just say this before I can't," he continued hurriedly. "I miss you. I miss us. Don't you remember all the good times we had together? I've been thinking about our summer in New York, the color of the leaves, and the way we felt so alive there. I think about you and how you'd come home and ask me about my day, my family, everything. We knew each other. We had plans—"

"And you threw those plans to the wind, don't you think? I believed you, Patrick. Past tense. I would have done anything for you, and you left. You fucking called me boring and you left. How do you think that made me feel?" Julie lowered her voice. Her gaze fell. She didn't want to do this anymore. "You know what? I'm fine. I'm actually, the happiest I've ever been, so just go."

Patrick raked his fingers through his hair. Color drained from his face and his posture collapsed.

"Just listen, Jules. Hear me out. I know you don't want to hear this, but you were never in the mood and you were going crazy with wedding plans and I...I felt left out."

She cocked her head to the side. "Are you fucking trying to blame this on me?" Disbelief twisted her expression.

"No, no." He scrambled now, his words choppy and hurried. By the urgency in his words, Julie could tell he'd been grappling with whatever he had to tell her, so she listened. Not really out of the kindness of her heart, but to set the situation straight.

That, and because Celeste needed to hear it, too, since she was standing near the door behind him, listening.

"Celeste came on to me at Shane's bar. I was there right after that Winston Company meeting and I'd had my ass handed to me and I needed to blow off some steam, you know? She was there and she was coming onto me hard. I know it was wrong, but she took me into the bathroom and made me feel wanted again. That's what I'm trying to say," he explained, his hands slicing a line in the air, as if that made it all better.

"It was just the one time and I thought it was no big deal, but then she told me she was pregnant. And you know how my family is. They would never let me live it down. I would have been disowned if I didn't do the right thing. You know it. So, I said you were boring. That was all I could come up with," he blurted out. Upturned eyes brimming with apologies bore down on Julie. "I'm getting a paternity test."

Behind him, Celeste glided one hand beneath her belly and rubbed it absentmindedly with the other. She had done this. Both of their actions had betrayed Julie, but Celeste had acted willingly, unapologetically, and with the intention to take what she wanted.

Patrick, on the other hand was the same weak-willed boy without the balls to keep her from taking advantage of him.

Julie looked straight ahead, with both Patrick and Celeste in her line of vision. Now, she knew why she had hesitated when she'd yes to his proposal. "Good luck with everything, Patrick," she said, edging her curves past him.

She walked slowly over to Nico as the weight of the world lifted from her heart and shoulders. From behind him, she hugged him and whispered, "Nico Farfalla. Butterfly. I'm so lucky. I'm in love with you."

At the softness in her voice, Nico attempted to twist his body in her arms, but Julie held him steady. "What is this?" she asked, her hand brushing over a hard, square-shaped lump in his jacket.

Julie stilled herself, her eyes widening. She could not move. Shock fused her feet to the floor as he turned himself in her embrace and reached into the breast pocket of his jacket.

In that moment, she freeze-framed him.

The same glorious snapshot of him looking down at her from his truck not too long ago came flooding back to her. He pulled out a small white box. "You know I've been waiting for the right time to give this to you." He tilted his head and looked at her with appraising eyes. "Is this the right time?" he asked.

His depthless brown eyes peered back at her. They were filled with what appeared to be hope and mischief as they pulled tight at the corners.

Suspiciously, she eyed him, furrowing her brows. "If it's another fitness band, I'm thinking no. But if you've got in there what I've been dreaming about since I was a kid playing dress-up, then yes. Yes, by all means, I don't think I could be any more ready," she admitted, half-heartedly preparing herself for the former and praying from the aching core of her heart for the latter.

With the small white box still in hand, Nico held Julie at arms-length, as if determining her sincerity. He took in their surround-ings, searching the room.

She followed his gaze. Derrick with Liz in his arms, their faces awash with anticipation and hopefulness. Her mom and Sophia with Aunt Helen huddled together, an iron curtain of strong women. And finally, Patrick and Celeste, their focus trained on Julie and Nico, so unaware of the fall that follows pride.

"I love you, Julie Laurich," Nico said, lowering himself onto one knee.

Her eyes welled with a flurry of emotions. Overwhelming love flooded her heart for the man who had made it forget that it had ever been broken. The man who loved her, flaws and all. And with the question in his eyes, she knew that she could imagine a million and one sunsets together. With Nico, she wanted to build a life.

She had no reservations. No uncertainty. Other than the whole losing her lunch in Nico's lap situation at Frankie's, she had no regrets.

Julie didn't hesitate this time.

She answered his question with a resounding "yes." And as the room erupted into cheers, they sealed their promise with a kiss. She held onto Nico, unwilling to let go.

When her lips parted, she tilted her head toward his ear and whispered. "I love you. You've made me so happy."

Once more, Nico pressed his lips softly against hers, then lowered his mouth to her ear and said, "red bluejay."

Thank you for spending your time with Julie and Nico. If you enjoyed Mixed Signals, please consider leaving a review.

Keep reading for an excerpt from Mixed Match.
See how Sophia turns her life around and finds instalove!

Join me in my reader group. I'd love to chat! That's where I connect with readers most.
Mia Heintzelman Reader Group

AN EXCERPT FROM MIXED MATCH

Sophia Kent dug her fingers under the sides of the box, and for a split second this move to Portland didn't feel as daunting as she made it out to be.

But then she steadied her legs, squatted for leverage, and strained to heft the box, determined to pry it off the floor...and the dang thing wouldn't budge.

"Come. On." She heaved and struggled some more. Not even an inch. She gritted her teeth, wiggled her butt to resettle, and dug her heels into the thick, cloudy gray carpet, pulling up with all her might. Still didn't budge.

"Ugh." She groaned, finally releasing her hold. She was about two seconds from pouting and stamping her feet. *Let go and let God.* She breathed. In and out. Again.

But it still frosted her cookies something awful. She could do this. She needed to do this. With both hands on her hips, she kicked the box with her sneaker-clad foot, stubbing her toe in the process. "Ow!!!. Sugar-Honey-Iced-Tea."

"Oh come on, you can do better than that. Give me a good, pissed-off 'fuck,' or an angry-ass 'dammit.'"

Sophia almost jumped out of her skin at the voice, but quickly recognized it and rolled her eyes instead. "Must you be so crass all the time?"

"And say it like you mean it, too. I don't want to hear anything about h-e-double hockey sticks, either."

Sophia finally turned to see her flawless, perky cousin Julie standing behind her.

Even for as labor-intensive an occasion as moving, Julie was fierce in fluorescent pink athleisure wear with her bale of glossy curls bound by an equally neon yellow bandana. A far cry from the high school volleyball shorts and dingy black T-shirt Sophia dug out of the box designated for donations because everything else was packed.

Behind Julie stood her shiny new Italian wet dream of a fiancé, Nico, who was biting back a grin. Apparently they'd been there just long enough to witness Sophia's little tantrum.

"Peachy. Just doggone peachy." Sophia plopped down on the gigantic box of books. "If y'all love me, don't say anything. Just...shut up." She waved them off.

"I see you're still holding on to your little facade. What'd you do, look up a list of Southern euphemisms and decide to insert one every other sentence?" Her cousin was definitely one of those high-anxiety, blunt people you either loved or hated.

Sometimes it took even Sophia a good long minute to remember Julie was a worrier *because* her love was so fierce. She was a good person she just lacked...tact.

Julie picked up a roll of tape and started over to a group of boxes in the corner. But not before Sophia noticed the telling look she gave Nico.

"What was that about?" She watched a mischievous grin toy at the corners of Julie's mouth, then she turned to Nico. "Well? The look, what did it mean?"

"This is between you guys." He stepped back, holding up his hands. A surefire sign Sophia hadn't misread the look.

She eyed him over the top of her nose. "Don't even try to sneak out. Tell me what's going on, because I know she won't."

A screech of tape jerked Sophia's attention back to Julie, who'd already sealed one box and moved on to another. "It means your mom is about to get hooked up, so now we've got to find someone new for you too. Whether it's here in Vegas or in Portland makes no difference. But hopefully it'll happen before you go falling into your mopey horror-movies-and-ice-cream phase."

"I do not have a horror-movies-and-ice-cream phase."

"You do. The first step to healing is acceptance. Now, accept you're not even from the South and please start acting like you again. I miss my crazy, sassy, foulmouthed cousin."

For a second Julie turned off the always-on, aggressive-boss-babe schtick. She was serious. "No more hold 'your horses,' or 'peachy,' or 'doggone peachy.' Just be you. You probably don't realize it, but you started this nonsense when you became a Harman.

"Since you're not anymore, I want you go to Portland tomorrow, live in your Barbie Dreamhouse there, and make it your own. I don't want it to be anything like this fucking lifeless, lonely show-piece with its cold grays and modern lines. It's an outdated, two-story museum without the benefit of pictures hanging on the wall, or any signs that love ever lived here. Don't look back at this place, or Assface (yet another lovely term of endearment for Sophia's ex-husband, Austin Harman, whose name Julie refused to say aloud). You don't need him *or* his money."

Of course her cousin was right. A ton of money had been thrown at the house but it never felt like Sophia's home.

Julie looked down at the box she was working on and scrawled on the side with permanent marker. With a long inhale she seemed to reset herself to playful mode. "And for fuck's sake, curse like you're a badass, knife-wielding chef with your big girl panties on, not an elementary school teacher." She winked.

Nico, who just so happened to educate a couple of dozen

second-graders every day, gave her a wounded look before he narrowed his eyes.

"No offense, babe." Julie flicked an apologetic pucker at him.

He winked in the totally smitten way people do only during the honeymoon phase. "None taken."

A roar of laughter from downstairs pinballed off the walls. Of course Sophia recognized the loudest, most high-pitched laugh was her mom. As expected, she'd proven to be as useless as ever—what with her ratio of two glasses of Pinot Grigio to one item of bubble-wrapped flatware.

But then a deep bass chortle joined the laughter.

Sophia bent her ear toward the hall. "Wait. Who all's downstairs?"

"My mom, Stan, and Aunt Helen. You know Aunt Helen sent us up here to help you see the 'merits' of staying." She laughed. "Oh, and your mom's boo is supposed to be on his way, and you know how that's going to go. It is going to be a straight-up shitshow. They've already been arguing about it." She was undoubtedly talking about their bickering mothers, who could come up with a bone of contention with anything and anyone.

"Already?"

"You know Aunt Helen is never going to let Mom live this down." Julie cocked her head. The knowing grin she gave Sophia said *you know you want to go watch this train wreck with me.*

She did.

Sophia sighed, let her head fall forward and her arms slump at her sides, still annoyed about her inability to move the box by herself.

Acceptance is key. Weakness is only temporary.

"Fine. Let's go downstairs." She popped up off the box and walked over to hug Julie and Nico.

"You all right?" Nico asked before releasing her. His big, kind brown eyes gleamed with empathy and concern. "You do realize we're here to help. It doesn't have to be a one-woman show." He flitted a glance toward the world's heaviest box.

Nico really was a good guy. Sophia couldn't be happier that her cousin was marrying him. And while she appreciated the thought behind his offer, she couldn't pretend a one-woman show wasn't exactly the new city circus her life was headed toward. "Actually, it does. I kind of need to get used to doing things for myself." *By myself.*

It's funny how things don't work out.

She wrung her hands, wishing she could rewind the conversation to just before she took that serious tone.

"But...no sense in sweating the small stuff, right?" She shrugged, going for nonchalant while she swallowed over the catch in her throat. *Lord, I'm speaking inspirational Instagram now. Maybe I do need someone new.*

The second the three of them reached the bottom of the marble stairs, Sophia's mom jumped up from the oversized leather sectional where she'd been completely in her element with a full wineglass in her bedazzling, bejeweled hand. As always, she was show-ready with expertly highlighted chestnut hair, a shiny sequined blouse, and glossy red lips, *just* in case someone happened to have a readily available mic. "We've got it covered down here. Don't worry about a *thing.*" Completely ignoring that she was still sitting next to the same two boxes she supposedly taped up an hour ago.

She set her glass down on the table, which clearly meant she was transitioning into business mode. Then she got up, walked over, and squared herself to Sophia, hands on each of her shoulders, her expression hopeful.

"Have you reconsidered yet? Given any thought to staying here in Las Vegas?" Her mom lowered her chin and deepened her gaze, as if she could somehow see inside Sophia's heart.

"No, Mom," Sophia's reply sounded strained since she couldn't believe she still needed to justify her actions to her mother at all. Somehow, some way, she knew her mom would turn everything around and make it about her instead of Sophia, but this was bigger than a move—bigger than running away from home. For Sophia this was about chasing a new life.

Lord, she needed a clean slate in the worst way.

Her mom's attention flicked to Julie and Nico. All the emotion and hope drained from her no-nonsense expression, the pained sigh and pursed lips directed at them a dead giveaway. Their inability to talk some sense into Sophia was clearly unacceptable in her eyes.

Look how cute Julie and Nico are.

By September they would be married in a crazy, fairy-tale wedding. And Aunt Marian and Stan? Adorable. It didn't get better than two sweet people holding hands after finding each other so late in life. Even their romance was a result of her mom's meddlesome matchmaking.

And then there was her mom. A stubborn mule with Sophia's shared fate. Mom made it clear she'd given love the old college try with Dad and it didn't work out, and that was that for her attempt at love. No three strikes rule, just a one-and-done.

Stubborn ass, more like.

"When is the guy getting here, Mom?"

"Don't try to change the subject. Besides, like I told Marian. I'm simply going meet the man and be cordial long enough to send him on his way. All this mushy foo-foo stuff? It simply isn't in the cards for me anymore."

"Oh cards, schmards. So get some new cards—a new dream—and move on. I am."

Sophia knew all about new dreams. Two years ago it seemed like she'd figured out the answers to all the age-old questions about love and life. She was married to a man who could give her the world, and blissfully on the verge of her motherhood and a picket fence dream—a royal flush in terms of possible hands to be dealt, considering her own upbringing.

But then everything was taken away. Again. She was meant to be alone. And finally she was okay with it.

The second she truly accepted it, she could breathe. All the walls came down, and she was free—to go and be wherever and whoever she wanted, without expectations and repeating cycles. The fact that the divorce was finalized and the Patton Place house was now hers confirmed she was right. It was time to get a new dream.

But those were Sophia's cards, not her mother's. Down to the very marrow of her bones, Sophia hoped her mom would find the courage to open up again, try again.

No matter how much it hurts, or how much you just want to curl up in a ball and rewind time to do it all over again in some alternate reality where things work out. Where you end up in a perfect marriage with a beautiful, healthy baby girl in your arms instead of only in your heart.

This move to Portland was as much to prove the benefits of new dreams to Mom as it was for Sophia. She had to try. If Sophia could relocate to another state and start all over again, her mom could go on a few dates.

A smile tugged at her mouth when she thought about the cute little old man from church Aunt Marian was setting her mom up with. But then she met her mom's unblinking look as she raised a brow.

"What?"

"You're running."

"I'm not running. I'm daring to imagine a new life. What about you? Have you considered giving this guy, this Otis, a *real* chance?"

For all of two minutes they stood there. The question charged the air. A dang face-off/stare-down brewed, complete with squinted eyes and a nonverbal bluff call before Mom shifted her weight and stuck out her hip. Sophia couldn't take the silence a second longer.

"Mom, what are you thinking about?" A sputter of laughter erupted from deep in her belly. She knew good and well her mom had a flare for dramatics. No matter what harebrained idea floated around beneath the tumbleweed atop her head, it couldn't be a good one.

She watched as Mom rubbed her forefinger over her top lip while she continued biting down on the bottom one.

"Uh-oh. That's the same look she gave me before fixing me up with Stanley," Aunt Marian snickered...because it's obvious that she's warning Sophia.

"The woman is ruthless in her pursuits." Stanley added. "Watch out, now."

Everyone laughed, including Sophia. She could feel the tension in the room evaporate. If anyone knew her mother was a ballbuster of a woman, it was Sophia. They were connected down to their DNA, inseparable and insufferable together when they were teamed up. But it was time they stopped leaning on each other.

"Okay, Mom. I know this face. Out with it." She snapped her fingers bringing her mom back to earth.

Mom's brows knitted together, as if she was struggling to find the right words. "This is what I'm talking about. I mentioned to Marian *one* time that this guy had a nice smile, and now she's setting me up. I mean, he's nice enough, but I don't *know* the guy. Still, you want me to find someone, or rather, give this guy a real chance, right?"

"Right," Sophia said, still not following where her mom was going with this line of reasoning.

"All I really want is for my only daughter to remain living in Las Vegas with me. So...how about we come to a little understanding?" She used her most velvety voice for this part. And sure enough, Mom was preparing for a total bomb drop. "So we both get what we want."

Sophia gaped. Then closed her mouth again. "Umm. I don't get it. I'm moving to Portland tomorrow, so..."

"So let's make a pact. Let's give it six months."

"Give what six months?"

"If you don't love it and you find there's nothing and no one there for you, come back to Vegas." The velvety voice again. As if this was a completely logical conclusion. "Meanwhile, I'll give this Otis a shot, or keep dating for the same amount of time. *But...*"

Uh-oh.

"If there's no one meaningful, fine. I don't have to continue searching for someone I know isn't out there for me." And there it was. This was classic Mom. Her special brand of putting a time limit on happiness. Her warped idea of compromise. But Sophia's plans did not include letting her mom get off easy.

Sophia was just about to let her know what she thought of her little plan when Aunt Marian weighed in with her two cents. "Six months? Why not three or nine? Helen, now you know that's just so damn random. Hell, why not a year?"

Not to be outdone by her mother, Julie couldn't resist having her say too—since this was apparently going to turn into a full-on extended family discussion. "No, three is definitely better. If it doesn't work out, she'll be back for the wedding." Because naturally everyone's lives revolved around her cousin's nuptials.

Precisely why I'm moving. To be left alone.

"Oh, I get it. This isn't my life or anything. Why don't you all take a number and everyone can line up to tell me what to do since I'm so pathetic? Since obviously I'm incapable of making good decisions." Sophia laughed. By now, her irritation had morphed into hysteria. This was insane. "I'm not smart enough. Not good enough for people to stick around. Right, Mom?"

She threw her hands up and whirled on the guys, who both flinched back. "Nico, Stan? Don't you guys have anything to add while we're at it?"

Neither of them looked at her, and both were dead silent as they shook their heads. If she wasn't mistaken, Sophia would have sworn she could see the indentation of Nico's teeth biting the inside of his cheek. Or maybe his tongue.

Mom held out her hand and let it hang in the air between them. "Deal, or not?"

Sophia searched every one of the few wrinkles on her mother's ageless face, but there wasn't a laugh line among them. She was dead serious.

And Sophia was dead serious about her mother getting a second chance.

Shit. Here goes nothing.

She narrowed her eyes at her mom again, gauging her intentions. Then she looked at Aunt Marian, took two fingers and pointed them at her own eyes first before turning them on her aunt. "Watch her when I leave to make sure she's holding up her end of the bargain."

With her aunt in place as her insurance policy, Sophia sighed and shook her mother's hand. "Fine. Six months. Deal."

OLD PATTON PLACE still looked and felt like home.

Everett Monroe sighed, taking a few steps back from the portico onto the weathered, brick-paved walkway. Shading his eyes from the afternoon sun, he took a good long look at his grandmother's home—his family's home for generations.

As much as he hated the Harmans, he had to admit they did maintain most of its original colonial elements. The four forward-facing dormers were tucked between twin chimneys, accented by the matching black front door and shutters flanked at each window. The contrast with the crisp white paint and lush green landscape made it a dream house, but it was the flaws he remembered that made it a home. The cracks he used to watch settle in the walls and the hardwood floors scuffed from years of childhood games.

He rang the old, familiar doorbell.

After a few minutes he leaned in and placed his ear on the door to see if he could hear someone walking around. When he heard muffled music or television, he knew someone was home.

He rang again.

Still no one answered.

"Hello!" He searched the windows for signs of life. "Sophia Harman?"

All his instincts urged him to grab the door handle and walk on in, but he couldn't just march in anymore.

Instead he held down the doorbell this time, dragging the pad of his finger over the button and letting it linger for a moment. It was both strange and almost haunting to stand on the steps of his childhood home and not be able to let himself in the way he'd done a million times.

He rested his forehead on the door and squeezed his eyes shut. Balling and un-balling his fist, he flattened his hand against the sun-warmed black wood. A soft breeze passed under his nose, teasing him as it swapped the robust scent of pine and wet grass with the rich, savory perfume of home cooking.

"Sophia Harman." His voice was just above a whisper.

He checked his watch once more. Dammit. Already one thirty. Mike would want a detailed account before he headed back to the courthouse for the filing. Everett took one more glance at the house. For good measure, he rang the bell one more time...then shrugged, prepared to walk away, until he heard a woman's voice.

"Who is it?"

He couldn't deny the way his shoulders lifted and relief flooded him as he replied to the closed door. "I'm looking for Sophia Harman."

"What do you want?" The woman asked.

"I have a package for her."

Come on. Let's just get this over with. I want to see the look on your face.

From behind the door, Everett heard the footsteps growing muffled and then looked over toward the rustle of blinds in the window to his left.

"Can you hold the package up, please?" the voice requested from the cracks between the blinds.

He jerked the hand holding the summons up to face the window. He opened his mouth to protest. Then closed it again.

The next thing he heard was the deadbolt being unlocked. A slim woman with a body for days appeared in the doorway with a phone glued to her ear. He gasped as a carnal urge shot to his groin, tightening every muscle.

This is Sophia Harman?

Get MIXED MATCH Now!

ABOUT MIA HEINTZELMAN

Mia Heintzelman is a graduate of the University of California, Berkeley and the University of Nevada, Las Vegas. She is a Chicago native who always has a book in her purse, loves to pair sweet and spicy tea with fluffy socks, and can't go wrong with polka dots and pearls. She lives in Las Vegas with her husband, two children, and a genius pup.

To learn more about Mia Heintzelman or to find out about upcoming books, follow on social media and visit miaheintzelman.com.